IN THE BROKEN PLACES

JACK GARRETY

FOR'SAIL PTY LTD

To Annie
For being the gold between my own broken places

"The world breaks everyone, and afterwards many are strong in the broken places."

Ernest Hemingway, *A Farewell to Arms*.

1

Chapter One

Death loitered beside bed sixteen.

Levi smelt it as soon as he entered the private room, its slow rot lurking beneath the caustic stench of disinfectant. The nightlight above bed sixteen and the bright digital readouts of the life support provided the room's only illumination.

Taking a deep breath, Levi held it for a count of three before exhaling slowly and approached, easing himself onto the chair beside the bed. Air escaped the vinyl padding with a hiss, mimicking the laboured breathing of the man on the bed.

The man looked worn, more used than old, receding hair still streaked with black, his pale skin gathered in slack pouches along the jawline. His eyes were shut but the thin lips moved, mouthing fervent, silent words. Perspiration sheened the etched lines of his forehead.

Levi reached out and gently covered the hand that wasn't intubated, trying to add warmth and comfort. The fingers were white, bloodless, and cold, their life force already shunted to the vital organs in a futile attempt at survival. The name Eric Layton was carelessly printed in blue marker on the whiteboard attached to the wall.

'Eric,' Levi whispered.

At his name, the man's eyelids fluttered.

Levi gently squeezed Eric's hand, mindful of the papyrus-thin skin and the blue veins snaking pale beneath it. 'Eric. My name is Levi Monk. I work with the hospice.'

Eric's breath came in irregular, shallow gasps, as if his body was having trouble remembering how to breathe. People became so hung up on death, but from Levi's experience the journey to there, the dying, was where the suffering dwelt.

Death itself was often a release. Levi reached over and dipped a tissue into a beaker of water by the bed, dabbing it at the corners of the man's mouth. It roused him a little.

'Would you like some water, Eric?'

The eyelids fluttered again. When Levi had first started sitting with the dying, he used to wonder about the cause of each pending death: accident, disease, illness, or simply neglect. After a time he'd realised it didn't matter; the need was just as urgent and the opportunity to sit with someone through their passing, the same rare privilege. Death was always a solitary journey, but support could often mitigate the fear. He'd worked out that much.

Levi picked up the water beaker, bending the plastic straw to slip into Eric's mouth. He sucked instinctively, and slowly the eyes opened, surprise-wide at first, then settling as realisation seeped in. They flicked sideways to see who was holding the water. Unlike the rest of him, the eyes were alert and alive. They narrowed when he saw Levi, as if struggling to place him.

Levi smiled and repeated, 'My name is Levi. I'm a carer here. Eric, is there anyone you'd like me to call? Someone to come and be with you now?' He already knew there wasn't, otherwise he, or someone like him, wouldn't need to be here, but it was an easy conversational bridge.

Eric looked wistful for a moment and then turned away, coughing to clear his throat.

'I'm dying, aren't I?' His voice cracked, turning the question into a statement.

'Yes.' There was no point in lying. Not about the obvious. This hospice was the last stop before death.

The pause stretched wide between them. Levi gently squeezed Eric's hand again, doing his best to expand support into it. This was always the most difficult moment.

'How long? No, don't tell me.' Eric paused, the skin around his eyes wrinkling into ready folds.

With difficulty, he turned his head back towards Levi. 'Will you do something for me?'

'If I can.'

'There's a letter—in my coat. I don't know where they put my clothes.' The words came out in a rush, as if at some cost.

Levi stood and opened the small closet beside the bed. Inside was a navy suit. Unhooking the hanger, he went to lay the suit across the bed.

'No. You'll have to do it... inside the coat's lining... near the hem. Rip... it.'

Levi fingered the cloth. It felt luxurious and expensive, the sort of lightweight finely spun wool that Italian tailors favoured.

'That will ruin the suit.'

'Just... do it. It's not... as if I'll be using... it again.' The last word was choked out, heralding a fit of deep, hacking coughs.

Levi slipped his arm around the man's shoulders, supporting him. When the fit passed, Levi eased him down onto the bank of pillows and handed him a tissue. The old man hawked into it, and the tissue came away mottled with pink froth.

Levi opened the suit coat, pushed the trousers aside, and reached down to withdraw a throwing knife from the sheath inside his boot. He made a long cut through the coat's lining. An envelope slipped free as if it had been waiting. Neither man acknowledged the knife as Levi slipped it back.

Eric tried to say something, but it was obvious that the effort to breathe was becoming increasingly difficult. His lips were blue. The heart monitor reading was all over the place. Levi reached for the emergency call button, but Eric stopped him. His long cold fingers wrapped themselves around Levi's wrist, shaking with effort. All the man's strength seemed to be directed into maintaining that grip. He was trying to say something, and Levi bent down to hear. Eric was gasping now, desperately trying to shape breath into words, his neck arching towards Levi's ear.

'Deliver it... for me.'

Eric gave a strangled gasp and flopped back. Levi eased his hand free of the death grip and walked to the door, closing it quietly.

The death ritual to ease the transition of Eric's spirit from the physical back to the Whole would look strange to anyone walking past. He returned to the bedside and closed his eyes, summoning energy. When it was vibrating sufficiently, he made the standard hand passes along the length of the body, head to feet and back again. The energy flowed from his hands, blue and vibrant. He paused and took several deep whooshing breaths through the mouth before moving to Eric's abdomen where he made a succession of fast scooping motions above the navel. Levi continued the rapid move-ment, following the outline of the of the body to the head, ending at the crown with a determined flourish. He waited, his breath heaving.

Nothing happened.

He took a step back and gazed into the space between him and Eric's body. *Something is wrong.* Slitting his eyes, Levi sensed the spirit's luminous pastel outline struggling to detach itself. He recalled Hiro telling him that sometimes the spirit remained tethered to the body, particularly when death came suddenly or the identification with the physical was too strong. Separation would happen eventu-ally, but in its own time.

THE SUN WAS ALREADY SMUDGING the haze surrounding Brisbane's skyline by the time the reports were completed, filed, and the body wheeled away. Bureaucracy always has a complicated and ongoing relationship with death.

Levi paused at the nurses' station, Eric's letter tucked inside his jacket, heavy with indecision. Eric had seemed so desperate to have Levi deliver it. It was against protocol, particularly as there were no known relatives. Levi wasn't sure why he'd agreed other than the desperation he'd witnessed in the man's eyes. *It's just a letter. Likely an apology too difficult to be spoken about.* Levi understood that; he'd even made a business out of it. The Last Word specialised in making, storing, and delivering post-mortem messages by text, video, or voice.

The matron saw him waiting at the desk and came over. 'Thanks for getting here so quickly, Levi. I realise you weren't supposed to be on roster tonight.'

He shrugged. 'I know what it's like. I'm only thankful I could get here in time. I assumed that the other Death Watchers all had urgent call-outs.'

The nurse's lips pursed before she added, 'Why, no. The patient asked for you by name. That's why we called you. I thought you knew.'

2

Chapter Two

The envelope stood on Levi's desk, leaning against the crystal bowl where he'd dumped his keys, wallet, and phone.

The unknown leaning into the familiar. Master Hiro would have remarked on it, as a way of underscoring a recurring theme in Levi's life.

Levi had been tempted to open the envelope as a way of dispelling the niggling feeling of having been manipulated. In the end, though, discipline had prevailed, electing instead to skate the narrow edge of uncertainty, of not knowing, his long legs sprawled over one of the padded arms of his favourite chair.

The only address:

Sara Montgomery c/o Misty Lady—*at mooring off Macleay Island* written across the front of the envelope in a perfect cursive script.

Macleay was one of a group of small islands just off the coast, midway between Brisbane and the Gold Coast. Anywhere else in the world, the islands would be webbed to the mainland by white arching bridges, becoming a mecca for millionaires and multiple marinas.

Instead, Levi remembered the islands as attracting those who valued separation and a quieter life, while there were others who remained islands unto themselves, desiring only to disappear below the near horizon, removed, yet not entirely cut off. There were no bridges.

He wondered where Sara Montgomery fitted in this. What could be so important that an old man would use his last breath to implore Levi to deliver the envelope personally? He could easily have used a courier.

And why pick me to deliver it for him?

He sighed and slid his legs to the floor, then used his phone to tap up the ferry timetable to Macleay Island.

Chapter Three

'Sara, it's Deb. There's a guy down at the ferry asking about you.'

Sara's fingers tightened around the phone, her eyes automatically darting to Maddy, who was happily playing with her dolls in the fore-peak. Sara lowered her voice. 'Who is he?'

'No idea. I was here collecting the day care kids from the Russell ferry and I overheard him say your name. It sounded like he had a letter or something for you.'

'A letter? What'd he look like?'

Sara could sense Deb's shrug through the phone.

'I dunno, tallish, well built, maybe late thirties, early forties. Really dark hair, rugged-looking, but kinda cute in a bad boy sort of way, if you get my drift. He's wearing jeans and a purple tee. Anyway, I thought you'd want to know.'

'Yeah, thanks.'

'Oh, and Sara.'

'What?'

'He was using your real name. Plus, he knew the name of your boat.'

Sara's hand trembled. She tried to keep her voice even. 'Thanks for the heads-up, Deb.' She clicked off, tugged out Tony's old binoculars from their cracked leather case, and scampered up the companionway. Tripod, roused from his sleep, followed, ears pricked and growling, sensing her heightened tension.

'Quiet boy, it's all right—I think.'

Kneeling in the cockpit, she brought the binoculars up and focused them, staying low.

Who is this guy, and how the hell does he know my real name? Not to mention how he found me. Misty Lady *is still registered under Tony's company.*

She scanned the foreshore. It was scattered with a variety of upturned skiffs and small tinnies used to access the yachts moored mid-channel.

There!

The bright flash of a purple tee stood out against the dun-coloured sand. She watched him push one of the tinnies to the water line, pausing only to kick off his shoes and toss them into the bottom of the boat before springing in when it was floating freely.

Beside her, Tripod growled again and scrambled up onto the moulded cockpit seat. Sara tracked the man, watching him fit the oars into the rowlocks before settling into an easy pull parallel to the long line of yachts moored in the centre of the channel. He appeared to be reading the names of each as he passed.

What to do? It's too late to run, even if I could sail the damn boat. Hide, so he'll think we're ashore? She eyed the inflatable dinghy bobbing on its painter at the stern. *No, too obvious we're not. Damn.*

When close enough, she watched him ship oars and cup a hand to his mouth.

'Ahoy, *Misty Lady*.'

Tripod barked once, as if in response.

~

LEVI HAILED THE BOAT AGAIN. The dog barked. It was black, with a German shepherd's muzzle and what looked to be a heeler's body. One massive front paw was draped over the rail.

The boat looked to be a forty-footer, white fibreglass, with two oversized helms on either side of the stern. A grey awning shaded the rear cockpit. The hatch was open, and an inflatable dinghy was bobbing on a line, so he imagined someone was at home.

A woman stood and trained a pair of oversized binoculars in his direction. He hoped it was Sara Montgomery. She looked to be in her mid to late thirties, with long brown hair that hung in a broad curtain around the binoculars. Levi used the heightened energetic senses that Master Hiro had helped him develop, sending a psychic enquiry towards the yacht. It returned, bouncing back like a sonar signal, bringing with it the bitter taste of suspicion, fear, and past trauma all roiling around beneath a thin layer of poorly applied bravado. There was also a strong wave of protectiveness, which he assumed was from the dog, and surprisingly the faint waft of innocence. He would have to use care in how he approached.

She put down the binoculars and brought a hand to her brow, shading her eyes against the glare bouncing off the water. 'What do you want?' Her voice carried easily across the space between them.

She didn't sound scared, but Levi knew that could be learned.

'My name is Levi Monk. I'm looking for Sara Montgomery.'

'I'll let her know you were here.'

Levi felt dismissed. His small dinghy was drifting, the current carrying him closer.

A small freckled face framed by red curly hair peeked through the woman's broad stance, one hand on either leg. 'Mummy, who's that?'

Ah, there's the innocence I picked up, and maybe the protectiveness was not just coming from the dog. It was like Master Hiro always said, emotions are energy; it takes time to sift through the layers.

Levi heard the woman speak to the child, her tone snappy. 'Maddy, I told you to wait below.'

'But he can't be bad, Mummy. See, Tripod isn't even barking.'

The little girl grinned at Levi, revealing small white teeth. She tilted her head to look up at her mother. 'Tripod only barks at the bad men, doesn't he, Mummy?'

'Maddy.' Her voice ratcheted up a tone.

Levi saw an opportunity. 'Your little girl is right, and if it means anything, so is the dog. I'm not here to harm any of you, only deliver a letter.'

'A letter? What are you? The water post?' A hint of amused relief flickered across her face.

'No. Just someone who made a promise to a dying man.'

She stared at him for a moment then pointed at the stern. 'You can tie up there. My dog may not be barking now, but he'll attack if I tell him to.'

Levi nodded and rowed around to the stern, lobbing her a line that she secured to a cleat on the yacht. He clambered over the transom, and she waved him to one of the moulded benches lining either side of the cockpit. The dog jumped down and sniffed Levi's legs before flopping at his feet, head resting on his one front paw.

'I see where he gets his name from,' Levi said, sitting down.

'He was in a fire,' the little girl said.

'Maddy. Go below, please.'

'But Mummy, Tripod–'

'Maddy. Now.'

The little girl turned, stomping her protest down the wooden steps. Sara came to stand in front of him, arms crossed, bare feet planted wide.

'So, who is this dying man?'

'Was. He's passed now. The name I knew him by was Eric. Eric Layton.'

Her lips firmed into a thin line before she spoke. 'Then you can keep whatever it was he gave you and row on back to wherever you came from.'

Levi held up his hand. 'Hey, I'm just the messenger. I was simply there when he died. Getting this letter to you—I assume that you are Sara?'

She nodded begrudgingly.

'Well, it seemed to be very important to him. He had it hidden inside the lining of his coat. I had to cut it out.'

'Are you a friend of his?'

'No. I work with the hospice. They call one of us to sit with the dying when there's no one else. It's distressing to die alone.'

'Not as distressing as having to live that way.' Before he could comment, she added. 'Monk, you said? What is that? A name or a vocation?'

He smiled. 'My name is *Levi* Monk. I'm part of a group who volunteer at the hospices and hospitals. We're called transitioners or final companions. We're part of a larger association called Death Watch.'

'Death Watch? Who are they? Some sort of God-bods?'

'God doesn't have all that much to do with my reasons.'

Sara looked down, the long curtain of hair masking one side of her face. It swung, as if undecided. Levi had a curious urge to lift the hair back out of the way, as if to reveal what it was hiding. From what he'd already seen, she was attractive with wide-spaced green eyes, a broad forehead, and cheekbones that lent a uniqueness to her face.

She glanced up sharply and caught him studying her. Levi had the disturbing feeling that the woman was far too sensitive.

To distract himself, he dug through his backpack and dragged out the letter, holding it out.

She backed away a step and sat on the seat opposite. 'You read it. I'd not trust him to give me the time of day; nor am I about to start taking anything from him now that he's dead. Go ahead. Read it out. Then you can say you did your, whatever you called yourself, Death Watch duty.'

'You want me to read your letter? Out loud? It could be personal.'

'From him? Never. Go on.'

He cleared his throat. 'Very well.' He ripped the top of the envelope and drew out what was inside, looking at it oddly.

'What is it?' Her voice was curious. Levi stared at the card, the torn envelope slipping from his fingers.

'It's a greeting card. It's one we use in my business.' He held it up.

She angled her head to read the printing on the front. '*The Last Word.* What, like "the" last words? You're really into death, aren't you, Monk?' She paused for a breath, then added, 'I thought you said you didn't know him?' The suspicion was back.

'I don't. My business is all online. People make recordings of their voice or video and upload it to my site. We send them instructions on how to access the record inside cards like this so all they need to do is get someone, usually their solicitor, to deliver it after their death. Whoever receives it then logs into our site, and the audio or video is available to download. Usually they're nice messages, things that people couldn't bring themselves say in life. Requests for forgiveness, statements of love, that sort of thing. What's curious for me in all this is that your friend Layton asked for me by name. At the hospital. And now this. I don't get what my involvement in all this is.'

'He obviously knew you.'

'It seems like it.'

'Well, let's hear what he has to say.' Sara said. 'I have a satellite connection if you want to log on, or in, or whatever you do.' She dragged an iPad from a waterproof pouch tucked next to one of the large steering wheels and passed it across. Levi opened the card and quickly loaded up his site, tapping in the code from the card. 'You may need to be over here to see it.'

She came to sit beside him, the iPad resting on the seat between them. Levi clicked Play, and the wasted features of Eric Layton appeared. Sara jerked away, though whether this was from the man himself or how he looked, Levi couldn't be sure. The date stamp running along the bottom of the screen read 16 November, only days before his death. Eric coughed wetly and began speaking.

"Hello, Sara. Long time no hear and all that. I won't apologise. Don't worry, this isn't some plea for forgiveness from the other side. I'm guessing you wouldn't accept it anyhow." The emaciated form gave a weary smile. *'I want you to collect something for me. Pull it off, and there's money to be had. For you—and Maddy.'* He coughed again, pausing as he struggled to catch his breath. It was painful to watch and took Levi back to the hospice earlier that morning.

Levi spied Maddy's wide green eyes peeking over the lower edge of the open hatch. She must have crept up the steps at the mention of her name. She brought her forefinger to her lips. Sara was angled away from the hatch, towards Levi, staring down at the screen, the corners of her mouth drawn back as if she'd inadvertently swallowed something distasteful. Levi nodded imperceptibly to the child, and she crept out, her movements low and slow like an oversized cat. Tripod's ears twitched toward the sound of the movement, but he didn't move from Levi's feet. Eric's voice continued.

'There's a guy called Hiro. Monk—I assume he's there with you— knows where to find him. Hiro said Monk has some... special talents. I guess by now, you'll be thinking "stuff you and your fucking favour, Eric," but you will do this for me, Sara, because if you don't, you'll only have a couple of months to live. What I'm infected with, what made me look like this so quick, has been impregnated into the envelope you just opened. Direct skin contact is the only way it can be passed on. It's very specific. The good news is that there's an antidote— you'll find it with the items I want you to retrieve. The choice, as I see it, is pretty simple: do what I ask and live a long, comfortable, rich life, or ignore me and you'll be dead before Easter.'

The image went black.

'Sick, perverted bastard.' Sara spat the words, shouting at the iPad. 'Well, your little trap backfired this time, buster, because I didn't touch your bloody envelope.'

A cold numbness crept up Levi's spine. 'But I did,' he said, staring at his fingers.

Sara turned to him, her expression moving from outrage and triumph through dawning awareness to apology. 'Look, don't worry. It's got to be a mistake. I mean, he's a bastard. Not only that, he's a *mean* bastard, but this? It's a new low. He was just a glorified drug dealer, for God's sake. Thank God he's dead.'

Neither said anything for a moment until Levi slowly became aware of a low humming.

His gaze tracked it automatically, and with a cry he bounded to his feet.

Sara, startled by his sudden movement, turned to see what he was looking at.

'Oh, God no.'

Maddy, cross-legged on the deck, quietly hummed, the small space between her eyebrows crinkled with concentration as she folded and smoothed the edges of the envelope into smaller squares.

4

Chapter Four

Levi bent to retrieve the folded envelope. Maddy stared up at him her mouth forming a small O. He ruffled her springy curls. 'Sorry, sweetie, I'm going to need this.'

Sara's face drained of colour, caught in the transition between shock and anger, the pieces of meaning refusing to join. It was all too incomprehensible. Finally, she spoke, pointing at Maddy but facing Levi. Her voice was pitched low, trembling with suppressed menace.

'You did this. You came here and did—this.'

'Please, Sara. Just wait. Remember you said yourself that we don't really know if it's true—'

'Just go. Now.'

'Sara—'

With a cry, she released the line tethering Levi's tinnie to the yacht and flung it at him.

'I said *leave*.'

Levi took a breath. It felt like a lifetime since he'd stepped aboard; so much had happened. So much had changed—for all of them. Even his movements as he leaned over the transom were slow as reality thunked home. If Layton was telling the truth, he was now dying, and what's more, his carelessness would also cost Sara her daughter. *Who was Layton? Is this real, or some mind game from beyond the grave? And what role does Master Hiro have in all this?*

Turgid emotions swirled within him: anger, regret, guilt cascading over one another. He drew the tinnie close and clambered in, using an oar to push off and back into the channel.

Sara stood at the rail, Maddy crushed to her chest, the child's legs hooked around her waist. Maddy's tiny face twisted in a tangle of confused emotions, unsure what she'd done to cause this.

Levi allowed the tinnie to drift. He felt drained. He stared back at *Misty Lady;* the tide was turning and now was slowly drawing them apart, yet they remained inextricably linked by events. Even Tripod seemed to sense it. The dog had clambered up onto the seat and was peering at Levi from beneath the rail. He cocked his head and gave a single inquisitive bark.

Levi began a slow stroke. With each pull on the oars, the two figures on the deck became smaller, the moment stretching between them, Sara shouting and shaking her fist. It took him several moments to realise that she was not raging but signalling furiously for him to return. Confused, he rowed back and tied up again. When he stepped aboard, no one spoke. It was as if they were replaying the previous scene in the bizarre hope that this time it might end differently. Only Tripod appeared pleased to see him, settling once more with a whumpf at Levi's feet. Sara took the seat opposite and drew Maddy onto her lap.

'The dog seems to like you,' she said finally. 'You're the first man he's approved of, much less taken to. That carries some weight.'

'I don't know what to say. Other than to emphasise that this could just be a dreadfully cruel joke. Some sort of payback on Layton's part. I desperately hope it is.'

'That's why I need you to give me that envelope. I want to have it tested. You took it when you… left.'

Levi nodded and pulled out the folded envelope from the breast pocket of his shirt and went to hand it across to her, pulling back his hand with a jerk. 'Sorry, I wasn't thinking. Do you have someone to do the test for you?'

She shook her head. 'Not really.'

Levi had thought as much, 'I do. He's quick and thorough. If you're okay with that?'

Levi sensed confusion forming a cloud around her. *She doesn't know whether to trust me. No, not just me.*

Finally, she nodded. 'All right. Yes. I wouldn't really know where to start.'

Their conversation was like taking turns in chess, using life-sized pieces, each move slow, requiring an effort. He glanced away, catching Maddy staring up at him with big eyes through tousled curls. He realised she hadn't said a word since he'd come back on board. An awareness slid through, and he softened his voice.

'Don't worry, Maddy. You've done nothing wrong. None of us here has. No one is mad at you. All right?' Levi tried a grin. Kids were sponges for other peoples' emotions. Anything they didn't have a reference point for often ended up in the box marked "my fault." Levi could personally vouch for that one. Maddy managed a brief smile in return.

Sara gathered the child up and bent forward to whisper in her ear, the curtain of hair re-creating the barrier. Again Levi sensed that it was hiding something. There was something about Sara that was troubling him, yet given the circumstances, he could only imagine what Sara must be going through, even if the threat wasn't real. *What a sick fuck Layton must have been.*

Sara stood. 'I'm going down to get Maddy something to eat.' She added begrudgingly, 'There's tea... in the galley. If you want.'

Tripod followed her down the steps. The dog appeared to have a three-legged technique that straddled a bounding hop and a controlled slide.

Levi stood and stretched, checking his body. He didn't feel any different. *How long before I notice anything, or is it really just some sick joke?*

Idly, he watched another ferry tie up at the jetty. It had come from the opposite direction, and he remembered the woman in the ticket office telling him that the ferries ran in a loop around the four islands to the mainland, alternating direction. He was about to go below when he noticed a man dressed in a black suit getting off. Unlike the rest of the disembarking passengers, he wasn't dragging a trolley or manhandling shopping bags, but running up the metal jetty empty-handed, looking around wildly as if searching for someone. He looked familiar. Levi picked up the binoculars and zoomed in. Earlier, when Levi's ferry arrived, he'd been daydreaming and almost missed the stop, only managing to disembark at the last moment. He vaguely remembered the man in black had tried to follow but it had been too late. Levi lowered the binoculars and narrowed his internal focus, sending a psychic probe across the water towards the man. Anger rolled back, like heat from a massive fire front, and Levi recoiled. The man took one more frantic look around and ran on, threading his way through the car park. Levi picked up the binoculars once more to watch the man stride up the hill. He had the distinct feeling that whoever the guy was, he was looking for him. He replaced the binoculars thoughtfully and went below.

The galley was compact. Nestled in the forward section was a corner banquette with white leather cushions flanking a polished wooden table. Opposite, a dinette provided two single seats. The hull's sides were reserved for recessed shelving finished in the same red polished wood as the tables. Many of the shelves were stacked tight with books. Above them long, narrow windows provided natural light. A door leading to the bow area was closed, as was another to the left. The air smelt slightly stuffy, overlaid with the smell of recently fried food.

Levi eased himself onto the banquette, nodding. 'Nice fit-out.'

Sara, in the galley, put a kettle on the stove with more force than was necessary. She leaned into her arms, hands against the bench, staring down. After a moment, she straightened and poured some juice into a cup, passing it to Maddy along with some biscuits.

'Sweetie, why don't you take your snack into the front cabin while I speak to Mr Levi about boring big-people things?'

Maddy looked like she might protest, but with a hint of a pout opened the forward door. Levi turned and gave her a grin as she entered what looked like the master cabin, built into the bow.

'I'm making tea. Do you want some?' Sara's voice sounded tired, or resigned, as if she'd decided on something. Or maybe Levi was reading too much into the determined arrangement of the tea things. He turned to face her. Tripod slurped noisily from a steel bucket mounted in the corner opposite the galley. Levi's mouth suddenly felt dry. 'Yes. Thanks.'

Sara brought everything over on a small tray. Two chipped mugs surrounded an old-fashioned teapot snugged inside a woollen tea cosy.

'This looks loved,' Levi said, touching the wool. 'My grandmother used to knit these. I remember she had one with red and yellow bands around—'

'Tell me the truth. Do you think Maddy is infected?'

Levi continued to stare at the teapot, buying time. After a moment he looked up. 'I'm hoping not. But you know Layton better than me. What sort of guy was he?'

Sara's hands came together, the fingers interlacing until they were clenched, white-tight. Her nails were short, enamelled with clear gloss. Levi noticed the one on the right index finger was bitten down. With what seemed an effort, she pulled the fingers free, placing her palms flat on the table as if deciding something. 'He's Maddy's father.'

Which was a bit like saying that the *Titanic* was a ship. Technically true but taking no account of what came afterwards. Levi had already sensed in her immense emotional icebergs, untold tragedy, and somewhere, buried beneath the sunken wreckage, incalculable loss, though of what he wasn't sure.

He waited in silence, meeting her gaze, drawing on his training, offering, he hoped, enough support and encouragement for her to continue. She looked away and picked up the heavy teapot, using a strainer atop her mug. Levi imagined it filtering out any leaves that might be tempted to form a patterned narrative of her life on the sides of her mug. His granny used to read tea leaves, and she'd often said he had the talent too. Master Hiro had echoed that and worked directly with it, apparently. Both of them, as far as Levi was concerned, had a curious interpretation of "talent."

When she spoke, Sara's voice was low and quiet. 'Eric Layton sold drugs, and not just in a small way. He was a major dealer. I was a... model, of sorts, back then. To a girl looking to escape the burbs, Layton was a catch: rich, exciting, and kind of dangerous. We were in Sydney together until I realised what he was really doing.'

Levi thought about the wizened old man in the hospital bed.

As if picking up on it, she added, 'He didn't look like that then. I didn't even recognise him on that video clip. He was always so conscious of what he looked like. It was one of the things that had attracted me to him. But that undercurrent in his voice was the same. I'd recognise that smarmy tone anywhere.'

'How old was he?'

She shrugged. 'Early forties, maybe. I don't know really. That was the thing—I could never tell when he was lying or not. At the beginning, I kind of liked that. It added to the intrigue and gave me permission to smudge the boring bits of me as well.'

'It must be some illness for him to end up looking like that so soon,' Levi mumbled, imagining the same bugs transiting to their new home inside him. 'He doesn't sound the type to let anyone just decide to leave him. Is that why you changed your name?'

She gave a disgusted snort. Her gaze was fixed on the teapot, but its focus was inward.

'He wasn't the forgiving sort, if that's what you mean. I tried to run. Lots of times, but he always found us. It became a kind of a game to him. He would delight in showing me who was in charge every time his thugs brought me back. Forcing himself on me. Maddy was the only good thing to come out of my time with him.'

'But you obviously managed to get away, eventually.'

'In the end I went to the police. I had plenty to tell them, but the prosecutor had been up against Eric and his barristers before. They needed hard evidence, so I managed to convince his accountant, Tony, to come over as well. He'd had enough of Layton too, and he was sweet on me. I used that. I'm not proud of it, but I was desperate. We all went into protective custody while they put the case together. They promised us new identities under Witness Protection, and to relocate us, as a family, to some other city.' Her wide mouth stretched to a sad smile. 'Right back where I'd started, the life I'd been trying so desperately to escape: living in the suburbs, hooked up with an accountant with a gorgeous kid in tow. Ironic, don't you think?'

It wasn't a question that needed answering.

'What happened?' he pressed.

'What else? Eric's people found us. They firebombed the so-called safe house we were in. No half measures for Eric. Both floors went up. I'd set Maddy up in the lounge room with a picture book while I made hot milk in the kitchen. Neither of us had been able to sleep that night. Sensitive kid; she always has been. This has all been really tough on her.'

Tears formed in the corners of her eyes. One escaped and trickled down her cheek unchecked, her gaze tracking inwards again. Levi felt her hurt cut deep and had to stop himself from reaching out.

Sara sucked in a ragged breath and went on. 'Tony was upstairs when it happened. He died in the fire. I could hear him screaming, trying to get to us through the flames. In the end he must have thrown himself out one of the bedroom windows, but by then it was too late. The fireman said his body was still smoking when they found him.'

The tears were flowing freely now. Levi poured more tea into her mug, adding a couple of sugars. The trauma was still real for her. He nudged the mug over, and she automatically picked it up. She had to use two hands to get it to her mouth.

'But you and Maddy obviously made it out okay,' he said, his own thoughts scrambling, trying to piece this all together. *What's going on here? And what's Master Hiro's involvement in it?*

The tone of her voice was flat as she answered, as if she were reciting. 'The downstairs firebomb came through the dining room window, between the kitchen and the lounge room. When I opened the kitchen door, there was fire, floor to ceiling. It was roaring, like it had a voice. At the time I could almost swear it was Eric's. It separated me from Maddy. I tried to get to her—over and over—yelling at her to run to the front door, but she was terrified. I could hear her sobbing and coughing, calling for me. Then someone, the guy from the house next door, burst through the kitchen door and dragged me outside.'

'And Maddy?'

Sara appeared not to hear him, the scene still playing in her mind.

'I ran around and tried to open the front door. The firemen stopped me. I fought. Bit someone, they told me later, as I tried to get past them back into the house. What I didn't know was that the upstairs fire had worked its way down and had blocked off the front. Maddy was stuck in the lounge.'

'How did she get out?'

'There was a cellar. It opened off the hall.'

'And Maddy got herself down there?'

Sara shook her head, looking over at the dog flopped beside his water bowl, her gaze kind. 'No. Tripod did.'

'Tripod?' Levi asked, the disbelief heavy in his voice. The dog started at the sound of his name, ears pricked, eyes watchful and wide.

'He was a stray when we found him. He started hanging out at the house, so Maddy fed him. She loved him on sight, and as so many things in her life had been upturned, I didn't see the harm. I even had a dog door put in down to the cellar where he slept on a pile of blankets. The firemen found them both there afterwards. That's how

Tripod lost his front leg. It was damaged so severely in the fire, the vet couldn't save it.'

'Yet, Maddy was unharmed.'

'That's the strangest thing. Maddy says Tripod had dragged a blanket up from the cellar. I don't know about that, but Maddy said she put it around herself and held Tripod's tail while he led her back to the cellar door.'

'What?'

'I don't care if it's true. If that's how Maddy wants to make sense of it, that's fine with me. So now you see why this dog has such a big influence around here. He started whimpering when you were rowing away. I trust that dog's instincts more than I do most people. Any people, for that matter. Including me, sometimes.'

Levi's mind struggled for a rational explanation and gave up. Strange things happened. He of all people knew that.

'And afterwards?'

Her brow creased in the middle, and she looked at him strangely.

'What do you mean?'

'Well, Layton obviously knew you were on this yacht. Did he try again?'

Sara shook her head. 'Without Tony's evidence, the police didn't have enough to make a case. I rang Eric and told him we wouldn't make any more trouble if he left us alone, and for some reason I'll never know, he agreed.'

'Why would he do that?'

'Why did Eric do anything? He is—was—totally unpredictable. A psychopath, I suppose you'd call him. He could be charming, then in the next instant horribly sadistic. He knew I couldn't hurt him without Tony's evidence and that the police were watching us, waiting for him to do anything. Maddy and I were too visible. I wanted to think he backed off because of Maddy, but they barely knew each other. I'd tried to keep them apart as best I could. Not that it was hard. Eric had no time for kids, even his own. I don't know what made him back off in the end, and quite frankly, I didn't care. I disappeared and drove us both up to Queensland under a false name. This is Tony's yacht. I should have known Eric wouldn't just drop it. Now I've seen that video, I realise he must already have been sick with that disease, too sick to do anything, and now he's given it to Maddy.' She paused. 'And you.'

He nodded, but more questions were lining up. 'How long ago was this?'

She shrugged. 'Two months. Before the fire, Tony gave me the keys to the boat and told me to meet him here if anything happened. It's owned by some shell company he set up. "Untraceable," he said. He always talked about sailing up the coast to the reef.' She grinned. 'Kind of a honeymoon, he called it, after Eric had been put away.'

'Did you love him?' The words fell out. Levi felt his face colouring, and he looked down at the tea things. 'I'm sorry, that's none of my business.'

'No. It's not.' She paused before adding, 'But here's something that is. What's your involvement in this, and who is that man Layton mentioned on the message? The one you are supposed to know. What was it—Miro something?'

'Hiro. Master Hiro, he's called.'

'And what is he a *master* of?'

Levi glanced back to check whether Maddy's door was still closed and cleared his throat.

'He's my mentor and teacher. As to what he's a master of, I guess you could say he specialises in speaking with the dead.'

5

Chapter Five

The next day started late for Sara.

Levi had stayed until the last ferry, promising to call as soon as he had any news on the test of the envelope. After that, she hadn't slept well and had spent most of the night trying to convince herself that all this was just another one of Eric's endless mind games. Yet she would never have imagined even he would go to this extreme. It was just way too bizarre and for what purpose?

She'd found out the long, hard way that you couldn't reason with Eric, but he must have been sicker than even she had thought. The only good news was that he was dead, so once Levi confirmed there was no contagion, she and Maddy would be able to go home.

Sara finished stacking the breakfast dishes and stared out through the narrow windows in the galley.

Where is home now anyway? Sydney? A birthplace doesn't necessarily make it home. All that's waiting for me there are really bad memories. No family. Maddy is all of that now. No, now we'll need to find someplace else to call home.

She heard the burbling drone of a large boat passing and automatically adjusted her weight as its bow wave lifted the yacht.

Some place that doesn't roll and pitch underfoot would be a good start. Yachts may be fine for a break, but as somewhere to live, forget it. But then I'm no sailor, not like Tony.

She filled the sink, sudsing up the water.

Funny how I arced up when Levi asked if I'd loved Tony. What does love even mean anymore? I thought I'd loved Eric—once—what was that? Infatuation? Excitement? Lust certainly, and, if I'm honest, more than a sprinkling of fear. How could that have been love? With Tony, it was the opposite. He cared—both for me and Maddy. He was there for us, literally, to the end. When I suggested he turn against Eric and come with us, he didn't hesitate. Was what I was able to offer in return enough? Was gratitude enough? And if it was, why do I feel so guilty when I think about what it finally cost him?

She washed the dishes, wiped down the galley bench, and squeezed the cloth into the sink, wishing it were as easy to sop up her guilt.

Levi was a mystery too. Everything about him seemed long—not gangly long, more like a coiled spring—powerful and contained. There was a sadness too around his brown eyes, like they'd already seen too much but were determined to remain vulnerable, still willing to take on more, and that intrigued her. It lent his face an openness that inspired trust, accentuated by a broad forehead made more prominent by startlingly black hair.

Where Eric had been all ego-strut and Tony was deferential, Levi gave the impression of quiet, strong confidence.

Until he started talking about that Hiro character. The "speak to the dead" master. Does he honestly believe all that? Obviously he's eccentric, possibly/probably weird. And what is it with him and death? He seems so hung up on it. Maybe he's just as crazy as Eric but in a different way—yet Tripod didn't react to him, and Maddy seemed to actually like him.

Sara left the dishes to drain, calling Maddy as she adjusted her wig in front of the small mirror. Her scalp was acting up today. She gingerly lifted the edge of the wig, revealing the angry, puckered skin on her scalp, and applied some hydrocortisone cream. The skin felt hot and rough beneath her fingertips, as if the flames that had caused it were still inside trying to burn their way out to finish the job. She'd been lucky. A miracle, they'd called it. With a breath, she settled the wig back and fluffed out the overly long brown wave on the left-hand side. It wasn't vanity so much as the need not to explain, to not see the pained looks or, even worse, not be seen at all in the studied see-past way reserved for the handicapped, homeless, or mentally ill. She turned away from the mirror and called to Maddy again. 'Come on, sweetie, get your bag. It's time to go to Debbie's.'

Maddy bounced out of the forward cabin, Tripod in tow. Sara helped her slide her arms through the pink backpack straps as she swayed, laughing. It was Thursday, one of the two days that Maddy went to Debbie's. Debbie was one of Sara's few friends on the island and ran a home day care. It was small, safe, and most important, Maddy loved going. Continuity was vital to kids, and while there hadn't been much of that in Maddy's short life so far, Sara was determined she would have it, and this was the start. She followed Maddy up the steps, calling over her shoulder.

'Tripod, stay.'

The dog slumped onto the floor below, his big eyes following them as they disappeared through the companionway hatch.

AN HOUR later she was shopping in the island's small grocery store, a carton of eggs in her hand. Her phone rang.

'Sara. Hi, it's Levi Monk.'

'Yes.' Her heart started thumping.

'Where are you?'

'Why?'

He was silent for a moment. 'Are you sitting down?'

Her chest tightened. 'It's real, isn't it? Oh God, no.'

'We don't know. Not yet. My guy says that there are spores on the envelope, but that proves nothing other than its fungal and not a virus. He needs more time to test, but he said based on the morphology, whatever that is, it doesn't look good. A potentially virulent strain, he called it. I think for now we have to assume the worst and that Layton was telling the truth.'

The eggs fell to the floor, spattering her sandalled feet. Sara's knees sagged, and she reached out to the display stand for support.

'What?' She could barely get the word out. Nothing was going in.

She heard Levi take a breath through the phone. When he spoke again, his voice was careful and kind, his words widely spaced.

'Sara. The tests came back on the envelope, and there are active spores on it. My guy has to run more tests to determine what they are, but I think we need to treat this threat seriously.'

'Maddy?' Her voice caught on the single horrible possibility.

'Is possibly infected. As am I. We need to do as Layton said and go see Hiro. See what he knows. I'm going there now. Do you want to meet me? He lives in the Valley.'

'No...'

'All right then, I'll—'

'No, wait. Yes. Yes, of course I'll come. I need to. God, I can't believe any of this.'

Someone from the store had appeared with a mop and bucket and was trying to clean up the splattered egg mess. Sara shuffled out of the way, her mind a flurry of thoughts threatening to bury her like fine volcanic ash. She straightened, firming her shoulders, abandoning the half-filled shopping trolley mid-aisle.

'Text me the address. I need to catch the next ferry.'

FORTITUDE VALLEY WAS in the final stages of transition from "better by night" seedy dives to trendy urban living, yet there were still whole blocks that the redevelopers hadn't touched. Hiro lived in one of these, pocketed between Chinatown and a glass-and-steel urban mall. The walls surrounding the simple wooden door were tagged all over, yet the door itself remained unmarked, free of graffiti. It lent the entrance a pristine feel. Levi pulled on a heavy chain hanging from the wooden archway. From inside, Sara heard a distant bell, its tone heavy, like that of an old-fashioned school or small church.

A camera mounted in the upper corner between the door and wall swivelled to take them in. Levi waved, and the door swung open, revealing a small, enclosed courtyard paved with black polished marble. In the centre was a round fishpond complete with large orange and white carp. Levi ushered Sara through, and the door closed softly behind them.

'This is a containment area. It's only big enough for a small number to enter at any one time.' He pointed up to a small camera in the corner. 'Hiro doesn't like surprises.'

A reluctant clunk followed, and a door on the opposite wall released from its jamb. Levi pushed it open and stalked through, Sara following.

It opened directly into a garden, Japanese inspired, a clever combination of smooth carved stone, water, and wood. It was quiet here, the noise from the constant traffic outside somehow shielded so that the only sound was water falling on itself from a small waterfall. It fed a meandering stream that divided the space, both sides joined by an arched wooden bridge. Seated on a large flat rock beside the waterfall was a man who seemed oddly out of place. Dressed in tight, none-too-clean jeans, checked flannel shirt, battered sweat-stained Akubra hat, and scuffed R.M. Williams riding boots, he looked like he'd come off a six-day cattle drive in Central Queensland and hadn't had time to hit the showers. He stood when they approached, grey eyes narrowing as he studied her.

'Master Hiro, this is the lady I spoke to you about. Her name is Sara.'

The man touched the brim of his hat.

Sara remained standing, hands moving to her hips.

'My daughter—'

Hiro held up his hand, cutting off her words like traffic at an intersection.

When he spoke, the words crunched from his mouth like boots through gravel. 'Levi told me. I'm sorry, and just so you know, I'm infected too, so I'm just as anxious as you that we get this fixed and do what he wants.'

'What does Layton want?' Levi asked.

Sara cut across Levi. 'We need to tell someone about this! Get help? There must be some cure that a university, or specialist doctors can come up with—'

Hiro slowly shook his head. 'To have a cure, this—whatever it is— has to have already been discovered. It hasn't. The spores of this thing are old—so old they might as well be brand-new. You saw what happened with Covid; vaccines or cures take time to develop and even more money. Even if we could find someone to do it, by the time they unpicked it and work up a batch of anti-whatevers, we'll be all be as stiff as this rock here.' He tapped the seat.

'I don't understand why—'

Hiro leant forward, large calloused hands gripping his knees. 'There's a time for whys, but not now. All right?'

A surge of heat flushed through her cheeks. 'No. It's not all right. We should go to the police. I want to save my daughter.'

Hiro's mouth drew down, forming small dimples at the corners. 'I know you do, and believe me, so do I. But what would we tell the police? That a dead man wants us to retrieve something for him, and to make sure we do, he's infected some of us with stuff that no one has ever heard of. That will all only burn through time and come to nothing, believe me. Time is our enemy here.'

Sara opened her mouth to say more, but Levi came in first.

'Layton said you would know where this thing he wants is.'

Hiro dug a battered tobacco pouch from his pocket and sprinkled some of the finely cut leaf onto a cigarette paper. He glanced up at Levi before running his tongue along the edge of the paper to seal it.

'The things he wants are called orbs. There are two of them, but no, I don't know where they are, but I—' He scratched a match to life and held it to the cigarette. It caught, flaring briefly. Hiro exhaled blue smoke through his narrow nostrils and licked his lips, daintily plucking a speck of stray tobacco from his tongue. '—I do know where we can find them.'

'Where?'

'Why don't we all go inside? It's getting hot out here.'

Hiro pushed himself to his feet. The man was a head taller than Levi, who already overshadowed Sara. Standing beside the older man's wiry frame, she felt like a child.

Hiro led the way, loping over the arched red bridge. They followed a weaving stone path through the garden to a low wooden deck adjoining the house. Hiro sat on the step, pinched out the glowing end of his cigarette, and tucked the stogy into the top pocket of his flannelette shirt before tugging off his boots and settling them neatly beside him. Levi took off his shoes too. Sara, fuming, kicked off her sandals too, still tacky with broken eggs, before following the two men inside.

It took several moments for her eyes to adjust from the brightness of the garden to the gloom. When they had, she realised that Hiro was no longer there. 'Where's he gone?'

Levi leant towards her and whispered, 'I should have told you. Hiro tends to come and go a lot. He's also likely to change every time you see him. It's best not to mention it.'

'Change? What do you mean? His clothes?' She barely recognised her own voice but intimately knew the anxiety crouching beneath the words.

Before Levi could answer, Hiro's voice rumbled from deeper inside the house.

'Come on through—better watch your step. Levi, you know where to go. Sorry about the light.'

While it had the same raspy tonality, Hiro's words sounded different, as if they were coming from a different-shaped mouth, more precise somehow. Levi led the way. The only light glowed from oil lamps set into moulded sconces that were mounted onto walls of polished timber panelling. As her eyes adjusted further other shapes emerged from the gloom. Low tables, but no chairs. Large, brightly coloured tapestries on the walls were woven with strange motifs that in this light appeared almost three dimensional. In other places, weapons, like an Asian sword, were mounted on a stand, seemingly more for ease of being snatched up rather than display.

From the dark corners she also had the disquieting sensation of unseen eyes staring out from the darkness, watching her. A shiver of something slithered up her spine.

'What is this place?' she hissed at Levi's back.

He stopped and swivelled to face her. When he spoke, his words were deliberate and quiet. 'Hiro's house is a bit of a maze. I know that sounds weird, but you can get lost in here. Hang on to the back of my shirt if you like, but make sure you keep up. I know where we're going. I've been here many times.'

They began walking again. Sara resisted the urge to snatch a handful of his shirt tail but kept close regardless. Despite the heat outside, in here it was almost too cool, the air undisturbed and close— like a crypt she'd visited once in Rome. In contrast, the smooth wooden floor remained warm against her bare feet.

An arched doorway loomed before them. Levi paused.

It was sectioned off by a heavy black curtain.

'We have to go through there,' he whispered. 'Best take my hand for this part.'

He reached out, and she reluctantly gripped his hand. It felt warm and rough.

'You don't have to hang on quite so tight.'

Sara consciously forced her fingers to relax a little. Her heart was pumping pure fear-fuelled adrenaline. 'Sorry.'

The edge of the heavy curtain fluttered, but there was no breeze.

Levi stepped forward, his hand rising to where the curtain was moving, and gently, as if testing the temperature, eased his fingers through. Seemingly satisfied, he followed with his hand, forearm, and finally upper arm. Again, he paused.

'Ready?' His voice sounded strained, as if he was struggling to lift a heavy weight.

'For what?'

'Don't let go of me.'

She felt his body move forward, his hand tugging her behind him. When her hand entered the space behind the curtain, it was like it had been plunged into icy water, yet the rest of her body remained at the ambient temperature of the outer chamber. She felt disoriented, as if she were in two places at once.

'Levi?'

He kept moving, easing himself further in, drawing her after him like the bobbing inflatable behind *Misty Lady*. Her mind leapt to Maddy and what would happen if she didn't return. Who would look after her?

'*Mum?*'

'Maddy?'

Maddy's voice was in her mind. It had to be. Maddy was safe back on the island. But she sounded so real, so close. Now Sara's upper arm and shoulder were immersed in the frigid coldness. Involuntary violent shivers overtook her, and she felt her grip on Levi's hand loosening. It was too cold to keep hold of it. She drifted. The brush of the velvety curtain against her face felt alive. There seemed to be no other side to the curtain, just a gauzy half-lit space that travelled on and on forever. And so cold. It stripped away everything, even the artifice and filters of everyday, until all that was left was an essence, something true and pristine. Her hand floated free. She was lost, insubstantial, yet somehow found too. A curious feeling of absolute freedom within the chilling, biting coldness seeped in, right down to her bones. And then gradually she became aware of a single patch of warmth returning, enveloping her hand. It felt strong, drawing her forward, like being towed through thick, viscous fluid. And she was out. Just like that. Dry and warm, the coldness sloughing from her beneath the light. Relief and a strange regret surged through her. She spun about. The edge of the black velvet curtain flapped shut, as if drawing itself together. Levi was standing in front of her, still holding her hand. She tried to speak, her mouth opening and closing until it found the words.

She pointed. 'What the hell was that?'

Levi released her and shrugged, his gaze apologetic. 'I told you not to let go.' He motioned behind him, and she looked over.

While the hard, sharp planes of Hiro's face and penetrating grey eyes were the same, the outback outfit had gone. In place of the jeans and hat, he wore an impeccable navy suit, pale blue silk tie, black socks, and shiny black shoes. Even his greying hair was brushed and styled back from his forehead. His mouth, top lip lined by a razor-thin moustache, held a slightly amused expression, as if daring her to say something. He looked up at her from a brown leather armchair, one of those big, winged, wrap-around numbers so popular in movies showing English men's clubs. She was still finding it difficult to say anything. When he spoke, Hiro's voice was inflected with an affected English accent, though a hint of the gravel-grate tone was still beneath it.

'My apologies. It's always difficult the first time, but I've found that trying to prepare one for it is as useless as trying to describe a Mozart sonata to someone who is deaf. They need to experience the vibration of the passage for themselves. It is different for everyone, as is music. Why don't you come over here by the fire and warm yourself, my dear. You look half frozen.'

Levi led her to the fire and slipped an oversized glass into her hand—a brandy snifter, one part of her mind told her. Inside its bulbous bowl was a brown spirit sloshing against the sides as if anxious to escape.

'Drink some of this. You'll feel better,' Levi said.

She lifted the glass to her mouth, the small opening butting against her nose, the warmed cognac releasing its aroma well before the spirit touched her lips. She drank rather than savoured, feeling the warmth worm its way through her insides.

'Better?' Levi asked. He looked concerned.

She nodded, handing back the glass. There was a sensation of landing, as if she'd been a in a hot air balloon that was in the process of being securely tied down.

Levi indicated the matching leather chair on the opposite side of the fire, positioned to face Hiro. She sank into it, feeling its comfort wrap around her. Levi chose to stand, his back to the fire. Before either of them could say anything, Hiro spoke.

'What you've just experienced, Sara, is what I like to call the in-between. Other belief cultures might call it limbo, or the bardo—but in simple terms it is the place between life and death.' He held up a finger as Sara was about to protest. 'No, Sara, it's better if you wait. This will make much more sense if you do.'

Levi nodded reassuringly at her before taking a deep inhale from the brandy snifter cupped in his hand.

Hiro continued. 'Levi asked me earlier if I knew where these orbs that Layton wants are, and I said no, but I knew where they could be found.' He lifted his hands and smiled at both of them, as if displaying something extraordinary. 'Well, this is the jumping-off point. Here we have time, because here, in the in-between, there is none. We are suspended, as I said, between life and death. If we stayed here all day and then went back through the veil, you would find that only seconds had passed. It doesn't matter if you believe me; I say this only as a means of reassurance because what follows will seem like many days, but if you are fortunate enough to return, then you will still have ample time to go collect your daughter from her day care.'

'What do you mean "if" we return?'

Hiro raised his eyebrows and shrugged.

6

Sara stiffened in her seat. 'I want some answers, or I'm going to leave. Right now.' She made to get up.

Levi came over and crouched in front of her, placing his large hand on her forearm, looking up into her eyes. 'You can't leave. Not yet, anyway. The passage,' he indicated the curtain behind him, 'takes time to settle. Why don't we hear what Hiro has to say first, and then if you still want to leave, we'll go. I'll take you.'

She remembered the feeling of the thick dry fluid, the sense of lostness within the drifting. She didn't want to experience that again. Not on her own. Tears welled at the corners of her eyes.

'I want to get out of this madhouse. Out of this horrible nightmare.'

'I know.' Levi glanced over at Hiro, a hard look in his eyes. 'And we will. I'll make sure of it. But you're here because of Maddy and what might happen to her. You didn't want to take that chance, remember?'

Sniffing, she nodded and wiped her eyes with the back of her hand. Levi handed her a folded linen napkin from the side table. She dabbed her eyes and tried to settle herself, failed, and lied, nodding anyway. 'I'm fine.' She faced Hiro, her voice steely, 'Well? What are these orbs he wants me to find?'

'The orbs are spheres about the size of a tennis ball. Made from gold and precious stones, very valuable—and not just for their monetary worth.'

'What use are they to Layton if he's dead?' Levi asked.

'One of the orbs represents life, the other eternity. It is said that once united, they can overcome death. Layton wants to be reborn, or reanimated, he called it.'

'Are you serious?' Sara spluttered.

'Quite, and considering that this is Maddy's only chance at survival, you should be too,' Hiro snapped.

'Should I now?' Sara sat forward, eyes narrowing. 'Do you honestly think I'm not? Maddy is my daughter, after all, so what I want... no, what I need to know right now is whether these damn things will cure her, and if so, how?'

Hiro stiffened as if he'd been struck. 'All I can tell you is that the ancient texts all agree. The orbs absorb and concentrate the life force that constantly swirls around us: prana, chi, qi, whatever you want to call it. Somehow the orbs beam that into the body, replenishing the cells and expelling any disease and toxins. Whether it will also reanimate Layton's dead flesh remains to be seen. But in answer to your question: Yes, I believe it will cure Maddy. And me.'

Levi cleared his throat. 'So putting reanimation questions aside, how do we get hold of these orbs?'

'I know where one is, and there is a map that provides directions to the other.'

'A map? To where?'

'Not so much to "where" as to "what." The map shows the way to the second orb. Layton was bringing the orb back when he heard that some of his own people were planning on stealing it, so he hid the second orb and created the map, presumably so he could go back later and recover it. However, he became sick soon after. You saw him. He was incapable of going anywhere and obviously couldn't trust his people to do it for him.'

'So where's the other one of these orbs?' Levi asked.

Hiro's dimples deepened, 'When Layton approached me, he told me to "hide the first orb and the map to the other where no one other than Sara can find them." Not even I know where they are.'

'I don't understand. How could you hide something and not know where you put it? This is making no sense,' Sara said.

Hiro glanced at her from under his hooded lids, saying nothing.

'Who are these people of Layton's you keep mentioning?' Levi tried.

Hiro sighed. 'Part of his cabal.'

'Cabal? What's that?' Sara repeated.

Hiro gazed into the fire as if he was listening to something.

'Hiro?' Levi prompted.

After a time, Hiro turned to face Sara. 'I don't know how much you knew about Layton, Sara, but he and his cabal sought power. Layton particularly had an obsession about obtaining it. That's how he came to me in the first place, several years back. I turned him away then.'

Sara was confused. 'Layton was just a drug dealer. People were terrified of him, and he was rich, but I don't know if you'd call that power.'

'Power runs much deeper than wealth or influence. They are only consequences of it. True power comes from using the will to shape the basic elements of nature and so bring about transformation. It allows energy to be manipulated that can then be used to change, create, or destroy.'

Sara straightened, her nostrils flaring as if smelling something objectionable. 'That sounds like magic.'

'Magic is a simple way of describing it. Believe me, it is far more intricate and layered than that. To call what Layton practised "magic" is like naming the ocean "water." It takes no account of its breadth, depth—or the inherent danger, because Layton and his group chose to follow the left-hand path, raising what some might call dark magic. It requires blood sacrifice to bring about transformation and is quite addictive. Hence the interest of his former cabal in these objects.'

Sara sat back into the chair, her mouth falling open. *Magic? These people are crazy. How could I have imagined they might be able to help Maddy?* Yet, memories intruded: locked rooms in Layton's house where she wasn't permitted, weird noises at night, screams sometimes, and afterwards, a terrifying, wild look in Layton's eyes when he returned. Once she'd glimpsed him emerge from the cellar with his hands and arms covered in what she now thought might have been blood. *Could any of what Hiro is suggesting be true?* She thought about the weird sensations coming through that curtain, that feeling of floating, drifting... even this maze of a house.

As if in answer, Hiro said, 'I appreciate that this all must seem very strange to you, Sara, and I cannot make you believe any of it. Nor do I wish to. Things are, quite simply, as they are. It's important for you to know, however, that despite being under Layton's influence, you still managed to break free from him, many times. You have a strong will. It's one of the reasons he chose you for this task.'

'But I don't understand why he would choose me at all. I hate him. He knew

that.' Sara thumped the cushion on her chair. 'God, *how* I hate him. Now, even more.'

'Most people did. And that's just it. He had no one else. That is why he spared you after the fire. To do this task for him. He told me you'd be coming to retrieve the orb and map. I gave him Mr Monk's details to facilitate that, not realising that I would be responsible for Levi becoming infected as well. Not to mention your poor daughter.'

Blame hung heavy in the air. No one said anything.

Levi broke the silence. 'Surely Layton can't be, what did you call it, reanimated?'

Hiro sighed heavily before answering. 'Part of my pact with

Layton was to tether his essence to the physical body until I could extract it. I have no idea whether the orbs can restore his essence to life.'

'His what?' Sara asked.

'Call it spirit or consciousness. He believed that once the two orbs are reunited, they will have the power to return him to life if the ritual is performed within three months of his death. I arranged for his corpse to be brought here. It's still in the cold store out the back.'

'That explains what I saw in the hospital,' Levi said quietly. 'His spirit appeared to be tied to the body, unable to move on.'

Sara was stuck on the shuddery idea of Layton's corpse laid out somewhere in the house. She laughed and shook her head, convinced now she was caught in a crazy nightmare. Someone else's. Surely, she couldn't have dreamed this up on her own?

Hiro turned his hypnotic gaze on her. She felt pinned to the seat. 'In order to be reanimated, his essence must be preserved in the in-between. Where we are now. Once it passes on, it is too late.'

'I don't believe any of this,' Sara said.

'The good news is that you don't have to. Beliefs are like the wind, Sara; they can change direction in an instant depending on the pressure systems around them. For this to proceed, your belief is not required. Larger forces will be at work.'

'What forces?'

'Layton had me hide the map and the orb where no one other than you could ever find them. I embedded them in what you might think of as a parallel or perhaps created world.'

'A what?' Sara spluttered.

'Consider it another stream of life operating at a different vibration to our own. Just because we can't see it, doesn't mean it's not there.'

'How will she get back?' Levi asked, seemingly unmoved by the news.

Hiro grinned. 'I've developed something which I call virtual enactment. It's similar to virtual reality, only the experience is fully lived. Essentially, Sara, you will be in two places at once. Your body will remain here, but your awareness will be in the other. You will have no memory of *here*, or even why you're *there*.'

'Sounds crazy,' Sara said.

Levi seemed hung up on the process. 'But if Sara has no memory of why she is there, how will she find this orb and the map?'

'She won't. I have set it up so that they will find Sara. However, I must warn you, Sara, that nothing else in that world is predetermined.'

'What do you mean?' Sara asked.

'Life, with all its myriad array of choices and consequences, will continue. Whatever happens inside that experience will also manifest here, in your physical body. Break a leg whilst in that state,' he tapped his thigh, 'then it will fracture here in this reality as well.'

'That's what you meant before when you said "if I return," isn't it?' Sara asked, not really wanting to know the answer.

Hiro's nod was solemn.

Levi shot to his feet. 'Are you kidding me, Hiro? You're saying Sara could die inside... wherever it is that you send her?'

'It's possible, yes,' Hiro said. 'But then she could also die walking across the road outside this house.'

'Then send me instead. Sara has a daughter to look after.'

'Noble as always, but unfortunately, Sara must be the one. The items are already tagged to her energetic signature. Neither the map nor the orb will respond to you, Levi.'

'Then I'll go with her. If there are two of us, there's a better chance anyway.' He left the rest unsaid.

Hiro sighed. 'That would be up to you. And Sara, of course.'

'I couldn't let you do that,' Sara said.

'It's already done. If I'd known what was in that letter'—he shot a glance across at Hiro—'or if I could change anything now by taking you back through that curtain, then I would. This way at least we'll be doubling our chances of one of us making it back with those, those things.'

'There is one further point,' Hiro said.

They both stared at the older man. 'If you both do go through in addition to not remembering why you are there, you will also not have a memory of the other... unless...'

'Unless what?' Sara spat out. This was like one of Layton's mind games, and she didn't like it.

'Unless there's a linkage. Something that connects your two fates. In this instance, it would have to be the spores.'

'But I didn't touch the envelope,' Sara said.

'No. But for the linkage to work, you would have to.'

'Now wait a minute, Hiro,' Levi said, jumping to his feet. 'This is all moving too fast. You're asking Sara now to, what, voluntarily infect herself?'

'No. I'm not. I'm saying that for you both to go that's the only way it will happen; otherwise you run the risk of having completely separate experiences.'

'I don't understand any of this.' Sara shook her head. 'Levi, you said you'd take me out of here. I want to leave. Now.'

Hiro leaned over and tapped her on the knee. 'As I said earlier, you are welcome to do that, Sara. The way is now open, but remember, this may be the only chance Maddy has, not to mention Levi and me. For what it's worth, I agree with Levi. There is a much better chance of one of you returning with the items if both of you go.' He sat back. 'But that is a choice only you and he can make. I've told you what it requires. The rest is up to you.'

Hiro's words whirled around her like so many satellites. She glanced at Levi, her heart racing with indecision and fear.

Hiro stood and stretched. 'Why don't I leave you two alone for a moment to talk about it? Call me when you've made a decision.' He made his way to a frosted glass-paned door at the rear of the room. He opened it and slipped through. The door closed behind him with a quiet click.

Levi came over and crouched beside her chair once more, his brown eyes sad.

'Sara, you can't infect yourself. It doesn't make sense.'

'No, what really doesn't make sense is for me not to do everything I can to save Maddy. If that means infecting myself so that it doubles the chances of bringing whatever these things are back, then I will.' Her gaze drifted to her lap; her voice when it came was quieter. 'Just before, I had a flash of what it would be like to sit by and watch Maddy die—slowly. She's all I have. If she isn't going to make it, then I don't want to either. Did your friend give you the envelope back after it was tested?'

Levi nodded.

'You'd best give it to me then.' She held out her hand.

Levi's eyes searched hers. 'You're a brave woman, Sara.'

'No, that's just it. I'm not. Not brave enough to watch Maddy die and then live on without her.'

He reached into his jacket pocket, then handed her the envelope.

Sara held it up between her thumb and forefinger, studying it for a moment. With something approaching resolve, she placed it between her palms and rubbed them together before handing it back.

'There. It's done.'

'Shall I call Hiro back in?' he asked.

'No. Not yet. I need a couple of moments. I find him quite intense.'

Levi grimaced. 'Hiro is eccentric, I'll say that, but he's also the real deal. I've worked as his assistant for the past couple of years. He's the original go-to fix-it guy. If you want something done or changed, then he's the man. I imagine that's why Layton came to him in the first place. In another century, Hiro would have been called a mage. What I do know is that he deals a straight hand. If he says we'll be back in time for lunch from wherever we're going, then I believe him.'

'If we don't die first.'

His smile faded. 'Well, there is that, yes.'

'You said you were his assistant.'

Levi paused before answering. 'Yes.'

'What do you assist with?'

He pushed himself to his feet and wandered back to the fire.

Sara persisted. 'Look, I don't know anything much about you and even less about Hiro. You're asking me to trust you both with the life of my daughter, and if you haven't picked up on it already, I don't do trust all that well.'

'Hiro is helping me develop particular skills and deal with the... consequences of others.'

'Such as?'

Levi was having trouble standing still. He paced. 'My work with the dying, for one. He's teaching me how to transition them.'

'Transition...?'

He hesitated, watching her face.

'You can tell me,' she prompted. 'It can't be any weirder than any of the other stuff I've heard today.'

'Some people find it difficult to pass over with peace into whatever next stage they move to. I am learning to help with that. I think of it as a kind of penance.'

'For those "consequences" you were talking about?'

'Spot on. I'm not proud of my past. I used to work Special Forces before following the money to a private security group contracted to the US military. "Deep cover strategic targeting," they called it. Assassin for short.'

'You killed people for a living?'

'That's what happens when you put on a uniform and have to take orders. It's the bit they don't mention in the recruitment ads.'

'That's awful. Were there... many?' Sara could see the pain scoring the corners of Levi's eyes and could only guess at what they'd seen.

He let out a deep sigh, squatting, elbows resting on his knees as he stared into the space before him.

'Does it sound worse if I say I don't know? Not exactly. But there were lots. I can't seem to see them all, not at the same time. They come at me in ones and twos, usually in the middle of the night, their faces looming out of the dark, their expressions not accusing exactly, but it's like they're looking for something, some reason, I don't know. It nearly sent me nuts. That's when Hiro found me, or I found him. I remember waking up in one of the bedrooms here, inside this crazy house. He gave me stuff to take. It took the edge off, and we started working from there. I owe him a lot.'

'So you trust him?'

'Yes. I do. Having said that, it was Hiro who gave my name to Layton, so while I trust him, he also works at different levels simultaneously. He sees the macro transposed over everything and keeps track of all the consequences each change will bring, so if something gets in his way, well, don't take it personally.'

'Like a yacht on a collision course with an aircraft carrier?'

'Yeah. Exactly.' His voice sounded hollow and distant, his attention caught on some unresolved hook.

He looked so alone, but Sara resisted the urge to reach over and touch his shoulder.

He glanced at her as if intuiting her impulse and shook his head. Another wry smile appeared, perhaps signalling he was okay.

What is it about this place? It seems to telegraph intent.

'Will Maddy be okay at day care?' she asked. 'Hiro said that time in this place is elastic, but I can't get my head around that. I mean, the woman who runs the day care centre is a friend; she'll look after Maddy, and I've been late picking her up before. Sometimes the ferries are delayed if there's weather. Maybe I should call her, just—' Sara knew she was rambling.

'There's no phone reception in here,' Levi replied, deadpan, his eyes wide with concern.

'Oh, because we're in the *in-between*, of course there isn't any reception, how could there be? Otherwise dead Uncle Henry could dial us up and—'

Levi cut her off. 'I can ask Hiro to leave a message with your day care friend back on the island that you may be late. How does that sound?'

Sara sucked on her bottom lip, as if to stop the words tumbling out. She gave him Deb's number, and Levi walked over to the glass-paned door and rapped twice. When it opened, she could hear him talking quietly and a muffled reply from outside. The door closed again.

'He'll only be a minute. There's another access to the house that way. It's a little rougher, but its transit time is much quicker. The phone call will take him a few minutes, so he told me to take you through to the next room. That's where this whatever it is, is going to happen.'

Sara, her stomach squirming, followed Levi through the door. It opened into a dim hallway, doors lining either side. More of the peculiar oil lamps were mounted sporadically.

'Electricity doesn't seem to have reached Hiro's house.' Sara reached out a hand, trailing her fingers along the wall's smooth surface.

Levi chuckled. 'It's something to do with the electrical field. It interferes with his work in this section of the house. Here we are. I think this is the one.'

'Are you sure? All these doors look the same.'

'I've been here a few times. Don't worry.'

He led the way through. Sara, cautious, remained in the doorway examining the room. Three of the walls were filled floor-to-ceiling with shallow wooden shelves, each stacked with a variety of ceramic bowls all seamed with curved slashes of lustrous gold.

In the centre of the room was a single piece of furniture, a high table, less than a metre square. Intrigued, Sara entered, examining the strange assortment of ceramic graded by size, from large salad bowls down to the small cups used for Japanese tea. In all cases, the broad gold slashes faced out, capturing and enhancing the warm glow from the lamps.

'What are all these?' she asked, lightly touching one of the gold-seamed bowls.

'The goldwork is called *kintsugi*. It makes an art form of imperfection through mending old broken ceramic pieces using a resin and powdered pure gold burnished to highlight the break line.'

Sara noticed one shelf nearest the floor held only shards, but even they were meticulously arranged, as if they'd burst apart like ripe fruit, their concave surfaces facing up, baring the vulnerability cupped within their sharp brokenness.

'There is a rich philosophy behind *kintsugi*—'

A tiny squeak from the old timber in the hallway interrupted Levi. They both turned as Hiro glided into the room. He had changed again. Now he was dressed in a floor-length robe slashed with gold, similar in look and lustre to the bowls lining the shelves.

'Ah, good, you found your way. Sara, I spoke to your friend and told her you've been delayed. She said to say your daughter is enjoying herself. I gave her my number just in case.' His voice had lost the affected accent but retained the same gravelly tone.

'Thank you.'

'Now we begin.' Hiro rubbed his hands together, the sound rough like two sheets of fine-grade glasspaper. He moved to the high table in the centre of the room. Waving them over, he positioned Sara and Levi on opposite sides of the table, then stood between them, gesturing behind him at the bowls lining the shelves.

'Mr Monk has undoubtedly told you something of these?'

Sara nodded.

'I have broadened the ancient *kintsugi* practice to incorporate relationship. Those relationships that are broken and wish to be re-joined, as well as those that, for whatever reason, need to be established. Each of these bowls has been dropped by a couple. I then attempt to re-join the pieces, seaming them with gold. If successful, this allows each to acknowledge and appreciate the imperfections of the other and move on. After that, they are bonded.'

'What about these on the bottom shelf?' Sara pointed. 'The ones in pieces.'

'Some relationships resist opening to the vulnerability required and cannot be joined.'

'So how does any of this help us find the orbs that Layton were talking about?' Levi asked.

'Shortly, I will give you both something to drink. You can think of it as a cross between a hallucinogen and edible software that will allow your awareness to separate from the body, which as I said, will remain here. I'll then bind you to the appropriate parallel world through a *kintsugi* ritual.'

'I don't like the sound of any of this,' Sara said. 'What about Maddy? What if something happens to me, over... wherever? What will happen to her?'

'Something already has happened, Sara.' Hiro's tone was patient. 'This,' he indicated the shelves around them, 'represents her only chance of saving her.'

Sara shuddered, silently cursing Layton again. On the other side of the table, Levi looked almost as conflicted.

'What is this *kintsugi* process?' Sara's voice was tight.

'Ah, good question, Sara. Allow me to demonstrate.' He reached into his cloak and withdrew a plain white bowl along with a thin-bladed knife. It looked sharp.

'Levi, give me your hand.' Hiro placed the tip of the knife on Levi's thumb pad. 'Now, I'll make small incision.'

A drop of crimson formed on the tip of Levi's thumb.

Hiro guided Levi's hand back, and a large droplet plopped, then rolled slowly down the curved inner surface of the white bowl.

Releasing Levi's hand, he pulled a small pad of cotton wadding from his pocket. 'Hold this tight until the bleeding stops.' He moved his attention to Sara.

After a moment's hesitation, she raised her hand, resting it against Hiro's open palm. There was a brief sting as the knife tip pricked her skin. Blood swelled to either side of the tempered steel. Hiro positioned her thumb over the opposite side of the white bowl. Unlike Levi's, her blood flowed boldly down the concave inner surface to join the rest.

Absently, Hiro handed her some of the cotton wadding. Careful not to disturb the scarlet pattern inside, he picked up the bowl.

'Now both of you, over here.' The pair followed him to the far corner of the room as he continued. 'The mixing of the blood in the bowl ensures you will both join the same parallel experience, while the spores ensure that you will be connected throughout even though you won't know or recognise one other.'

'I still don't understand,' Sara snapped, becoming frustrated.

Infuriatingly, Hiro smiled and patted her hand. 'Trust is both as strong as a steel cable and as delicate as a strand of gossamer in a web, Sara. Only you have the power to break it. What do they say nowadays? Ah, yes. "Trust the process." Can you do that?' He fixed his intense gaze on her and she felt exposed, but also strangely seen.

She finally answered, surprised at her honesty. 'I don't know.'

He stared at her for another moment before saying, 'Then you will find out.'

'Hiro, how do we get back?' Levi's tone was as dry as if asking for directions to the closest servo. Sara desperately wanted to know as well.

'The needs of your physical body mean that this experience will only last a certain amount of time, which is unpredictable. You'll return when needed, regardless of whether you have recovered the items or not; however, as it progresses you will become aware of a deadline emerging. This will match how much time you have left. In an emergency, I may be able to bring you back if you exhibit signs of having integrated too far.'

'What do you mean?' Levi asked.

'Sometimes the psyche becomes too entrenched in the experience and consciousness will not return to the physical body.'

'You mean we'll be stuck wherever with our bodies still over here?' Sara's voice pitched high.

Hiro nodded. 'It's possible. Until the physical body dies from dehydration, anyway.'

'This gets better and better,' Levi said. 'I think you'd better give me that magic juice, Hiro, before I change my mind.'

Sara's mouth was dry. She mentally repeated, *This is to save Maddy's life. This is to save Maddy's life.* Anything else—any other thought—would only send her running from the room.

Hiro took a bottle from the shelf behind him. The liquid inside captured the flickering light from the lamps, appearing at once green, then blue before becoming a bright flashing combination of both. He poured a measure of the liquid into two of the small Japanese teacups and handed one to each of them.

'Drink it all.'

Levi tossed it down.

Sara stared into her cup. The blue-green shade was mesmerising, the viscosity difficult to judge. It looked thick on top but moved easily at the sides. It had no discernible smell.

'You must drink it, Sara. Otherwise your body will transition as well, and I won't be able to bring you back.' Hiro's voice sounded a long way off. Her hand moved towards her mouth. It was like watching herself from a distance. The cup touched her lip, tipped, and the liquid trickled in. Swallowing. No taste but a squirming sensation of something swimming.

'What?' Hiro was saying something, holding out the bowl with the blood in it.

Surely he's not expecting me to drink that too?

'Hold your hands out and bring them to the level of your chest. Sara, allow your fingertips to touch Levi's.' His voice was muffled, as if coming from inside a hollow tree.

Hiro rested the bowl into the nest formed by their outstretched hands.

'Meet the bowl with the fullness of your heart. Allow everything you feel for each other, me, and Layton to flow into your fingers.'

'Layton?' Sara said, startled.

'We are here because of him, and we are all linked by these spores.'

Sara jerked her hand back. Hiro caught it and encircled one of her wrists. 'If he is over there, you won't know, but his energy may seem vaguely familiar. Someone to avoid.'

Sara registered a distant knocking. From the look on his face, Levi did as well, but Hiro seemed to be unaware of it.

'One.'

The knocking became more urgent. Levi looked around the room.

She saw the tip of Hiro's tongue travel along his upper lip, like a snake taste-testing for danger.

'Two.'

The knocking became more insistent. She wanted to ask what it was, but her tongue felt too thick to form the words.

'Three. Separate your hands.'

Their hands moved apart in unison. The bowl appeared to hesitate before surrendering to the fall, shattering into two large pieces and a succession of smaller ones, some smeared and splattered with red.

Sara felt herself falling as well, not so much down but into something. Moving towards the knocking. Getting louder.

7

Chapter Seven

The sounds at the door became an aggressive pounding. She heard someone yelling in the corridor outside, the words distorted through the thick oak.

Sara swore.

Where are my ladies? Remembering then that she had dismissed them earlier, chasing them out like so many clucking chickens, she swept in from the wide balcony, holding her skirts in one hand, the other reaching for the key hooked to her waist by a red plaited cord.

'Wait a moment,' she shouted, her voice imperious enough to quieten the noise outside.

The lock was stiff. She hadn't had cause to use it since Anthony's death six months previous. Finally, the large key clunked home, and Sara jumped aside as the heavy door burst open, travelling on its hinged arc to thump against the stone wall behind.

Nicolai stormed in, all outraged drama and snapping cloak.

'Grand Duke Nicolai. How good of you to make an appointment.' She could get away with the sarcasm when they were alone.

Breaking court rules didn't matter when no one was there to witness it.

'I received your note,' he said, spinning on one of his expensive heels to face her, flinging the parchment to the floor. It lay there, as impotent as the message it contained.

'Excellent. Then there is no need for any further discussion.'

'Sara. Your refusal is unacceptable. I demand that you be reasonable.'

'Reasonable?' Sara closed her eyes, measuring her words. 'My husband—your brother—has only been dead four months. How can you ask... how can you demand this betrayal of his memory? I am still in my widows' robes.' She touched her black gown.

'And I wouldn't if it weren't a matter of urgency. You know that. But there have already been skirmishes along the border. Invasion is imminent, and you're the only one who can prevent it.'

'How? By marrying a man—a beast, by all accounts—that I have never met?'

'Yes. But he is a beast with a large army,' Nicolai countered, the corners of his mouth curling in the same supercilious way that her husband's had when silently relishing his own cleverness.

'You say that as if it is enough.'

'Isn't it? This is your country now. Do you want it to be enslaved? Its people tortured? The ruling class ridiculed? If the barbarians are permitted to reach the capital, they won't kill you—or me—or anyone with royal blood. Not straight away. They are said to have a taste for it. They believe the blood of their enemies gives them strength. They'll milk us, like cows, and in between punish and torture our children. Do you want that for Madison?'

'Leave my son out of this. He is your future king. Have some respect.'

'It is him I am thinking of. As his regent, it is my responsibility to ensure he continues to grow past his fourth year.' Nicolai paused, his voice dropping a notch. 'As regent, I can compel you. You do realise that?'

Sara trembled with rage and stalked out to the balcony. Nicolai had become unbearable since Anthony's death. He was like another person. Gorge rose in her throat. She centred her attention on the view before her. Temper wasn't what was needed now.

The city spilled in disorderly rows down the hillsides to the port. The wind kicking up from the distant harbour was cool, and she folded her arms, allowing her anger to evaporate and so quell the fear that threatened to break through. At this time of day, the breeze always carried the sweet overlay of decay and exotic spices lifted from the warehouses and open holds of ships bobbing at anchor. Other vessels, their hatches closed and topsails set, cut through the swell beneath the fort cannons, taunting her with faint hope.

Why didn't I escape on one of those ships when I could?

Down there, everything seemed so simple. The same as it had always been. People battling to survive, to find love and comfort where they could. It was only here, inside the palace, where greed supplanted need and threatened to overturn her world. *I should have returned to the mountains and taken Madison with me.* She turned and stalked back inside.

'I refuse to discuss this any further. I want you to leave my chambers. Now.'

The outrage welled up again. Later, there would be tears, but she would not give Nicolai the satisfaction of witnessing those. Not again. 'I will not be the mop for a mess you created.'

'What are you talking about?' he spluttered.

'If you hadn't raided the barbarians' lands, ransacked their crops, and killed their people, then perhaps they wouldn't be so intent on invading us now. You are the grand duke. You control the army and were entrusted with the Marshall's Key. That carries responsibility as well as reward.'

Nicolai's face flushed, and he took a step towards her. Sara wondered whether she'd gone too far and cursed again her decision not to flee the country when her ladies had urged her to. A widow's future was limited to either religious devotion, remarriage, or death. The only difference was in the colour, weave, and cut of the cloth.

He stalked to the side table and snatched up a crystal flask, sloshing red wine into a goblet. He quaffed it in one gulp, paused for a moment before placing it gently back onto the table. The quiet click as the glass made contact with the marble was loud in the charged silence.

Plucking a kerchief from his puffed sleeve, he brushed at a wine streak on his white vest. To Sara, it seemed like blood.

Finally, he spoke. 'You will leave the day after tomorrow. That should give you ample time to assemble your trousseau. I suggest the current fashion will not favour black.'

He strode to the door, removing the key that Sara had left in the lock. 'And do not concern yourself, lady. You will be well protected from now on. I have already posted men outside your door. We can't have our sacrificial cow getting hurt wandering around the castle before she's delivered to her new prize bull, now can we?'

His dark eyes remained cold, the corners of his mouth turning up. He left, closing the door behind him. Sara heard the lock turn and clunk from the outside. She stalked across the room, picked up the goblet from the table, and hurled it after him, its form shattering against the door.

8

Chapter Eight

Levi registered a distant knocking from the front door of the shop.

Ignoring it, he released the man's wrist, handing him a small pad of cotton wadding before turning to the young wife.

'Now you.'

The woman's lips firmed, more with resolve, Levi sensed, than disquiet.

After a moment's hesitation, she stepped closer to the table and raised her hand. Levi pricked the skin with the thin blade and positioned the wound over the bowl.

The old man was still in the corner, his focus riveted on the bowl. If not for the brilliant gold streaks slashed across the dark weave of his robe, he would have blended with the long shadows. A thick candle sputtered, bringing Levi's attention back, and he picked up the bowl, careful not to disturb the pattern of the blood inside.

'Stand here, at either side of the table.'

The pair shuffled into position, facing each other. She, calm, grey eyes seeking those of her husband; he, gaze slippery, sweat beading his upper lip. There was something about the young man that bothered Levi. His lineage was printed boldly on blue silk, sashed diagonally from shoulder to hip around his torso. The sash was pinned by an ostentatious silver clasp emblazoned with the crest of the grand duke. Though that in itself proved nothing. Many in the city wore the fealty seal.

Even Levi had. For a time.

Reluctantly, he acknowledged his rising dislike and recalled the old man's words: "You are an agent only. Your personal feelings are unhelpful here."

Levi glanced at the shelves of white bowls similar in size to the one before him. Most wore the marks of *kintsugi,* their broken joins seamed with gold.

'Take the bowl lightly—use both hands, bring it to the level of your chest. Meet it with the fullness of your heart. Allow everything you feel for each other, regardless of what that might be, to flow through your fingers. Imagine it filling the bowl,' Levi intoned.

The young man hurried to comply. He was nervous.

Levi lightly settled the bowl into the nest of their fingers.

'I'm going to count. When I get to three, I want you to remove your hands, opening them like this at the same time.' He separated his own in demonstration. 'The bowl will smash. It is vital that you release together. Do you understand?'

They nodded.

The knocking outside became louder, more urgent. The man's dark eyes darted, following the sound.

'One.'

It was important to allow sufficient time for the emotions to travel down the arms, into the hands and seep in.

The knocking became a pounding.

The old master, no more substantial than a dark shadow, glided past, his house sandals lightly slapping the wooden floor, black robe swirling about his feet. He slipped soundlessly through the beaded curtain, heading toward the front of the shop.

The young man's eyes danced after him.

What is going on?

'Two.'

The grating sound of the latch. The bell at the top of the door tinkling, offset now by a loud, authoritative voice. Levi thought he heard his own name. It was followed by the old man's high, piping tones.

'We have clients. The *kintsugi* ritual must not be disturbed...'

'Three.'

The couple's hands separated. The bowl smashed.

The beaded curtain clattered apart, its strings swinging wildly about the intruder.

'Levi Monk.'

The man was on the threatening side of big and wore authority like a too-small cloak.

'Levi Monk,' he repeated, louder this time.

'Yes. That's me.'

The man drew a crushed parchment from inside his straining jacket and thrust it at Levi. Taking the document, Levi flicked it open.

The script was elaborate, the letters small. The three candles in the treatment room were not up to the task, and he angled it to catch some of the full afternoon light from the front of the shop. The document seemed to be from the Bailiff's Office and was demanding payment of...

'This must be some mistake,' Levi spluttered.

The big man grinned, revealing discoloured teeth. They looked surprisingly sharp. 'They all say that. Failure to pay means you'll be indentured as a journeyman and on-sold to satisfy your debt.'

Levi looked at the man as if he'd spoken in an unknown tongue.

'You are not authorised to—'

'Your arm!'

The big man made a frustrated grunt and snatched Levi's hand, dragging it towards him, crumpling the paper. Levi tensed his powerful biceps but did not resist, instead going with the movement, readying his other fist to drive deep into the man's massive belly.

'Levi.' The old man's voice cut through Levi's conditioned response. He exhaled the stored tension away from his limbs and allowed himself to be dragged forward before saying, 'I repeat. You are not authorised. I am an invested noble. Only someone of rank can serve this on me. That is the law. I demand you release me.'

A look was exchanged between the bailiff and the young man at the table. Levi felt the movement of air behind him as the young noble moved to stand beside them.

'I am of rank.'

The bailiff drew what looked like a small club, or nightstick, from a holster at his belt and touched the end of it to the back of Levi's captured hand. The stick felt wet and cold like a slab of mortified flesh.

When he looked down, the back of his hand sported a stain of vibrant yellow. The colour was spreading under his skin. He knew what it was. Within an hour, it would cover him completely.

'The debtor's mark,' the young man said with satisfaction as the bailiff carefully reholstered the club. 'By order of the Grand Duke, Regent of Battavia, your debt is to be satisfied by midnight tomorrow. You are reminded that yellow skins are not permitted to leave the city. Any attempt to do so will see you immediately sent to market as a life indentured slave—not a fixed-term journeyman if the debit is not paid. Is that understood?'

Levi could only stare at the encroaching stain as it flowed past his elbow and up his arm, cold and damp.

'We understand.' The old man's voice filled the silence.

'Gino?'

It was the woman. She wasn't part of the trap. She hadn't known. Perhaps it was only now gradually dawning on her that the young man's agreement to be here today was a ruse and that the pieces of their relationship were destined to lie unjoined at the end of the shelves.

The master shuffled the two men back through the curtain, the woman bobbing in their wake. She looked back over her shoulder, grey eyes wide with fear and confusion before the beaded curtain closed behind her with a clatter.

The door slammed. The latch slid across. A final confused tinkle from the bell, and they were gone. Levi had a sense of his own future disappearing with them.

Chapter Nine

Levi shifted on the wooden bench leading to the audience chamber. Other petitioners on similar benches lined the opposite side of the palace's Grand Passage. Their resigned patience triggered memories of other times he'd been here in a different capacity. Memories he did not cherish.

'What's keeping him? The sun is about to set. We've been here for hours already.'

Beside him, eyes half-lidded, Master Hiro stared at a spot midway between him and the opposite wall. When the words came, the thin lips barely made space to let them pass.

'Patience is more than the ability to wait, Levi. It is how the time is met that counts.'

Levi exhaled and tried to settle himself. He wondered again at his suitability for the contemplative life and tried to focus his mind, managing only to replay the scene at the shop earlier in the day.

How did they find me? And as for the unfounded debt and this accursed yellow skin...

The elaborately carved doors swung inwards, and the grand duke's ageing personal assistant appeared. Levi straightened expectantly. He was the only noble waiting. Surely, he would be next. The personal assistant whispered something behind the back of his hand to one of the two guards flanking the doors before waddling down the corridor.

The guard took a step away from his post to announce, 'Petitions have closed for today. Everyone is instructed to leave the palace. Come back tomorrow.'

Levi bounded to his feet and stalked across the hall. The guard was not young but appeared fit. A sergeant. Whitened, raised battle scars bristled his hands. One of the fingers was stiff and bent off to the right, as if trying to escape the rest.

'Halt. Or you will be arrested, yellow skin.'

Levi kept coming.

'Levi.'

He heard his old master's thin voice piping behind him, but this time he ignored it. Coming back tomorrow would be too late. Levi knew how these things worked.

The other guard joined the sergeant. They took a wide stance as Levi approached, hands on the pommels of their swords, readied but yet undrawn. Nearing them, Levi feinted to the left as if he might dodge past. The two men lunged into the space where he ought to be, but instead Levi pivoted right. Catching up the sword arm of the grizzled sergeant, he whipped it up, then down and around, feeling a grim satisfaction as the shoulder joint popped. The sword clattered against the flagstones. Levi spun to confront the other guard, who stared in horror at the old sergeant staggering, calling for help—his misshapen arm hanging uselessly at his side. Before the second guard could draw his sword, Levi drove his fist deep into the guard's solar plexus. There was a whoosh of air and a strangled attempt to inhale before the man sank to his knees and doubled over, his breath drawn in with a laboured wheeze.

The remaining petitioners stared at the scene in front of them, a mute audience frozen by fear. They would cause no trouble.

Levi kicked open the double doors and entered, immediately closing them and ramming the stout bar into the doors' iron cradles. They were doors built to withstand invaders and palace intrigue. Nothing would be coming through them tonight without Levi's invitation.

Inside the audience chamber was dim. The afternoon sunlight that usually flooded through the wide windows to backlight the raised dais was muted red and bled into long angular shadows cast by the tall, intricately carved throne. The seat was empty, save for a red velvet cushion.

An agitated hammering and a babble of urgent voices floated from the doors behind him.

'Nicolai,' Levi yelled, the word swallowed by the immensity of the space. 'Nicolai! I know you're here. Show yourself.'

The scratch of a flint drew his attention to the massive fireplace built into one wall. The grand duke emerged from behind one of the high-backed chairs that flanked the fireplace, dusting his hands together. Behind him, kindling flared into life, licking at the heavier logs resting across the maw of the grate.

'I see the title that I gifted you with has not tempered your manners, Levi, any more than that rather striking new skin tone does justice to your wardrobe.'

'It was chosen for me. Yet another gift that I have to thank you for.' Levi paused in front of the grand duke, a mere sword's thrust from his chest.

The fire provided the only light inside the grand chamber. Its glow revealed one side of the grand duke's face, the other lost to shadow. So much like the man himself.

'And that is why you're here? Surely. Why else would you risk liberties so far beyond your station? Breaking into the audience chamber and holding your regent against his will. These are treasonous acts.' Nicolai smiled and patted Levi's cheek. 'But we are old comrades. Let's not allow titles or formalities to stand between us.'

'Titles didn't come between us when we were children, Nicolai, or even later when I did your bloody bidding.'

'Duty is an insatiable mistress, Levi. We are bound to serve her whenever she demands. Surely you still agree?' Nicolai moved back to the fire, using the heavy poker to move one of the larger logs into a better position.

Levi followed. 'I have no time for any of your convolutions, Nicolai. We *have* an arrangement. Keeping that is part of your duty to me.'

Nicolai straightened, the poker in his hand, his fingers gripping it like the hilt of a sword.

'No. We *had* an agreement. Until you disappeared, to become what? Some sort of mystical matchmaker?' He flipped the edge of Levi's robe. 'I gave you a title. It carries responsibilities.'

'To what? Murder strangers?'

'Enemies of the state.'

'Enemies of Grand Duke Nicolai, more precisely.'

'Same thing. Especially now.'

'Except, now you will need someone else to do it for you. Why have you done this?' He thrust out his yellowed hands.

'Sharelle came to me for a loan. Quite a large one. She wanted to make a new start for herself. In Samaria.'

'What? Don't tell me you gave it to her? You know as well as I that she is... unwell.'

Nicolai gave an exaggerated shrug. 'You could not be found, and she was in trouble. Debt collectors, merchants, even her landlord was after her. What was I to do? Besides, she offered your chop as security. It's as good as your signature, so I had my chancellor draw up the loan.'

'Sharelle is no longer my wife.'

'Then she should not have had access to your chop.'

Foreboding slithered through Levi's gut.

'She didn't.'

Nicolai's smile stretched across his cheeks. He dug through the purse at his belt and produced a wooden block. He turned it so that Levi could see the distinctive metal scrollwork at the base. It was unmistakably his.

'When did this happen?'

'Two, perhaps three weeks ago.'

Levi paced. Thoughts, turgid and dark, roiled through him, competing, overlapping each other. He could do nothing more for Sharelle. She had to help herself, and to do that she must sink to the bottom of her own misery, one tavern and gaming house at a time, as she ran from her guilt over Andrew.

Their guilt.

He stomped on the thought before its fibrous threads wound back through his head.

'How much did you advance her?'

'Ten talents.'

'What? My entire portfolio is only worth fifteen.'

Nicolai did his best to feign incredulity. 'That's what I thought, but secure enough, no less. I managed to retain your good name. I paid out all the debts before I advanced her the few talents that remained. However, that was then. Events have overtaken us all, and I now need the loan repaid. Tonight.'

Levi's molars ground together. 'You know I'm good for it.'

'Well, that's the problem, Levi, you aren't. Not anymore. I was examining the securities under your chop, and they are mostly in land, arable farmlands between here and the border.'

'So?'

Nicolai shook his head. 'You have been in isolation, haven't you? A war is looming. The barbarians are due to invade us within the next lunar, perhaps sooner. To reach the capital, they will have to ride across land—your farmland. What they cannot steal or pillage from it they will burn, leaving the buildings in ruins, the crops spoiled. Even if the Battavian army manages to drive them back, your land and the assets on it will be worthless for years to come.'

How had Sharelle known where he'd kept his chop? Or... perhaps she'd had some help. The realisation thunked into Levi, the pieces clicking and clacking into place. Each of them with Nicolai's face smeared across it.

'What do you really want, Nicolai?'

'Want?' Nicolai asked, setting down the poker. He wiped a smudge of black soot from his palm onto his white hose.

'I know you, remember? You don't take a shit without making a plan for how big the turds will be and how long they'll take to drop. So what do you want?'

The grand duke smirked, rubbing the well-cropped beard bristling the edge of his jaw.

'You. I want you, Levi.'

∼

SARA TUGGED on the bell cord for the third time, hearing again the distant empty tinkle from the small suite of rooms next door.

Where are they?

She hadn't seen her ladies since Nicolai had locked her in. Her face burned at the memory of his smug face. Did he really expect her to undress herself as well? This dress alone took two people to release the stays.

Outside, the night shimmered, speckled with light from the city sprawling beneath. The heavy evening drapes had not yet been drawn nor the fire lit, and Sara shivered, hugging herself. The heat generated by the argument with Nicolai had dissipated, and her lime crushed-silk day dress was proving totally inadequate.

The cold was coming early.

Earlier today, before all this had started, she'd pointed at the far ridges and commented that the higher peaks were already white dusted. It had reminded her of the times she'd accompanied her father to the northern boundary of their lands. Her mind travelled there now, where the cold would steal along the sheer rocky slopes to lurk in frigid patches of the high grazing plateau. The high-pitched calls of the shepherds who guided the famed herds of long-haired mammoths echoed off the rocky cliffs, down the ancient trails to the relative warmth of the valleys below.

Sara had always identified with winter. Winter was patient, focused. It knew its time always came, and each year it seemed to hang on and rule a little longer, putting off spring, which once started could never wait. Spring reminded her of her younger brother, gambolling around like a newborn colt, all legs and eagerness—but lacking stamina or guile.

Dead now, like the rest of her family.

She turned from the thought and lay on the bed, unmindful of the dress, dragging up one of the heavy quilts to cover her, drawing it over her head like she'd done as a child. As if this might protect her, if not permanently, then at least deferring thoughts of what might come. Cocooned, she drifted, turning onto her back. The quilt settled across her nose. *That smell!* She flung the duvet away with a disgusted cry, gagging on the smell and the memories chained to it.

Her dead husband's cologne.

Some must have soaked into the densely packed feathers or been absorbed and caught within the quilt's close weave until the warmed air beneath the duvet had released it.

Can I never be free of him?

Sara rolled off the bed and froze.

Someone was at the door. The clank of keys jangling was simultaneously exciting and terrifying. For a bizarre moment, she imagined it might be her husband, but his spectre would have no need for keys.

The lock turned, and the door flew open, hitting the wall behind with a solid thud. Nicolai strode through. Reluctantly in his wake was another man who for one blinked instant looked familiar, like catching a glimpse of someone as they rounded a corner. But that was impossible. This man had the yellow skin of a felon.

Sara stepped forward, her chin leading. It was one of the characteristic traits she had unconsciously adopted from her father. 'What is the meaning of this? How dare you bring this wretch into my chamber? Get out, both of you.'

Nicolai ignored her protests. Instead he dragged the man towards the middle of the room to make space for two others. They had been obscured behind the bulk of the yellow skin, but now she saw what they were.

The kingdom's class boundaries were flexible; some said slippery. Sara's father used to say there wasn't a social position in Battavia that couldn't be bought. Except for melders, who, regardless of anything else, always remained at the bottom—both feared and despised in equal measure.

Sara drew back. 'Nicolai. What is this? These people, they're—'

'Melders. That's right.'

He flicked one of the melders' ears. 'Shut the door, and then we'll get on with it. Set yourselves up over there in that corner. God's breath, it's freezing in here.' He puffed air into his cupped hands, then pointed at the younger of the melders. 'You, get a fire started in that grate, otherwise we'll all freeze before the job gets done.'

One of the two men assembled a pyre of wood in the hearth atop last night's ashes, flinting it into life while the other unpacked a strange assortment of copper dishes, glass tubes, and implements from two hessian sacks.

'Nicolai. I demand you give me an explanation of why you have invaded my personal chambers.'

'I needed somewhere private and for you to be present. This,' he indicated the room with a sweep of his arm, 'just seemed easier.' He hacked out a laugh. 'Why do you always think there's a conspiracy at work, dear sister-in-law?'

'How do I always *know* that dog's waste stinks, *brother*.'

The corner of the yellow-skinned man's mouth jerked up in what could have been the start of a grin. Sara chose to ignore him, though that was hard. Even in the middle of her generous chamber, he took up a lot of space. Not that he was all that bulky—it was more the energy pulsing from him. It felt angry, though not dangerous—at least not towards her. The black robe he wore was curious. *Is he some sort of priest? A bastardised version of the melders?*

His large brown eyes seemed intelligent and calculating. They put her in mind of a corralled stallion planning an escape. *With the colour of his skin, it would have to be a palomino.*

'Ah, finally.' Nicolai clapped his hands. 'You have recovered your sense of humour.'

Sara realised she had been about to smile at her thought. She turned her attention to the melders, who now stood back from what they had assembled as if to admire it. To her it looked like a series of bowls supported in the air by long metal rods. All of the bowls were connected to at least one other by glass tubes. The older melder spoke, his voice oily and obsequious.

'We are ready, Excellency. Please present the subject.'

Nicolai urged the yellow skin towards the bowls. The man resisted, and Nicolai whispered something in his ear.

'Who is this, Nicolai? I don't understand what this is all about,' Sara said.

Nicolai ignored her and instead guided the yellow skin forward to the contraption of bowls and tubes. The melders swarmed over. One secured his hands and legs with iron manacles before tugging down his trousers, leaving them pooled around his ankles. The man's legs were like cords of muscles, tightly bound. The younger melder then fished into a small pail, drawing out several large leeches that he placed over the primary arteries of the yellow skin's inner arms and thighs.

Sara's stomach heaved, her mind gouging out memories of her beloved father's prolonged death. She had watched his once vibrant life force being gradually be drained by the wasting sickness and the physics application of these blood-sucking parasites.

She stormed over to face Nicolai, standing between him and the yellow skin. The surging outrage that had been simmering in her stomach since the grand duke's intrusion now bubbled over.

'I want you to stop whatever ghoulish thing you have planned here and tell me. Now. What is going on?'

Rubbing the stubble along his jawline, Nicolai gave a mock bow. She could tell he was enjoying this.

'Forgive me, sister. This gentleman is called Levi by his friends. As you can see from his skin colour, he has been the victim of an unfortunate circumstance, a debt that he now wishes to make amends for.'

'And what has any of this to do with me?'

'Oh, I am sorry. I'm being obtuse, aren't I?' He grinned, the wolfish teeth white and sharp. 'Levi is, or rather was, an assassin. He worked tirelessly for your late husband and the kingdom, dispatching its enemies as required.'

She flashed a disdainful look at the big man. There was still that hint of familiarity about him, which vanished when he had the audacity to meet her gaze. The leeches on his arms had already doubled in size, a trickle of red rolling down one forearm. She swallowed the bile rising into her throat and turned back to Nicolai.

'I repeat. What has this to do with me?'

'Why, I thought that would have been obvious, my dear. He is to be bound to you as your journeyman. From today, Levi will become your personal bodyguard and will escort you to your new husband's lands. What better bodyguard than an assassin? After which, as a gesture of goodwill, he will remain with you for the term of his indenture to ensure your... security.'

LEVI STARED STRAIGHT AHEAD, trying to ignore the cut of the cold metal at his wrists. He knew the slimy-feathery feel of the leeches against his skin was in his imagination, as the creatures somehow numbed the nerves while they gorged.

Somewhat like Nicolai.

As for Sara, he'd sighted her occasionally, and then only from a distance. The court had dubbed her the ice queen, and not only because of her fragile white beauty. Even now a resentful frigidity rolled off her, tempering her anger like a steaming, hissing new blade fresh from the water of a smithy's forge. Levi recalled her sitting alongside the late king upon the royal dais at seasonal feasts, her back ramrod straight, mouth severe even when forced to smile. He'd never been this close to her, and yet that glimpse of frustrated outrage beneath the regal façade felt somehow known... He shook the feeling away. He hadn't been born into the nobility; Nicolai had thrust it on him, effectively binding him to silence beneath the royal code on pain of death or exile. In reality, the title was just that—a parchment. It carried negligible privilege and even less influence, barely warranting an unpadded seat at the furthest table in the great hall, where together with the other lesser nobles he could eat his royal roast beef cold, the last in the room to be served. He had no love of entitlement and didn't know why he'd accepted the title. Respectability? Perhaps. Validation? Probably. Belonging? Almost certainly, but after Andrew's death, even that had evaporated like morning mist before an uncompromising sun.

Unlike this woman who, now he examined her more closely, dripped entitlement and grandiosity. There she stood, small fists clenched against her sides, glaring at him.

Him.

As if this was all his fault and it was she who was about to lose five years of her life.

'How dare you? How dare you think that I would agree to this? I would not have this... this criminal anywhere near my kennels, much less my presence. I will not have it. Do you hear me? Bundle up your, your... contraption over there and these low lifes and get out. All of you.'

Nicolai glided across to stand over Sara. Using a calm, quiet voice that Levi recognised as his most dangerous, he spoke slowly. 'You will, and you most certainly *will do* exactly as I tell you. There are those who would seek to block this alliance with your future husband

—not the least of whom would be you, Sara. Levi's only job is to ensure you arrive safely, intact, and remain so. He will be your constant bodyguard.'

Levi said nothing. He didn't intend to be around this woman any longer than the time it took for him to clear the city gates.

The woman shot Levi a venomous look. 'Bodyguard. Watch dog, you mean. How much more humiliation do you intend to heap on me? I am your sister-in-law. The widow of your king and the mother of his heir. I will not be treated like this, to be shadowed and watched over by some criminal. God only knows what he has done.' She waved wildly at Levi's face. 'Look at him. The whole world will know it from the colour of his skin. You will hear the laughter from the Stevonian court from here. And it won't only be me they will be mocking, not if I have any say in it.'

'I doubt that. Not once you remember that Madison will be remaining here. Your son will be safe behind the very thick walls of this castle under my *personal* protection. We must take care to secure his throne. And as for poor Levi's skin colour, look, even now it fades. The leeches were soaked in the antidote before being administered. By tomorrow, Levi will be just another handsome retainer.' Nicolai reached up to give Levi's cheek two quick pats.

Two of the leeches, engorged with blood, dropped to the floor with soft plops. The melders scooped them up, placing them with care into a gleaming copper bowl. The rest followed. Levi could feel several warm drops form on his arm and join the red trails down the inside of his forearms and thighs. The young melder tried to splotch them with a filthy cotton rag, and Levi thrust him aside. He'd been on too many battlefields not to know the result of soiled linen on open wounds. He ripped his own shirt into strips and thrust those at the melder, who reluctantly tied them around Levi's arms and legs. Levi bent down and tried to drag his trousers up. The older melder stepped over and rapped his wrist with one of the long metal rods.

'Not yet.'

Levi straightened slowly, weighing up whether it would be worth it to use his bound wrists to slam the loathsome man's jaw. Ragged tatters of his shirt hung from him like white streamers strung from a stout yellowish tree. He felt a curious mix of vulnerability and shame standing there in his smalls in front of strangers yet was relieved at the news that the yellow shading would fade. A draft blowing from under the heavy drapes found him and played about his legs, prickling his skin.

'Excellency. The binding?' the older melder asked, his hands squirming as if they might strangle each another.

'Of course. Proceed. Proceed.'

The melder nodded to his assistant, who, picking up a pestle, crushed and ground the leeches in the bowl. Blood spurted as they burst apart, spraying the younger man's face and hooded robe, but he seemed oblivious. When they were reduced to a dirty red liquid, he poured the foul mixture into the uppermost bowl of the assembly they had constructed. He then added a handful of yellow powder and several careful drops from a bottle that smoked when he removed the stopper. The resultant brew reeked like week-old fish. The melder tipped the contents into the bowl below it, adding more powders before opening the small tap on the glass tube attached to the bottom. Thicker now, the mixture globbed down until it reached the lowest dish on the apparatus.

'The mistress?' he asked.

Nicolai nodded. He wrapped his arm around Sara and dragged her towards the old man. She struggled, pummelling Nicolai with her white-knuckled fist.

'No. What are you doing, Nicolai? Stop it. I will not have this. Unhand me.'

Levi allowed himself a grim smile. He felt no compassion for her.

The melder gripped Sara's hand, turning it so that the inside of the arm was exposed. Using a sharp metal instrument, he pricked one of the arteries on the inside of her arm and attached a narrow glass tube to the flow. When it was full, less than a couple of thimbles' worth as far as Levi could tell, the melder placed one of the unused strips from Levi's shirt over the small wound, then tipped the contents into the bowl.

'Present the journeyman,' the old man intoned, holding the bowl above his head as if in offering.

Levi remained where he was. The younger one shoved him from behind, and Levi staggered forward, the manacles around his ankles threatening to topple him. Both melders then dipped their fingers into the bowl and smeared the foul-smelling gunk over his exposed arms and legs, ending on his cheeks, forehead, and neck.

Levi tried to flinch away, but something stronger seemed to be holding him, preventing struggle. He found he was only able to grudgingly accept. Something in the tincture was seeping through his skin and into his body. As the mixture dried, he could feel it encircling his will. Internally, he struggled against it, trying to move his arms, legs, even his head. Nothing worked.

Except his eyes. They darted from one face to the other. Nicolai was staring at him open-mouthed, a smile playing at the corners as if he wasn't quite sure of the joke, but certain in the expectation that there was one coming. Sara's mouth gaped with horror.

What are they seeing?

Few people other than melders were ever allowed to witness binding ceremonies. Obviously, there were good reasons.

The older melder put down the bowl. Levi was able to lower his eyes enough to see that a small amount of the sludge remained at the bottom. This the old man was scraping into a funnel sitting atop a fine blown-glass bottle. When it was full, he tapped in a stopper and covered it with the bottle's delicately crafted lid. Encased within its fine new container, the remaining mixture looked grey—innocuous. The melder handed it to Nicolai.

'Here is the release, Highness. When the journeyman's sentence is complete, under the law he is entitled to ask for this to be returned to him. Once the container is smashed, the binding link will be broken. Until that time, he is bound fully to this lady. Their blood is now joined. If she dies, so does he. If they are separated more than several leagues, he will sicken. The greater the distance between them, so too the level of distress. Too far, and both will die.'

The melder turned his attention to Levi.

'Do you understand this, journeyman? You must protect this woman with your life, for if you do not, you will die. You must remain within call at all times, otherwise you will sicken. From this moment, you are bound to the death.'

Chapter Ten

'My lady.'

The voice again. More insistent this time. Sara stirred beneath the covers and groaned, her mind reluctant, consciousness trailing.

'What is it?' Sara raised herself onto her elbows as too many hands tried to stack and arrange feathered pillows behind her. She waved them away, reaching around to do it herself. Her ladies had flocked in last night when Nicolai had left, and after they'd finally unlaced the damned dress, she had ordered them out once more. They fussed and clucked about so, more eager to peck up gossip than to comfort her about what had happened.

'The royal guard is forming outside, my lady. The grand... er, his highness, the regent, has requested you be ready to join it by mid-morning. While you slept, we have packed your wedding trousseau and travelling clothes.'

Sara glanced toward the balcony, squinting against the early sunlight. From the angle of the beams, it looked to be barely two hours since dawn.

A hesitant knock sounded at the door, and one of the ladies scurried to open it, the hem of her skirt swishing against the pile of the silk rug.

'Your breakfast, my lady,' she called back over her shoulder, putting out her hands to receive the tray.

A dark shape appeared beside the kitchen maid. 'One moment.'

It took Sara several seconds to recognise the man without his yellow pallor. He had the gall to lift the lid covering her food and bend over the plate, sniffing at it like some great hound.

'What are you doing?' Her voice held an early morning edge, shrill even to her.

Ignoring her, he extracted a small vial from his belt and sprinkled something over the food. Evidently satisfied, he grunted and nodded for the tray to be passed across. He had the impudence to ignore her again, instead speaking directly to her ladies.

'Everything for your mistress comes through me first. I am her new bodyguard, Commander Levi. My nose has been sensitised to recognise most poisons. I have condiments to identify others.'

He pulled the door to before she could say anything further, the sound of the lock clunking home from the outside a further reminder of her new status. Royal prisoner.

She felt a light pressure on her legs. Bernadette had placed the tray down. Beside her, Louise snapped open a starched white serviette and gently draped it across her chest. Finally, Elena lifted away the gleaming gold lid of the main platter with a flourish.

Why did it take three of them to feed her?

Small specks of purplish dust spotted the peeled doves' eggs. More floated atop the silver chalice of orange juice.

Remains of the thief's condiments.

The breakfast looked contaminated. She fancied it smelt of crushed leeches and spent blood overlaid with the stench from the grey-robed men. A rush of last night's memories cascaded over her. Her son doomed to grow into adolescence and majority without her.

Something ripped through her chest, leaving in its wake a gaping hole, the edges jagged, sharp with guilt and helplessness. She gasped at its power, her hand hovering at her throat over what felt like an emptiness inside. Later, she knew, the anger would fill it, and then, like oil floating atop its surface, she would pour out a calculated plan of revenge.

The prospect of marriage to yet another despicable creature "for the sake of the state" was of no concern, because whatever else happened, those unfortunate nuptials would not happen—despite Nicolai's trained beast crouched outside her door. The purple specks on her eggs seemed to mock her, and with a frustrated curse, Sara flung the tray to the floor, her future clattering and shattering against the flagstones.

BY MID-MORNING, the unseasonal heat was sweltering. Without cloud cover, the sun blazed with a glaring intensity, in defiance of winter's approach.

Valour, Levi's massive white stallion, snorted and danced sideways. Levi, standing beside the horse, tightened his bunched grip on the reins and drew him back. 'Easy, easy, fella. I know it's hot.'

As usual with courtly etiquette, efficiency and common sense had been sacrificed to ceremony. The regent had not yet appeared on the balcony above to give them his blessing and allow the convoy to proceed.

Perspiration trickled down Levi's spine, and he sipped from his water flask, glancing enviously at the officers smoking and lounging beneath the shade of the broad-leafed trees that flanked the palace's carriage drive. While Sara remained in her carriage (being fanned by two pageboys), Levi was bound to remain here, without shelter or any hope of relief from the heat.

The colonel charged with heading up the escort trotted past the royal coach. Sara's hot, flushed face appeared at the carriage window.

'Colonel. A word.' The command was a whip crack, cutting across all other conversations.

The colonel reined in sharply, touching the brim of his plumed cap as his mount skittered.

'Why are we trapped here in this heat?'

Levi couldn't hear the colonel's guarded reply, but there was a lot of gesturing in the general direction of the balcony.

'I don't give a fig what the protocol demands. I'm getting out.'

She rattled the handle of the door, and as if he had been waiting for this, Nicolai emerged onto the wide viewing balcony above, his hand waving vaguely as if shooing a persistent fly.

Relief flooded the colonel's features as he once again touched his hat and turned away, yelling, 'Mount up. Mount up.'

The officers in the shade snapped to their feet, hurriedly tapping red-glowing embers from their tobacco tubes as they ran to rejoin their units.

'At last,' Levi muttered, swinging up into the saddle. He tucked Valour in behind the royal carriage. He would eat dust in this position, but it would allow him equal access to either side of the carriage should an attack come. Not that he expected it. Who would care whether this spoiled and pampered brat made it to her next marital victim? Certainly not him. But Nicolai had been right about one thing. Duty was an unforgiving bitch. He needed to be seen serving her—at least until tonight. As soon as they made camp, he would use the darkness to slip away. There was nothing left for him in Battavia. Not anymore. He'd start again. War created opportunities as well as widows, and he had no fear of the so-called melders' curse. Curses were held in place by fear and superstition. It would take more than two men with filthy feet and grey-stained robes to do that.

Nevertheless, last night's experience lingered. Even after he'd flushed and scrubbed the caked foulness away, something remained, like parasites fluttering beneath his skin. He fancied he could feel it even now. Levi shook the unease away. *I've been through worse.*

Much worse. The ritual had been meant to disgust and terrify him. That's how such charlatans bound you. Levi had little time for either.

THEY MADE camp as the sun was setting. An advance party of fast-moving supply wagons had been sent ahead much earlier in the day. By the time the main party arrived, the royal pavilion had already been pitched. Pennants atop each support pole snapped and fluttered in a rising wind that, after the heat of the day, was pulling cold air in from the south. Further away, huge iron tureens were suspended over cooking fires, the rich smell of mutton broth and freshly baked loaves drawing the hungry men forward.

One of the coachmen jumped down to open the doors of the royal carriage.

'Hold there, man. I have to check inside the tent first,' Levi said.

The coachman, his hand already on the door's elaborate handle, nodded and held it shut. There was a fumble from inside, and then one of the windows thumped down. He heard Sara's imperious voice demand that the door be opened. The coachman doffed his cap and mumbled something up through the window.

Levi heard Sara's outraged cry. He smiled grimly as he reached the tent.

Tossing Valour's reins to one of the guards stationed outside, Levi slid to the ground. The man caught them clumsily, trying to maintain his hold on a long pike.

'Watch him. He bites. And make sure no one else enters until I check the quarters are clear. No one.' He indicated the coach with a toss of his head. The man's eyes flickered, and he licked his lips. Everyone could hear the strident protests of the royal passenger.

Slipping between the tent flaps, Levi went inside, sword drawn. The oil lamps had already been lit, one suspended on either side of a vast bed. He ran his fingers idly across the thick pelts covering it and grunted, thinking of his own thin bedroll.

But after tonight, at least I'll be free to choose whenever and wherever to unroll it.

That was something.

A large hanging drapery sectioned off an area of the room that obviously was intended to provide privacy whilst dressing. He snorted, imagining Sara's white scrawny body bobbing behind it. As if anyone would care if they caught a glimpse of the royal titties. He guaranteed they'd be a damn sight less impressive than those on display at the nearest tavern.

He paused at a small table where someone had laid out a carafe of wine. He poured a measure into one of the polished wooden goblets and swirled the contents, sniffing deeply. He nodded in appreciation. Privilege did hold some advantages, after all. He took a sip and then walked over to the dressing area, using the tip of his sword to ease the drapery aside.

Garments. Some hung from cords strung between tent poles, while others were draped across the lids of open travelling trunks. It looked much like a dress shop that Sharelle used to visit... before.

Andrew's death had become the place marker of their lives. The death of a son dividing their lives into before and after. He, turning inwards and away from her futile attempt to anaesthetise loss with firstly wine and then wild gambling.

He drained the wine. Its aftertaste had turned sour, and he was about to spit it out when he paused.

Something doesn't feel right.

Gently, he set the goblet on the table and eased past the separating curtain into the dressing area. The heavy material swung to behind him. In the smaller space, the air was close with the smell of freshly rammed earth and stale perfume.

The sword's long blade would be difficult to swing in this confined space, so sheathing it, he drew his two daggers. Their blades were long, finely tempered steel, set into hilts that had been moulded to fit his grip. Whenever there was cause to use them, the daggers became extensions of his arms.

He waited, motionless, steel extending from both hands. There was definitely something here... it was hidden, he knew that much. The only way to uncover it was to wait and watch and be ready when it showed itself. Whoever it was would make a mistake—

'...Alice, I told you I don't care what that fool thief said, we've been sitting in that damn coach all day, and if you think I'm going to be ordered around by some criminal, then—'

Levi cursed loudly and shoved his way back into the main area, still holding the two blades. The two women screamed and jumped back.

'Get out of here. It isn't secure yet.'

Sara's face, usually pale and contained, flushed, her throat red. When she spoke, her voice was low and loud.

'How dare you draw steel in my presence. Guard!'

The two sentries pushed inside, the iron points of their pikes bearing down at the sight of Levi's weapons.

'Stand down and search the dressing area,' he snapped.

'Arrest him. Do you hear me? Arrest him.'

'Goddammit, do as I say, now. My job is to protect your queen.'

The guards exchanged an uncertain look, torn between rank and discipline. The older one mumbled something and took several steps towards the drapery while the other adopted a wary defensive position in front of Sara, his pike levelled at Levi.

Two quiet *phat* sounds followed. The guard standing in front of Sara jerked back, his hand moving to a small yellow dart in his neck before crumpling to the floor.

Levi threw his weapons aside and launched himself at the two women, arms wide, using his momentum to take them all to the floor, scrambling to cover the queen with his own body. Sara struggled beneath him, her teeth sinking into the unprotected muscle between his neck and shoulder.

More *phat* sounds followed. Levi felt something hit and bounce off the chainmail on his back. Gripping Sara's shoulders, he used the weight of his body to roll them both across the floor until they reached the protection of the massive bed.

'Stay down.'

Pinning her by the shoulder, he eased himself up and peeked over the top of the mattress. The second sentry was sprawled in front of the drapery, as was Alice, the ladies' maid; both had yellow darts sticking from their necks.

Sara was struggling to get free, cursing him in between yelling for more guards.

Levi knew that for an assassin to survive, they had to constantly monitor the fluctuating ratio between risk and reward. More guards meant higher risk with a lower likelihood of reward.

The darts had stopped. Whoever it was had gone.

Levi struggled to his feet and sprinted forward, pausing only to retrieve his daggers before crashing past the edge of the drapery divide. The hanging dresses were in disarray; several lay in muddy, trampled piles on the floor. Others, still hanging, swayed gently in the breeze puffing in through a man-sized slit in the back wall of the tent.

THE CAMP HAD SETTLED into silence by the third watch, and Levi, staring up at the stars, was still undecided. If he was going to leave, then it would have to be now. Yet the attempt on the queen's life had been real. The prissied-up colonel had refused to believe it wasn't a one-off attack from bandits even after Levi had explained that the dart tips smelt of a compound he recognised, one that was designed to kill quickly. Bandits weren't usually that sophisticated. It was possible but unlikely.

Who did the fool think the killer was if it wasn't one of the men who'd set up the camp? Bandits indeed.

Blowpipes weren't their preferred weapons, and bandits were neither fools nor overly brave—but they were greedy, and none of the jewellery was missing. That would have been the first thing they would have gone for—just before the exit. Bandits only turned aggressive when they were cornered. And as for killing innocents? Unarmed women? No way; they needed to maintain the good will of the common folk too much to risk that.

Levi rolled onto his side, grunting as another sharp rock dug into him.

Get up and go.

The words had been a chant in his head for the past couple of hours.

It wasn't as if anyone wanted him to stay. Sara would certainly be pleased to see the back of him.

Maybe if she'd offered me a word of thanks. She knew I was press-ganged into being here.

But even after he'd saved her life, she'd threatened him with execution *and* imprisonment for the "impertinence" of laying his grubby hands on her. Forget that three others, including one of her ladies, lay dead at her feet.

I have to think about my needs from here on in. I never asked for this. I've taken a vow to leave violence behind. Besides, the damn woman has almost a full regiment of soldiers to look after her, and despite everything, the colonel isn't so much of a fool not to realise what would happen if the queen is killed on his watch. Selfish wench. At least she has a son who is still alive, not that she seems to give a shit about leaving him behind in Nicolai's tender care. But that's not my problem. That's it. I'm going.

Before he could change his mind, he sprang up and gathered up his bedroll. Slipping past the sentry line, he picked his way down to the small creek where he'd tethered Valour earlier.

The horse looked up as he approached, making a snuffling sound as Levi patted his neck before throwing on the saddle and tightening the cinch. He paused, hearing only the lonely strident challenge from a night bird and the sound of water gliding around rocks.

He swung up and urged Valour into the middle of the shallow stream. The stallion snorted at the chill of the water, or perhaps it was the uncertain shifting feel of the river sand beneath his hooves. Levi patted the horse's neck again.

'It won't be long.'

He'd use the stream to hide their tracks for a league or so and then gallop through the final hours before dawn. Not that he expected anyone would bother following.

But the thoughts wouldn't quit. He still felt guilty. Levi shook his head.

Let the colonel look after her, and good riddance to royal shrews and prideful idiots...

HE JERKED AWAKE, checking his sideways slide by clutching at the saddle's pommel. Watery sunlight was only now clearing the top of the mountains, picking out streams of white mist caught in cold pockets on the banks of the stream.

Was I dozing? How long have we been moving downstream? I should be well across country by now.

A sandy stretch snaked through the damp black rocks on one bank, and he clucked Valour over to it. His head felt like it was over-stuffed with cotton waste. Dirty cotton waste, by the feel of the sticky foulness inside his mouth. He tried to spit and found he had none, ending up coughing instead. Even the sound of that was wheezy.

What the devil is wrong with me? I'm so thirsty.

He reined Valour in and slid off, collapsing into an untidy heap when his legs buckled beneath him. The edge of the water was so close he could smell it, clear and fresh, barely two strides away. Summoning strength, he tried to stand and failed. Instead, he levered himself up onto all fours and crawled, hauling himself between Valour's front and hind legs, methodically moving one arm forward and dragging its opposite knee through the coarse sand, the tantalising gurgle of water drawing him on. When his hands reached the edge, he allowed himself to collapse into its delightful wetness. Chin submerged, he turned his head to one side and sucked water through the corner of his mouth.

When he came to, water was lapping the edge of one nostril. He coughed and with a tremendous effort pushed himself up back onto all fours, looking around. His vision was blurred and unable to focus, as if his eyes were coated with oil. He blinked several times to clear them, finally managing to make out Valour's bulk off to one side, picking and pulling clumps of lush grass along the bank. The sun was now almost directly overhead.

What's wrong with me? How had it gotten so late?

He managed to shuffle out of the water, shivering now despite the warmth of the day, and propped his back against a large black boulder. Squinting up at the sun, he tried to estimate the time, his mind sluggish, mired in mud. By the sun's position, it was hours since he'd last checked.

How far have I come—and which way?

The light was too much to bear, and he shut his eyes against it, immediately feeling himself sliding off the edge of consciousness once more.

'WAKE HIM UP. Throw him in the water if you have to. In fact, do that. He'll stink for days otherwise.'

Two guards hastened to carry out Sara's command, one taking hold of Levi's ankles, the other his wrists, the bulk of him sagging between them. The men hauled him to the stream, grunting with the effort. With a half-hearted swing, they allowed him to drop unceremoniously into the water. Sara, watching, smiled in grim satisfaction as Levi woke with a start, spluttering and swearing.

She looked away before he noticed her staring and used a limp ostrich feather to fan the air about her face. It was insufferably hot out here—the afternoon sun was now level with her eyes—though at least the nausea and headache had eased off. She wondered whether that was a coincidence.

'Help him onto his horse. He looks incapable of doing it himself. I want to be back at camp before dark.'

Orders came easily to her. She'd given them all her life, and no one argued with her orders—well, not for long anyway. No, it was relationships she found challenging, suspended within the spans of multi-layered intrigue that flowed in deep and unpredictable currents throughout the court. These were impossible to navigate, so she used coldness as a foil, fostering the image of the ice queen, though no one would dare call her that to her face. That was one thing about the thief. While he obviously had a problem with listening to orders, he appeared to have little tolerance for subtlety either.

'How did you find me?' he asked, swiping water from his eyes, flicking wet curls from his face, the droplets spattering Sara's hands.

She arched back yet relished the chilliness of the water. Her words bristled, sharp with scorn. 'Surely you mean, thank you, Highness, for rescuing me.'

The man has the gall to look at me directly.

'No, I didn't mean that at all, but if you can't tell me how you came to find me, I'd be interested in knowing. And why.'

Sara turned her head, avoiding his insolent gaze.

'It was not my decision.'

'Whose, then? Surely not my friend the colonel's.'

Sara checked the smile that threatened to flutter the corners of her mouth, remembering the colonel's aghast look when she suggested they send out a party to find the thief.

She firmed her expression before turning to face him. 'Have you been well?'

'What? You enquire after my health, madam? Are *you* avoiding *my* questions?'

Sara reined in and, using her knees, brought the dappled mare around so that she blocked Levi's way. His white stallion reared in surprise, front hooves pawing the ground with annoyance.

Like man, like horse. Sara ignored their bravado and leaned in close so she could speak directly to Levi without being overheard by the guards.

'I want you to listen very carefully, thief, and then think well before you answer. Since you left the camp very early this morning, have you felt... well?'

His reply was reluctant. 'No, but what has that—'

Sara held up her hand, palm out, halting him. 'And there is your "why," because I too have felt wretched. I'll admit when I heard you had ridden off, I was pleased. Yesterday's "incident" was deeply... disturbing. But you did well. I realised later that I had no desire to punish you. Not for that, anyway. Then the nausea and headaches started. The more time that passed, the worse I felt. Eventually I remembered the disgusting melders' curse and equated each step you travelled with a worsening of my symptoms. That's when I ordered the colonel to put a detachment of men together in order to find you. He is a fool, of course, with no idea of where to look, and, I suspect, even less desire, but for some reason I seemed to know which way to go, so I told him to follow me, and here we are. So, there is your precious "how." The curse, it seems, works for us both. I imagine you are also feeling recovered now?'

Levi's eyes hardened, but he said nothing.

'Good. Then until we can get this yoke of a curse lifted—at least from me—I suggest you remain close in my company.'

'I will not be your slave.'

Sara dug her heels into the mare's ribs and tugged her back onto the trail.

'I have no further need to speak with you. Stay close, thief.'

'Wait.'

Sara cantered to the head of the column, reining in beside the dapper colonel. Let the thief stew. His frustration could cook for a little while yet before she offered him a way out.

Chapter Eleven

By the time they returned to camp, the sun was nudging the jagged peaks of the western mountains and preparations were being made for the evening meal. Levi made a quick inspection of the queen's pavilion before waving her inside. The guard patrols around the royal pavilion had been increased since what she insisted on calling the "incident." He didn't expect a repeat attack, but assumptions were risky.

Tired, angry, and a little ashamed at being dragged back, he led Valour away from the main camp. Beside a copse of trees, he removed the saddle and began brushing the stallion down. The easy repeated strokes settled him, allowing some of the tension to drain away. He was gradually surrendering to the realisation that he was inextricably tied to this damned woman, even to death. A lesser man may consider whether that might be a simpler solution: let the assassin have her and be with it. He dismissed the thought. It was not his way.

A movement of colour from the royal pavilion caught his attention.

Sara.

Standing in the entrance.

A guard pointed in his direction, and he swore softly to himself.

Is there to be no peace?

She strode toward him, her guards attempting to accompany her until she waved them away like bothersome insects. They hovered regardless, uncertain, a dozen paces back. Levi empathised. If anything happened, they would be blamed first. He, of course, would be next. He cast a practised eye across the camp, mentally marking men taking too much interest. He shifted his attention back to the queen.

She moved with a fluid motion, as if everything was in balance. Her hair, unbound, swayed, brushing the tops of her shoulders. Something stirred in his memory at the way her hair swung across her face, like a curtain. It was both a familiarity and an idea that he had forgotten something. Something important. Pausing several steps away, she shaded her eyes against the sun.

'You have an easy way with him.'

'We both enjoy the brushing.'

He kept the horse between them as an excuse to avoid her gaze, willing her to leave. She stepped around Valour, making it harder for him to pretend she wasn't there.

'You shouldn't be out here alone,' he said.

'I'm not. You're with me. And there's them, of course.' She pointed at the two nervous guards a dozen paces away.

'Did you want something?'

'Highness.'

'What?'

'I think you forgot to add "Highness." Or Majesty. Either will suffice.'

'Consider it added. What do you want? *Majesty*.'

'A thank you might be appropriate.'

Levi guffawed. 'For what?'

He knew he was goading her and was rewarded with a firming of her mouth. 'You would have died today if I hadn't found you.'

He leaned in close. 'As would you if I'd stayed hidden.'

She laughed. 'Hidden? You were barely able to raise your head when I tracked you down.'

He sighed. 'What do you really want, Sara?'

He took some pleasure in watching her cheeks crimson. How much she managed to choke back would be a keen measure of her need. *She wants something, that is certain.*

She closed her eyes. Levi heard the control in the deep breath she took before answering.

'Very well. Given that there is no one here to witness your impertinence, I'll forgive it—this time.' A pause. Then, with a rush, 'I want you to help me.'

'Do what?'

'Rescue my son.'

'Oh, is that all?' Levi chuckled and began brushing the coarse hair of the horse once more. 'You do know that Nicolai will have him under close guard in the most secure section of the palace?'

'I'm not underestimating the challenges, and before you say anything else, your freedom is held there as well. Remember that vial, made by the melders? Once it's broken, our blood bond goes with it. I know where Nicolai would keep it. Help me, and I'll help you—us— to go our separate ways.'

'That carrot comes with a wicked-looking stick for me if we are caught. All you risk is being sent back to your beastly betrothed with a slap on the wrist and a redoubled guard.'

Her voice turned cold and hard, heavy with vehemence. 'No, you are wrong. I risk losing *my son*. He is everything to me. Though I doubt someone like *you* could even comprehend what that means.' She turned away, arms folding beneath a heaving chest.

The verbal barb buried itself deep inside his gut, releasing memories of his own son, Andrew. *What wouldn't I do to have him returned alive to me?*

Recriminations followed. The should-have-dones. They followed him everywhere, like flies around a butcher's wagon. His reflex response was always to draw back, swallow the pain whole and cover it beneath a mantle of cold indifference or blistering belligerence.

He surprised himself when he found himself saying, 'You're wrong. I had a son, once. He died, and I blame myself. I wouldn't wish that on anyone. Even you.'

The clatter and noise from the camp drifted away, leaving them stranded within a deep silence penetrated only by the soft warble of a nearby bird and the light brush of the wind through the tree canopy. After a time, he realised she was crying. Hesitantly, he reached out a hand to touch her back, and she jerked away.

When she turned, the tears ran unchecked down her cheeks. 'Then you will help me get him back?'

He sighed. 'All right. Yes.'

She tightened her lips, her face strained, and nodded her thanks. As she turned to go, he stopped her with a touch to her shoulder.

'Meet me here at the second watch. Instruct your ladies not to disturb you in the morning.'

CLOUDS HAD SCUDDED in from the south, effectively blocking most of the moonlight. He heard her coming before sighting her silhouette against the orange glow of the camp's fires.

The horse he'd chosen for Sara skittered when she appeared beside him. Levi tightened his grip on the bridle, touched his finger to his lips, and gestured for her to follow, leading the horses away through the copse of trees until they were a safe distance from the camp.

'Here, put these on,' he whispered, handing her a bundle of clothes.

She shook them out. 'What? These are men's clothes.'

'Sssh. There are no side-saddles out here. You'll have to ride astride. Besides, you'll be less conspicuous in an army uniform. Make sure you tuck your hair under that hat. When they figure out you're gone, they'll be looking for a man and a woman.'

Grumbling, Sara walked away several paces and concealed herself as best she could behind a spindly bush. The moon broke through as she tugged off her simple dress, and Levi caught a silvered flash of bare leg.

He turned away, pretending to cinch the saddle tighter on the queen's horse. When she returned, he hoisted her into the saddle, stuffing her dress into one of his saddlebags before raising his arm. 'Hand me the cloak.'

She threw it down, and he ground it into the mud before handing it back.

Sara held it at arm's length. 'Why did you do that? It's filthy.'

'Only on the outside. I want us to look like a couple of travel-stained soldiers by the time we reach the castle. Which we will after a night's hard riding. You'll be thankful for its warmth, filthy or not.'

He vaulted onto Valour's back. 'I want to make the castle before dawn. There's always a queue of merchants' wagons waiting to get in then. Plus, it's the end of the night guards' watch. They'll be cold, tired, and hungry. It's still risky, but that's our best chance of slipping through unnoticed—but we have to make it there by dawn. Did you tell your ladies not to disturb you?'

'Yes. I told them I was tired and not to wake me until eight. Unless the colonel insists. He said he wanted to make an early start to make up time.'

'I'm betting he won't run the risk of upsetting you any more than he has so far. You're intimidating, did you know that?'

'It's my gift. Can we go now?'

⁓

THE INSIDES of Sara's thighs were burning. Every other part of her body ached with a deep, penetrating fatigue. She was unused to riding astride, and once they'd circled back to join the road, Levi had set a solid pace. An hour ago, she had given in and stopped trying to ride the horse, allowing herself to bounce around on the mare's back, her mind fixed only on not falling off. It had slowed their pace considerably.

Levi appeared unaffected by the gruelling ride. He'd spent the night racing the dawn, but now the eastern horizon was showing the first flush of pink. Sara estimated they were still an hour from the castle. It would be more risky if they arrived now. The guards would be fresh and vigilant, according to the thief. She supposed a thief would know about risk. The only thought in her head was reaching the castle and rescuing her son, but she had no intention of using any of the gates. She couldn't take the chance that they'd be discovered.

Sara had no illusions about Madison's security. He was the only obstacle between her brother-in-law and the throne, and Nicolai didn't tolerate obstacles for long.

Levi rubbed the stubble on his chin. 'The dawn has beaten us. We won't make the castle before full light.'

'I know. I haven't told you, but I know of another way in. One that few people do and isn't guarded.'

'Where?'

'Get me closer, and I'll show you.'

They followed the main road for another thirty minutes. Early sunlight slanted through the trees, casting long shadows across the trail. Levi slowed his pace, allowing Sara's mare to draw up beside him.

'Why are have you slowed down? The turnoff isn't far now.' 'We're being followed.'

'What?' She made to look around, and he reached over, gripping her wrist.

'Stay calm. I don't want to alert whoever it is. I suspect it's the same one who tried to assassinate you in your tent.'

'Is that likely? They've had all night to have another try.'

'We were simply dark shapes then. That was the point of the

uniforms, to make us look like dispatch messengers. But now the sun is up, it will become more obvious who you are. I'm going to have to flush whoever it is out before we reach this secret entrance of yours.'

'How?'

'You can start by taking off your clothes.'

SARA STRUGGLED BACK into her brown travelling dress. It was badly wrinkled from Levi's saddlebag, but at least it was a straight line without corsets and required no help to wriggle into. She stepped out from behind the shelter of a large tree, smoothing her palms against the crinkles in the soft material.

'Did you leave the leggings on? You'll find it hard to ride if you didn't.'

Sara resisted telling him that it was hard to ride with them on. *Now I know why some men walk bow-legged.* 'Yes. Is he out there?' There was an edge to her voice that underscored her nervousness. Understandable, given that someone wanted her dead. 'Can you see him?'

'No. But we will soon enough. Do you need a hand mounting?'

She nodded, and he slid to the ground, bringing her mare over and interlacing his fingers beneath the stirrup. Sara lifted her skirts with one hand, and using the other to pull herself up, sprang from Levi's fingers into the saddle. She hiked up the skirt of the dress bunching it in her lap.

'Now what?'

'We hope that he hasn't been practising his blowgun skills. Now he has a target in sight that should bring him closer.'

'That's very reassuring.'

'I'm pleased.' Levi's brow furrowed as he searched the forest.

'What will you do?' Sara asked, remembering the cursed link between them. *If he dies here, what happens to me?*

'Keep your eyes open. I'm looking for colour. The feather flights

on the darts are bright and should stick out when he loads... there.'
The final word barely carried before he spurred away, catching her
by surprise.

'Wait!' The word escaped, her anxiety about what would happen
to Madison bubbling over should he be killed.

Levi's stallion barged through the dense woodlands and disappeared behind a stand of trees. Sara heard what could be a startled
cry followed by several thumps. Moments later, Levi emerged from
the wood leading a small pony. A figure lay prone across its back.

'Is he dead?'

'He wouldn't be much use that way.'

Levi dragged the man from the saddle onto the ground, exposing
his face, bruised and smeared with blood. When Levi rolled him over,
Sara gasped. 'I recognise him. He used to work in the castle. One of
the king's guards, I think.'

'He's Nicolai's man dressed as a barbarian. I thought as much
when he failed to hit you with the dart. Barbarians are experts with
the blowpipe. They rarely miss, and never from close range. I'm
guessing that's why our friend here didn't try anything when you
came to "rescue" me, or last night for that matter.'

'Nicolai? But that doesn't make any sense. He organised this
wedding alliance. Why would he want to kill me?'

'To make it look like the barbarians assassinated you. Ask yourself
what would motivate a prospective ally more: a reluctant bride who
showed her disgust every time she looked at her new husband, or his
beautiful fiancée slaughtered on her way to her intended. Murdered
by a common enemy.'

'My God. You're right, that sounds like Nicolai all over. What
will you do with this man?'

'Take him with us. We can't allow him to be found. Besides, he
might be able to tell us where your son is being held.' Levi bound the
man's limbs and mouth before tossing him face down across the
pommel of Valour's saddle like a bag of millet and mounting up

behind him. He let the assassin's pony go. 'Now, *Highness*, why don't you lead us to that secret entrance of yours?'

They travelled for another forty minutes before Sara turned her mare, nudging her down a slope away from the road and to a thickly wooded area. Her mind was busy, remembering. It had been a few years, and the woods looked different, more overgrown. She was having difficulty recognising landmarks. At least it was taking her attention off her chafed thighs. Attempted assassinations were another thing. The more she thought about it, the more it didn't make sense. *If Nicolai is so intent on getting the throne, why didn't he send Madison with me and have both of us killed? No, Nicolai has some other purpose for my son. Please God, let us be in time.*

'Where are we going?' Levi called, interrupting her thoughts. From what little she'd observed, he hated not being in control, and following her must feel like chewing on creek sand.

Sara smiled and encouraged her horse forward into the trees. She ducked to avoid a low bough, calling over her shoulder "Mind your head" a fraction too late and was rewarded with a solid *thunk* and muffled curse. Ahead, she could hear running water and headed for it.

The stream was bordered by black gravel over white river sand. Her horse paused to drink from the clear running water.

'Don't let her take too much,' Levi snapped, drawing up beside her, an angry red bump on his forehead.

'I know that much.' She dragged on the reins, pulling up the mare's head, and urged her on.

They kept to the middle of the stream for another hour, the methodical splash from the horses' hooves setting a rhythmic cadence that gradually settled Sara. After a time, she reined in, and Levi drew up beside her.

She pointed at a distant range of mountains. 'See what looks like a pass between those two peaks, where it dips down?'

Levi nodded.

'When the middle of it lines up to that large, pointed boulder over there'—she moved her arm down and a little to the right—'we will have our way into the castle. My former husband showed me the landmark once. It's a secret entrance leading to the palace. Come on.'

Sara could sense Levi's frustration at following her building like a storm front. *Serves him right.*

They rode on, moving closer to the shallow edge of the stream. Fed by other tributaries, the stream was broadening into a small river. In the distance, she could hear the echoing rush and fall of rapids. *We're close.* She waved Levi forward. Ahead, the river forged a swift passage between high cliffs. When she checked the alignment of the landmark pass to the pointed rock, it was almost directly in the centre.

'It's just ahead, on the left, I think. The entrance is almost impossible to see if you aren't looking for it. Come on, and keep your eyes open.'

She used her heels on the tired mare, and they started forward, Levi swinging further over to the left, staring into the deep shadows thrown by the gorge walls.

'See anything?' Her voice sounded hollow against the sound of the rushing water.

He'd stopped in front of what looked like a shadowed cleft in the rocks.

It looked vaguely familiar, but she couldn't be sure from this angle. On a whim, she jumped down. The water surged around her calves and down into her boots, cold and foamy, easing the burn of her muscles as she waded forward, using the reins to drag her horse behind her.

As she moved past Levi, the shallow cleft opened out. Water streaming from her leggings, she clambered between slippery rocks and through a dark entrance. Levi dismounted and fell in behind, leaving the bound man draped across Valour.

Inside, the sound of the rushing water faded, and they found themselves in a natural passageway. Light filtered in through the narrow gap, giving the first few metres an eerie feel before dissolving into darkness. Moving to one side, she ran her hand along a high ledge, her fingers finally closing around a dusty oil lamp. She dragged it down and handed it to Levi, who took out a flint and flared it. The light when it came was uncertain, flickering and dancing off the uneven surfaces.

'The oil is old,' he said shaking the lamp, 'but at least we can now see where we are, if not where we're headed.'

'It's not that far, perhaps ten minutes. We can leave the horses here. There's a hitching rail a little further on. This passage used to be the natural underground river course in the old days. As the city grew, the water was diverted to supply the greater population and this entrance was sealed off. My late husband's grandfather had it secretly re-opened to provide a safe exit for the family in the event of a siege.'

They started forward, the horses' hooves clattering against rock, the sharp sounds bouncing off the walls until they came to the rail. Levi secured the horses and then slid the assassin off Valour and onto the stone floor. When he removed the face covering and gag, the man's eyes were wide with fright, his head thrashing to either side as he tried to make sense of where he was. Levi gripped the man's chin and brought his face down close.

'Where is the prince being held?'

'I don't—'

Levi placed his foot against the man's throat and pressed down.

'Tell me and you'll be alive when we come back.'

He eased his foot off.

'What if you don't come back?'

Levi shrugged. 'If you're clever, you'll have these ropes off in half a day and two horses to get a head start on Nicolai's men.'

Levi withdrew a long dagger from the sheath at his waist.

The man's eyes tracked the tip of the dagger, jerking when it came to rest lightly at the base of his throat.

'The way I see it, you have two options. Tell me and I'll free you when we return. Say nothing, and you can die now.'

The man licked his lips and nodded. 'The prince is being held in the east wing. The regent's annexe.'

Levi turned to Sara. 'Do you know where that is?'

'Yes. It will be heavily guarded.'

'I think I already had that in mind.' Levi reattached the gag and rolled the man over to face the wall. 'Come on.'

The watercourse twisted and turned back in on itself, blocking out the light from the entrance.

'How many others know about this place?'

'Nicolai, almost certainly. No one else, I shouldn't think. The workmen are all long gone. My husband's father installed a seal on the entry to the castle to forestall invaders. I think I remember how it works. It should be unguarded.'

'Or it will be until Nicolai hears that you've gone missing. But I'm guessing no one will be in a hurry to deliver that particular piece of news. I'd say we probably have a good two hours to get this done and another three to get the hell away.' Levi's voice trailed off before adding, 'You know, if this comes off, Nicolai will be livid. He'll come after you. Do you know where you'll go?'

'To my homeland—the high country. My people will protect me.'

Levi snorted. 'That'll be the first place he'll look.'

'Then it will be the last place he'll see.' Her father had been king of the northern peaks and the fertile plains beyond until he'd been tricked and killed by her husband. She, in turn, had been dragged back as bounty to "seal" the peace between their two lands. To her people though, she was still their true queen, and if Nicolai wanted a fight, they would give it him. He couldn't wage a war on two fronts.

The darkness beyond the sputtering lamp was oppressive, seemingly endless. The uneven floor sloped down and felt like they were walking into a pit. Behind them she could hear the horses snorting, their hooves moving uncertainly against the loose rocks.

In front, Levi stopped, holding up the lamp and pointing. 'What is that?'

The pale light danced across a solid wall made from the flat black rocks of the river course.

'That's it. The entrance.' Hurrying forward, she reached up, feeling for the keystone. They all looked the same.

'What are you doing?'

'One of these rocks is the way in. I can't quite remember which one it is though.'

'You'd better hurry. The oil in this lamp is about gone.'

Sara's fingers slid across the smooth coldness of the rocks.

They all feel the same.

The light from the lamp flared briefly, then, with a sputtering hiss, went out.

Chapter Twelve

'Is there another lamp?' Levi's voice sounded hollow and loud within the deep silence.

'Don't you think I would have lit it if there was?' Sara's voice whipped back, sharp, shaking with constricted fear.

'Try not to move around too much,' Levi continued. 'It would be easy to become disoriented in here. If we can't get in, we'll have to be able to find our way out again.'

'I'm not leaving without Madison.'

'Let's focus on staying together and getting this door to open. Reach your arm out.'

Sara bit down on her lower lip, smothering the sobs that were threatening to escape. She raised her free arm. It was shaking. It felt like she was reaching into a void—

A stifled cry escaped her mouth as Levi's large fingers closed around her wrist.

'Got you. Your hands are freezing.'

She slowed her words, spacing them carefully, finding enough gaps between her chattering teeth to sound normal. 'You should feel them from my side.'

'Are you sure you're all right?' Levi's tone suggested she was not.

In the distance a horse whinnied, followed by the sound of hooves coming down hard on the cavern floor along with a muffled curse.

'What is that?' Sara asked, her voice echoing off the stonewalls.

A hand came out of the dark and clamped itself over her mouth, the calloused fingers hard against her lips. A strong arm encircled her waist and pulled her against a well-muscled torso. The smell of stale sweat filled her nostrils. Rough whiskers rasped her throat.

'Quiet,' Levi whispered, his lips warm and damp against her ear. She slumped against him briefly before thumping at his restraining arm with her fist.

He tightened his grip. 'The assassin is more wily than I thought. My guess is he's worked his way loose. Stay here.'

Levi slipped away, and the darkness surged over her like a stifling black cloak. She sank to the floor and hugged her knees, hating Levi for leaving, cursing her need for him to stay, curious at her willing-ness to almost trust this thief. As if she knew something more, some-thing deeper. She hunkered down, leaning into the stone wall.

After a time, she heard him return shuffling and feeling his way along the wall. *At least I hope it's him. What if the assassin—*

'Sara?'

Relief flooded through her. 'Over here.'

He stumbled against her. She clambered to her feet.

'Sorry. The guy has gone. He must have had a concealed knife, or he's better at knots than me. Regardless, he's on foot; that's one good thing. Valour wouldn't let him near your mare.'

'It's an hour's walk. I did it once. If he raises the alarm before we get out—'

'We'll need to get in first.'

Levi helped her up. 'It might be better to use both hands to find the keystone.'

She reached up, fingers stretching into the dark until they found the line of rocks at the top of the wall. They were all flat, cold, and hard. 'I don't know. They all feel the same.'

'Tell me what you remember from the last time you were here. It might help. Where was your husband standing when he opened it? Tell me exactly.'

Sara closed her eyes. The darkness behind her eyelids seemed more contained, less threatening. 'I remember when we came down from the palace side, he touched something at the top of the wall—in the middle—and a section swung open, then we walked through to this side.' Sara focused on the memory.

'Good. Stay here.'

His reassuring hand slipped from her shoulder and she heard him stumble off.

'Where are you going?'

'I'm at one end of the wall. Now I'm going to come back towards you.'

He started counting. When he reached her, she made space for him to pass until he spoke again.

'It's eighteen paces from one end to the other. I'm coming back now. Move towards my voice. One, two, three... are you moving?'

'Yes.' Sara's fingers trailed along the wall. She was scared of losing contact with it.

'...seven, eight nine. All right, I'm in the middle—ah, there you are. Now try from here. You said the keystone was at the top of the wall?'

'Yes. Anthony wasn't tall. I remember he had to stretch right up to reach it.'

She sensed Levi reaching up. 'How does the stone move?'

'It turns. Yes, I remember him saying it was stiff and wouldn't turn easily.'

'You try working your way along one way and I'll try the other direction. Ready?'

'Yes.'

They started from the same rock. On the uneven surface, Sara had to stand on her toes to reach the top row in places, leaning against the wall to keep her balance in the dark. It was slow progress. Her fingers were so cold, she found it hard to grip and hold each rock, much less try to turn them.

'Find anything?' he called.

'Don't you think I would have told you if I had?' Her disembodied voice sounded harsh. 'Sorry, I'm not very good at handling the dark.'

'I'm at my end now. I'll work my way back and try again.'

Despite the wall, Sara was becoming disoriented. *What if the assassin hadn't run away? What if he was even now working his way through the darkness to kill her?* She shut out the thought and focused on the task, her fingers flinching from the rough edges of yet another unyielding rock. The tops were flat and smooth, but the edges were flint sharp. Her hands were raw as they closed over the next and applied pressure first one way and then... *is it giving a little?* She tried harder.

'Levi, I think I've found something. But I can't shift it. Can you help?'

She heard him skitter along the wall and appear immediately beside her. His hands followed her outstretched arm, fingers finding her hand atop the wall.

'This one?'

She stepped away. 'Yes. I thought it moved to the right.'

Levi's grunt was followed by a loud clunk and a section of the wall, previously solid and unyielding, swung inwards. Sara, using her hands to guide her, stepped through. Behind her, she could feel Levi following.

'There used to be a lamp on this side too. Where the wall ends,' she said.

'Got it. It's full of oil too.'

A flint flared, and the wick caught. The lamp's brilliance was out of all proportion to its soft light after her time in absolute darkness.

Sara turned away until her eyes adjusted. When she opened them, she recognised the archway leading to the palace.

He handed her the lamp. 'Lead the way.'

Sara moved through the arch and up the narrow spiral steps. The spill of light from the lamp flickered against the rough-hewn walls.

The air tasted stale, leached of life. Each small movement disturbed flurries of dust that hung suspended around the lamp's yellow halo. The spiral stairs rose steeply and ended abruptly at a wooden door. Sara tried the latch. It resisted but groaned open when Levi put his shoulder to it, revealing a dark passageway.

Cautious, she peered down the corridor as far as the lamp's light reached before speaking over her shoulder. 'It's clear. I recall that this was an old service access for the servants. It connects both wings of the palace.'

'Which way is the east wing?'

'Left. No, right.'

They walked. This part of the palace was unused. The rooms branching off either side of the passage were empty, their open door-ways laced by ancient spiderwebs. Frantic scuttling in dark corners followed them.

'Rats,' Levi said, and Sara shivered, thankful for the lamp light. She hadn't remembered it like this. She increased her stride. Rounding a corner, they came to a solid wooden door.

Locked.

Levi knelt beside the door and fiddled at the lock with some thin metal strips that he'd taken from a pouch at his belt. There was a distinct click, and he eased the door open a crack, leaving a small arc in the dust on the floor.

'How did you do that?'

'Practice.' He opened the door a little more, and Sara peeked through. The passageway beyond was wider and much cleaner, the smells of cooking wafting up from the kitchens.

Sara's mouth watered. *How long has it been since I ate?* 'The kitchens are down to the left. This is the main service corridor, and it's almost lunchtime.' She pushed the door shut at the sound of muted voices and approaching footsteps.

They waited until they'd passed before Levi whispered. 'Do you know the way from here?'

'Yes.'

'I estimate we have less than a half hour to get in and out again, unless our friendly assassin found himself a ride on the way to the palace, in which case that margin will be significantly less.' He raised an eyebrow and gave her a grim smile. 'Highness.'

She closed her eyes, weary with pretentious memory. What had seemed so important only days before was now overwritten and completely unreal. Everything had changed. All that mattered now was saving Madison. She eased the door open. 'It's clear.'

They both slipped through and eased the door shut behind them. On this side there was a beautifully carved fresco. The door itself was concealed within the clever timber lines. They hurried down the corridor. In their travel-stained uniforms, Sara imagined they looked like two tired guards at the end of their watch.

The hallway spilled into a vast covered courtyard peppered with tinkling fountains and manicured shrubs in the shape of animals. People were everywhere. Levi pretended to be in conversation with Sara, hoping their uniforms would help them blend in.

'This is the People's Courtyard. All the royal apartments are up there,' she whispered. Sara motioned with her eyes towards a grand marble staircase that curved up to the next level.

Levi moved towards, them and Sara caught his arm. 'Not that way. The main stairs are only for nobles and guests. We need to use the servants' steps. Over there.'

She led him to a broad arch. Once inside, the walls turned from smooth whitewash interspersed with beautiful frescos to rough, unfinished timber. A wide set of wooden stairs, much steeper than those outside, led up. Levi took the steps two at a time. Sara's followed, the long night dragging on her. She pushed herself to keep going, sensing Levi's impatience.

Levi waited for her at the first landing. 'I suggest you try and keep up. Soldiers in a hurry are assumed to have a mission and so are asked fewer questions.'

'Coming.' Sara summoned her strength and hurried after him. Above, she heard someone clattering down the wooden steps. She made way, glancing up at the last moment. The girl paused on the step above her.

'Milady?'

Levi stepped between them, effectively blocking the girl's view. 'What is it, girl?' he said. 'Can't you see we're on the regent's business?'

'I'm... I'm sorry. For a moment, I thought...' The girl's face was creased with confusion as she tried to see past Levi.

'About your business now. I have no time to spend making up lies to bed the likes of you. Maybe later.' Levi gave her a leer, and she fled, face aflame.

'You do seem to have a way with women,' Sara muttered as she followed him up the final flight of steps. 'The regent's annexe is the third set of double doors past the next turn.'

They rounded the corner and stopped suddenly.

'That would be the double doors with the two guards outside?' he muttered.

The guards lounged back against the white-and-gold-trimmed doors, looking decidedly bored, their long decorative pikes loosely held. Levi straightened his uniform and stalked across the space, his voice lancing out while still three strides distant. 'Why are you men still here?'

The soldiers snapped to attention when Levi shot his cuffs, revealing the three gold officer flashes on his sleeves.

'We were told—'

'You were told, along with every other man on duty, to get down to the central courtyard. There's a battle drill on. Now!'

'But the prince—'

'Is downstairs in the courtyard with the rest of the *men*. What are you two defending? His royal robes? Get down there before I put you both on report.'

The men looked at each other and, as if by mutual agreement, hurried away.

'Battle drill tempo,' Levi shouted after them. 'I have a way with men too, it seems,' he said to Sara, watching the two men jog along the corridor and down the external stairs. 'Come on, we're not home yet.'

He tested the door. It was locked. He rapped on it twice. The latch clicked, and Levi used his shoulder to barge his way into the bedroom, sending the soldier on the other side sprawling.

Levi threw himself on top of the guard, striking him hard on the jaw. The man went limp.

'Call for your son, Sara. Hurry up. Those men were thick, but it won't take them long to realise something is wrong when they find no guard formation in the square.'

Sara ran into the bedroom and heaved a sigh heavy with relief. Madison was standing between two women who were curling his hair into the latest court style.

He saw her in the mirror first, his face confused at the way she was dressed.

'Madison.'

When she spoke, the puzzled look vanished, and he rushed over, the two servants trailing. She caught him in her arms, twirling him around. He felt right in her arms, as if some elemental part of her had been missing up to now.

'Sara, we need to go. You,' Levi motioned to one of the servants, 'get the boy a travelling cloak to put over this red thing he has on, something dark that preferably doesn't have gold on it—or that glitters or shines.'

The woman looked at Sara, who nodded.

They bundled the boy into a brown cloak, and Levi, removing a cloth hat from one of the women, jammed it over Madison's curls. He looked strange, but more important, he didn't look like the heir.

Levi wagged his finger at the servants. 'Tell the regent you were attacked by six men. Got it? And tell that fool in the other room to say the same. He might avoid getting killed for his stupidity.'

'I wanted my son,' Sara added, flashing a smile at the two servants.

They shuffled their feet, looking down, caught midway between a curtsey and a scream, still unsure whether this strangely dressed woman was the wife of the former king. Sara shook out her hair and assembled her best imperious stare. The faces of the women cleared, and they bobbed their heads and bent low.

'Say nothing about the queen's presence here. To anyone. Say it was a kidnapping.' Levi tossed two silver pieces at them, and the women scrambled after the rolling coins as he ushered Sara out.

Sara guided them on a circuitous route along little-used corridors, avoiding as many people as they could on their way back to the wide hallway. When they reached it, the smell of roasted fowl and baking pastries was even stronger.

They waited while two serving maids laden with heavy platters hurried towards them. Sara pulled her cloak over Madison, silencing him with a quick squeeze and shake of her head.

Levi stepped into the path of the two servants.

'What do we have here?' He reached over and lifted the lid off one of the platters. Sara spied bread and mutton with some sort of gravy, and her mouth watered.

'This is for the officers' mess, sir.'

'And what are we if we are not a fine example of an officer's mess?' He guffawed before helping himself to two flats of bread and a slab of steaming meat for each. He winked at the girls, and they giggled. 'Off with you now. No one will miss it and, what's more important, we won't miss our main meal. Not today at least.'

Levi bit into the bread and meat, a runnel of hot gravy trickling down his chin. Levi flicked it away, licking his finger as he watched the girls turn the corner. 'Give me the boy so you have a hand free to eat yours.' Sara exchanged Madison for the slice of bread and mutton.

She ate it while hurrying back to the carved fresco. Levi pushed it open. As Sara followed him through, she heard the distant, strident call of a bugle.

'Is that about us?' she asked.

'I hope not. We're in no position to make a chase of it.'

'We?'

'Well, I can't go anywhere where you aren't, remember? Our timeline didn't allow me to find the vial of that foul mixture that would free us of each other. It would likely be somewhere in Nicolai's rooms. I was a fool to think I could have found it in time.'

'Oh, Levi, I'm so sorry. In all the rush to get Madison, I forgot our arrangement.'

'Forget it. Your son's life is more important.' He looked away, but she saw the defeat in his face. 'I know I would do the same for my boy if he were still with us.' Sighing, he turned back and tried a smile. 'We may need to be stuck with each other for a way yet, at least until I can get you both safely to your home country.' His expression hardened. 'Once the child is safe, getting free of you will be my priority, so do not worry your royal head.'

Sara frowned and turned away, annoyed at the relief that had washed through her, though whether it was for Madison or that she wouldn't have to make the long journey alone, she couldn't tell.

Chapter Thirteen

It was well past noon when they emerged from the cave into brilliant sunshine.

'My eyes hurt, Mummy.' Madison turned his face into Sara's chest. Sara hugged him closer, repositioning his weight across the mare.

'I know, sweetie. Give it a moment.'

Levi was scanning the stream and the bank beyond. He turned in his saddle to face her. 'Do you need me to take the boy?'

His voice sounded different, or perhaps more indifferent.

'No, he's fine. Is everything all right?'

Before he could answer, Madison said, 'Mummy, I can hear your heart. It's loud.'

Sara smiled. 'It's telling you how much I love you. Rest now. We have a long way to go.'

Levi was moving upstream, back the way they'd come. She used her heels to encourage her mare to catch up.

Drawing level, she looked over. He was frowning, and she was fairly certain it wasn't only because of the strong sunlight.

'You didn't answer me before. About being all right,' she said.

'Perhaps you only want answers that you want to hear.'

She reached over and tugged hard on Valour's nearside bridle strap. The stallion snorted and tossed his head, one eye wide and wild. Levi cursed and balanced him, patting the big horse's neck.

'I don't understand,' Sara said before he could say anything. 'Inside the palace you seemed, well, not happy but resigned to come with us, and now you're acting like we're a burden and it's all my fault.'

'Well, it's certainly not mine. It's not me who's supposed to marry the goon who will save the cursed kingdom. I didn't ask for this. Any of it. You're not my responsibility. I had years of being trapped inside someone else's personal drama, believing I could make a difference, and in the end it didn't. My son—'

Madison wriggled around to face Levi. 'What's his name?'

'What?' Levi's tone softened under the child's curious scrutiny.

'You said you have a son. What is his name?'

'Andrew. He would have been about your age now.'

'Where is he?'

Levi looked away, knuckles slowly whitening across the pommel of his saddle. When he turned back, Sara noticed his eyes were glassy.

'He's waiting for us somewhere, I hope.' Levi looked at Sara over Madison's head, his gaze meaningful.

Bugles and the unmistakable baying of hounds and jackals floated down the stream towards them.

Levi took a breath, and the moment passed. 'We'll keep to the stream for a bit,' he said. 'That barking is from Nicolai's hunting pack. The longer we can stay in the water, the better.' He spurred Valour into a trot, moving through the shallow water, away from the palace. Sara was ready for him this time and kept pace.

'Won't that slow us down?' she asked.

'It's a trade-off. I noticed a fork in the stream on our way in earlier. I'll lay a false trail along that bank and then double back along the stream to join you. It may buy us a little time. Nicolai's hounds are bred to be relentless, not smart.'

～

THEY MADE CAMP AT SUNSET. The sounds of the pursuing pack had faded after they left the safety of the water. Levi had then set a course for the distant mountains that Sara called home.

She turned over, the ground hard and unyielding against her back. The saddle beneath her head was even less comfortable than when she was astride it, and the muscles in her arms were weak from holding Madison upright. He'd fallen asleep earlier in the afternoon and had flopped to one side, so she'd had to support his full weight. He hadn't yet woken. Sara draped the red cloak over him and tucked it in firmly. The night was rapidly gulping the heat from the day, and Levi had refused to light a fire in case it could be seen. She shivered and hunkered further into the old stained travelling cloak. It smelt of dried swamp mud and other people's sweat, but it was a welcome layer against the cold.

Levi crunched back into the camp and flopped down opposite, his long legs stretched out towards her.

'I found a small rise over to the left. From the top I could make out two or three fire glows off to the east. If they're cooking fires, it means they've split up to cover more ground. That could be a sign that the hounds haven't picked up our scent yet. Once one of them does, that's when the race will really start. How far off are these mythical lands of yours anyway?'

'Surely you mean mystical?'

'I mean how far off are they?'

Sara sighed, then glanced at Madison's sleeping figure before shuffling over to Levi, saying quietly, 'I'm only going to say this once.' She jabbed his arm, punctuating her words with her index finger.

'Despite everything, I'm grateful you're here, but sniping at every-thing I say is pointless. We both know why you're here, but I'll repeat it anyway, so we're both clear—because you'll die otherwise. It's as simple as that.'

Sara took a breath before continuing, her voice quieter. 'As to the other issue, that my son is alive and yours is not is not my fault, or yours either from what you've told me. Fair or unfair, that's the way it is. Now, I don't know how this will all end. We may die anyway but, regardless, I will do everything I can to keep Madison and myself safe and together. What you do is your business. Kindly keep your self-pity to yourself or find somewhere else to sleep. Tomorrow we should be close enough to the highland territories to get a message to my people. You won't be any freer to leave, but hopefully your disposi-tion will have improved in order to make the best of our situation. If we make it, I can ask our physic to see if he knows of a cure. He has access to many old remedies that the lowlanders don't. Other than that, I'll support you with horses and enough men to infiltrate the palace and steal back the vial.'

Levi glared at her with his large brown eyes. He grunted what might have been assent before rolling onto his side, leaving her to stare at his back.

After a time, she muttered, 'And a jolly good night to you too.'

'SARA. WAKE UP.' Levi shook her shoulder again, his attention riveted on the eastern horizon and the thin line of light that preceded the dawn. The isolated decaying sound of a dog's bark floated towards them.

'What is it?'

'Get up. Nicolai's men are on the move. They must have worked the hounds and jackals in shifts through the night. I'm guessing one of them has stumbled onto our trail.' He gathered the loose night traces of the horses and drew them from their easy grazing back into the camp.

'God, so soon? Madison, wake up, quickly, we have to go.' Sara struggled to her feet and lifted the child, holding him against her. 'It's all right.'

'Mummy, I'm tired.'

'I know, sweetheart. You can rest on the way.'

Levi clamped down the desire to tell her she'd have all the time she wanted to rest if they were caught, however, he was mindful of what she'd said last night and grudgingly acknowledged to himself that most of it was true. Besides, smart comments wouldn't get her up on the horse any faster.

He hoisted the heavy saddles onto the horses and cinched them tight. Sara mounted, and Levi handed up a sleepy-eyed Madison to her. She gathered the red cloak around him, but by now he was fully awake and struggled to face the front, his eyes wide and curious.

'It's still dark,' he said.

'We're getting an early start, sweetie. We're going to my old home. Your home now too. In the mountains. You'll be able to see them better when the sun comes up.'

Levi sprang into the saddle and used the ends of the reins to flick Valour's neck lightly. The stallion sprang forward. It was risky cantering while it was still dark, but they had to create distance. The time for caution had passed. This was now a race.

THE HORSES WERE BLOWING hard by the time they took a break for a quick meal. Levi signalled a halt and slid to the ground, holding up his arms for Madison. They all drank deeply from the water bladder.

He gave both horses a measure of the remaining water and shaded his eyes against the glare of the sun to watch the remorseless dust cloud as it inched closer, mentally measuring the distance to the peaks against the speed of the pack. He came up short. *We aren't going to make it.* Leaving the horses to graze, he walked over to Sara and Madison. 'We'll ride to the top of that next rise and then split up. The hounds are following the horses' scent. They won't be able to tell which is you, so it should divide their number. You keep going hard towards the mountains—and put on that army uniform again. From a distance they might think it's me and break off.'

He looked into the sky. 'There's still about six hours until sunset. If you can stay ahead of them until it gets dark, then you'll have a chance.'

'What about you? Remember what happened last time we got too far apart—'

'I know, but there are too many for me to fight.'

He waited, watching Sara weigh it up, followed her gaze towards the mountains. Even at this distance, they soared above them in wavering shimmers of blue and green topped with a dusting of snow. They did look mystical.

'There may be another way. I was going to wait until we were much closer, but this will have to do. Come, help me light a fire.'

'What?'

'A fire. Madison, gather some dry sticks for Mummy, like this one.'

When Madison had moved a few paces away, Sara whispered, 'There's a signal we use in the high country to call for help. It's a slow-burning flammable powder that creates clouds of coloured smoke. There's a chance it may be seen by some of my people.'

'And then what? These are armed men behind us. Even if one of your shepherds does see it and comes to investigate, he'd be killed.'

Sara shook her head. 'The royal family has a different coloured powder that produces thick purple smoke. Because my people live in isolated communities where communication is difficult, we needed a way to gather them quickly in the face of an external threat. This is what I'll use.' She tugged off her large moonstone ring and pressed the side of the stone. It flipped open revealing a compressed purple powder inside. 'It's essentially a call to arms and tells them to drop everything, bring their weapons, and follow the smoke.'

Levi was dubious at the amount of powder beneath the moonstone. 'It hardly seems enough.'

'It doesn't take much. The powder expands when ignited and burns slowly.'

Levi looked back at the dust cloud. 'How long will it take?'

'It depends on where the migrating herds are. What I do know is that purple smoke hasn't been used since my father was killed, and no one outside our kingdom knows its true purpose. My people will come, and what's more, they'll know it's me who's calling. We only need time.'

'That's the one thing we're short on, but you've given me another idea. Let's gather some wood for your fire anyway.'

Levi squatted down and bundled strands of dry grass and twigs while Sara dragged over some larger branches. He flinted the dry tinder into a tiny flame, blowing on it and adding fuel until he had a decent fire.

'Watch.' She shook the contents onto the flames, and immediately thick purple smoke billowed into the sky. 'Once it gets high enough, the cool air will make it spread. See? It's designed to be seen for many miles.'

'It's pretty, Mummy,' Madison said.

Levi watched the smoke. She was right. It seemed to be staining the sky.

Now he had a plan of his own. It was feasible as long as the wind held. He squatted down and lit a taper from the main blaze. Shielding it, he moved a dozen paces away in the direction of the approaching pack. Once the wind was at his back, he touched the taper to the dry grass. It sizzled for a moment before crackling into a flame. He fanned it and added twigs and sticks until it was burning nicely, then he repeated the process a few paces further to the right until there were a dozen fires, all burning fiercely. The wind fanned them and they began to move, eating the dry prairie grass, turning it into white smoke and heat, leaving only a blackened trail in its wake as it advanced towards their pursuers, spreading and growing stronger as it did so. Soon there was a roaring wall of fire that spread across the plain like spilt water across a stone floor.

'That should slow them down. Come on, let's ride.'

They mounted and spurred towards the mountains. Levi allowed Valour his head, every few moments glancing behind him at the wall of burning prairie grass, the billowing white smoke setting off the bright purple burn of Sara's powder. She'd been right, it could be seen for many miles, and more so from the vantage of the high steep cliffs in front of them, but Levi knew that even with the best intent her fastest riders would not be able to reach them in time. His best hope was that the pack would have to go around the fire front or wait until it had passed. Either option gained them precious leagues, but would they be enough?

'Levi.'

He turned in his saddle. Sara was pointing wildly behind her. Two hounds were bounding across the blackened grass towards them.

He recognised them instantly. They bore the distinctive black-and-white markings and protective leather jackets of pursuit jackals. Thaumaturgically mated with savage wolfhounds, they were trained to track and kill. Fortunately, these two were on their own. They must have been scouting wide when the fire front went through.

Wheeling Valour around, Levi raced over. In war, the jackals were capable of bringing down a battle stallion by tearing out its belly, after which the infantry would deal with the unseated knight. Sliding from his saddle, he drew his sword and took a defensive position between Sara's mare and the charging jackals. The snarling duo paused when they saw the sword. They paced a cautious circle around him, waiting for an opportunity to strike. Valour snorted, pawing the ground.

'Sara. Hold on to Valour's bridle. If I go down, let him loose. Battle stallions and hunter jackals hate each other.'

'Can't he help you now?'

'No. They'll both turn on him. They're trained to bring down horses.'

Levi feinted towards one and then the other, keeping their focus on him. When they attacked, he knew they would come from opposite sides. He would have to be ready.

He crouched down and snatched a handful of fine grey dust. The animals were at polar ends of their pacing circle, and he had to keep turning his head to keep both in sight. He'd watched some of these beasts being trained a lifetime ago when he'd been in Nicolai's service. The trainer had taught one of a pair to give the impression it was about to spring to attract the prey's attention. At the last moment, it would stop while the other ran in low from behind to tear out the victim's Achilles tendons. Once the target was down, the first jackal would spring, going straight for the throat.

Or the tactic may be reversed, depending on who trained them and how.

If I guess wrong, then I'm dead.

Levi was betting everything that these two were trained the way he'd observed. They were Nicolai's beasts, after all.

The attack came with a snarling growl from the left. Levi turned his back to it. He heard Sara shout a warning, but by then the real attack had begun coming in fast and low, as he'd anticipated. Levi was ready. He jumped aside, hurling the handful of dust into the beast's eyes as it shot past, the long sword taking a chunk out of the animal's haunches. Blinded with the dust and incapacitated by the wound, it stumbled, tumbling across the ground.

'Release Valour. Now.'

Levi dived and rolled onto his back. The second jackal had sprung only seconds before and was now airborne, coming straight for him, teeth bared. It was so close, he could see the saliva dripping from its mouth. He ducked and drove his sword up, deep into its unprotected belly. The beast yelped and dropped, landing in a shaggy heap, its fetid breath coming in laboured pants as it snapped, still trying to bite him.

He pushed himself to his feet and used the sword to finish it.

Behind him, Valour whinnied, snorting in triumph as he continued to trample the first attacker.

Levi wiped his blade clean against the coarse hair of the dead animal.

Sara's face was white, her mouth open in shock. She held Madison to her chest so he couldn't see.

'We have to move, Sara. There may be others.'

She looked exhausted. He reached out. 'Here, let me take the boy. He's heavy.'

Clutching him tighter, she shook her head.

Levi rested his hand lightly on her shoulder. 'It's over. Come on. Let me hold him for a while. Give your mare a break from carrying the both of you.'

Reluctantly, she released her hold on the boy and passed him across. Levi hoisted him to the front of his saddle and mounted behind. Valour snorted at the extra weight. Levi hooked his arm around Madison's middle, surprised at how familiar it felt. Memories of early morning rides with Andrew overlaid themselves on the present, but he shook them away, and they set off once more, the smell of smoke now heavy in the air.

The wind had shifted. Now the fire would back burn until it consumed itself and went out—along with their slight advantage.

THEY PUSHED on until early afternoon, when Levi called another halt to spell the horses. The mountains seemed just as distant as they had that morning, but the deeper ravines were now in shadow.

Behind them, he could make out the moving smudge of their pursuers. Whenever the wind gusted, it carried with it the faint clank of armed men on the move and their baying hounds and jackals. While still some distance away, there was no question they were catching up.

He scoured the sheer cliff face in front of them. 'How much longer before your people come?'

Sara pointed at a high ledge. 'Up there, look.' Two small purple dots were barely visible. 'They're scouts. They'll be relaying what they see.'

'Good for them, but I don't see how they can help us from way up there.'

'Trust me, help is coming.'

'I don't doubt that, it's the "when" that has me worried. Those men behind us haven't even stopped for a break. At this rate they, or a pack of those war jackals, will be on us within the hour. I think we should split now like I said earlier, before they can tell which of us has the boy. Madison is who they really want.'

'If you want to go, then go. I'm not keeping you here.'

'Are you leaving us to the bad men?' the small voice interrupted. Levi closed his eyes and gripped the narrow shoulder in front of him.

'No, Madison, I'm not. But I'm hoping to make them follow me rather than you. We can meet up later. All right?'

The boy turned his face and looked at Levi. 'Later? Promise?'

'I promise to... do my best. Okay?'

Madison nodded, and Levi lowered him to the ground before dismounting and leading the boy over to his mother. 'Do you still have that red outfit he was wearing in the palace?'

She nodded and handed it to him.

He took it and set about pulling tufts of the dried prairie grass. 'I'll stuff his outfit with grass and rope it to my back. Hopefully they'll think I have the boy and give chase. Put on the soldier's uniform and cloak again. Make sure to keep Madison in front of you, like I did today. With any luck, most of them will chase the red outfit; plus, Valour has more stamina than your mare. We'll at least make them earn their meal tonight. Hopefully it will provide enough time for your people to reach you.'

'Reach *us*. Remember, you need to stay close enough not to fall out of the saddle this time.'

'The melders' bloody curse. I get it.'

Sara ducked behind her horse and changed out of her dress. When she reappeared, her expression was contrite.

'Levi.'

He looked at her, clutching a tuft of prairie grass.

'I wanted to thank you. For everything.'

Levi rammed the dried grass into the red cloak and cinched it shut before tying the cloak to his back. 'Consider me thanked. But remember, we're both in this. The separation curse affects you too. I'm not all that sure how much distance I'll be able to put between us before it disables me or you, so don't be too hasty with your gratitude just yet.'

She nodded, glancing at the mountains. 'The scouts are gone. I expect help will come before sunset.'

'Well, that's something to aim for.' He waved and rode off, spearing away at an angle to their original course. Glancing across, he saw Sara had continued on, their respective dust plumes charting separate courses towards the mountains.

The discomfort intensified as the distance increased. It started as an ache behind his eyes, spreading rapidly across the forehead to wedge itself between the back of his skull and spine before radiating throughout his body. Each additional metre of separation forged a higher threshold of suffering. He rode its unrelenting edge, disorientated, pushing the separation to its extreme, daring it to claim him. New thresholds of tolerance carved through him, his vision blackening, then he remembered that Sara would also be suffering the same symptoms and wheeled back in, conceding one metre, two, relishing the tiny gush of relief as the pain came off a notch. To the left he could see Sara doing her best to ride like a man. He hoped she could handle the curse's discomfort. He eased Valour in another two metres and chanced a quick look behind. The majority of the hunting party had chosen to stay on his tail, as he'd hoped. A few straggled after Sara, but he guessed they were not as motivated. The prize Nicolai would have promised was for the woman and the boy, not the body-guard who wouldn't even be worth the trouble of bringing back.

They rode for another hour, until the sun was well into its final arc. It had disappeared behind the mountains and was now casting long shadows across the plain, making it difficult to see the burrows dug by the small furry rodents that abounded in this part of the country. Valour had stumbled in them twice but had thankfully recovered. He wondered how many of his pursuers might fall victim to them. Their horses were smaller, bred for endurance, not speed. He wondered whether this would make them more or less vulnerable to the prairie holes.

Valour was tiring. Levi could feel the stallion's stride shortening, his breathing becoming laboured. He patted the side of his mount's neck, whispering into his mane. 'Just a bit longer, old friend. One way or the other, it'll soon be over.'

The sun had not yet set, but nevertheless, it was time.

He eased Valour over, setting him on a course to intersect with Sara.

Behind him he heard the excited baying of the jackals. He was no longer running from them but travelling diagonally across the plain, decreasing the interception vector. He'd given Sara and her people as much time as he was able.

What is she doing? She's slowing down. Surely she isn't going to try and wait for me to catch up? The men behind her will make short work—

No. Something was appearing, rising out of the plain, like a massive drawbridge lifting into the air, tugged up on long struts. Beneath it, mounted men in purple and red uniforms were coming straight out of the ground like ants from some giant disturbed mound.

A tunnel with a gigantic hatch.

The uniformed men reached Sara and formed a protective ring about her. Her pursuers reined in, uncertain, the jackals snarling and snapping at the ends of their leashes.

Levi spared a glance behind him and urged Valour towards the tunnel.

His pursuers had stopped too, unsure of what was happening, calling back their hounds and jackals with whistles and loud, discordant shouts. Sara pointed animatedly in his direction.

He took off his hat and wearily waved his arm in response. A detachment of brightly uniformed men veered off and rode towards him. He'd never been more pleased to see soldiers. He gripped the pommel of his saddle with white-knuckled hands, lest he slide, exhausted, to the ground.

14

Chapter Fourteen

Levi followed the line of purple-uniformed men into the tunnel. When everyone was inside, the last soldier pulled a large lever on the wall and two thick ropes, looped to the roof of the tunnel, ran out as the great hatch lowered and closed with a resounding thump.

If Levi hadn't been so exhausted, he would have been over there inspecting the mechanism that controlled the drawbridge. He glanced at Sara, shaking his head at the enormity of it.

She gave him a tired smile. 'It's raised by one of our mammoths. The cables are connected to that ratchet wheel over there. The mammoth is trained to walk in a circle that then pulls the ropes around the wheel. The same principle is used to raise and lower the elevators. You'll see soon.'

'You knew all this but didn't tell me? I assumed they would have to climb down that cliff face.'

'As I said, I didn't know where the herd migration was up to. There is no reason for the tunnel to be manned otherwise. It could have taken longer.'

'Thank the gods it didn't. I've never seen tired men move so fast as when your soldiers gave chase,' he said.

'Those men and their cursed dogs were only trackers and mercenaries. They would have had no chance against my trained cavalry.' The commander of the men rode up and bowed, whispering into Sara's ear. She nodded and turned to Levi.

'There's a welcoming waiting. Madison and I should be at the front. Would you like to accompany us?' She paused before adding, 'You'll have to ride a horse length behind.'

Levi said nothing, conscious of the wave of resentment at being relegated to the role of servant once more, despite all they had been through.

Sara flushed. 'I'm sorry, it's just—'

'I understand, and I still am your personal bodyguard —Highness.'

She took a breath and gave him a resigned smile before urging her horse into a trot. Levi fell in a horse length behind.

The tunnel sloped down and was wide enough to accommodate four horses abreast. As they reached the front, Levi could see a large open area, brilliantly lit, the light spilling into the tunnel augmenting the intermittent yellowish glow from the oil lamps. As they emerged, a huge cheer echoed throughout the chamber. Sara smiled, acknowledging her people. Madison too was waving at the crowd, mostly soldiers, bright in their distinctive uniforms. Many tossed their puffed multi-coloured hats into the air.

Sara drew her horse to a stop, and Levi came up beside her, leaning in towards her. 'They seem pleased to see you.'

'It's been far too long. They have never even seen Madison.'

By the length of the tunnel, Levi estimated they must now be under the mountains. Beyond the half circle of soldiers was the mammoth Sara had referred to. The beast was four times the height of Valour and eight times as broad. A broad leather harness stretched across its massive chest and was connected to two thick ropes that wound about a wheel. The muscles rippling beneath the mammoth's hide made the shaggy brown coat appear alive. It stomped and snorted, impatient to be moving, and when it bellowed, the sound reverberated around the hollowed-out space.

Sara handed Levi her reins, leaving Madison in the saddle, and dismounted. 'Can you watch him?'

Levi nodded and caught Madison's eye, indicating the mammoth. 'He's big, isn't he?'

The boy, eyes wide with wonder mixed with a generous dollop of fear, nodded. Levi winked, and Madison gave him a tremulous smile.

'Why don't we go explore for a bit while your mother gets reacquainted with her army?'

Madison nodded.

'Hold tight then.' Levi nudged Valour with his knees, leading Madison on Sara's mare. They gave the mammoth a wide berth on the way to the next section, a natural cavern. It stretched up. Near the top, light was visible through what appeared to be a large hole carved out of the rock wall. Levi could make out men leaning over a wooden barricade, looking down. On the floor of the cavern was a huge platform with a wooden railing, similar to a rectangular raft. More of the thick ropes were attached to its four corners, coming together in an intricate splice above its deck before looping around a series of pulleys. These connected in turn to the ratcheted wheel and ultimately the mammoth. Levi craned his neck, looking up, then back down at the raft, trying to work it out.

'We call it an elevator.'

He turned in his saddle. One of the officers was standing beside him, grinning.

'Is that how you all got down here so quickly? The hairy monster over there pulls that thing up and down?'

'That's probably the short version, but yes. I see you have the queen's heir with you.' The man bowed, extending one leg in front of him. 'My name is Captain Lake, commander of the company you see here.'

Madison didn't bat an eyelash.

He must be used to it. Levi felt a little uncomfortable. 'Levi Monk. I'm, er, the queen's personal bodyguard.'

'From what I've heard, you have done an excellent job of keeping them both safe until you reached here.'

'We had some interesting challenges,' Levi said, anxious to get these formalities over. He could feel the creeping numbness of exhaustion coupled with the dank cold of the cavern spreading up from his feet and into his legs.

'Ah, the queen is coming. Now you can experience the elevator for yourself.'

∼

THE CONTRAPTION ROSE in a series of jerky movements. Levi imagined the huge beast below circling the pillar and with each rotation the thick rope spooling around the column and up through the series of pulleys hoisting the groaning timber platform higher into the mountain.

He found looking up to be more settling than watching the ground get further and further away with each lurching creak. Light spilled from the large hole he'd seen earlier, and he realised it was a landing area. As they rose higher, he could make out men's faces peering down at them. They shouted in an unfamiliar dialect, unfurling ropes that were quickly secured by those on the platform, allowing it to be guided close to the landing. Once it was secure, Sara led her mare off and out onto a wide flagstone promenade that must have been hacked out of the mountain. It was obvious that some of the excavated rock had then been used to construct a waist-high stone balustrade on one side, which would afford a panoramic view out across the plain in daylight. Now, with night rolling in, the drop off into black emptiness appeared endless. Levi edged his horse between Madison and the opening, concerned that the young boy may get vertigo on top of Sara's horse if he came too close to what must seem like a dark abyss spiralling below.

However, when he looked across, Madison was sitting straight and still, the training and discipline necessary for a future monarch evident even at this age, though Levi noted the boy's small fingers gripping the pommel of the saddle were tight with tension. Levi didn't blame him. He wasn't one for heights either.

Sara saw him looking down as she lifted Madison off the horse. 'The elevator is an easier way of getting down there.'

'I don't intend finding out.'

'So you're not going back? Not even for the melders' antidote?'

'When I do, I'm sure Valour would feel much more comfortable taking the track.'

'I'm sure *he* would.' The ghost of a smile briefly lifted the corners of her mouth. 'Well, naturally you're both welcome to stay here as long as you wish, and once this business with Nicolai is settled for the soldiers, I promised you to retrieve the remedy.'

A diminutive man bustled towards them, his outfit heavy with crimson, purple, and gold. He drew to a stop in front of Sara and bowed as deeply as the stiff, voluminous clothing allowed him. On straightening, his small frame remained lost within his robes.

'Highness. Your return is welcomed by all your subjects, but none more than I.'

Sara held out her fingers, and the small man pressed her moonstone ring to his forehead.

'Rabine. I take pleasure in seeing you again, and I thank you for taking care of affairs in my absence.' She made a presenting motion between Madison and Rabine. 'And of course, this is Prince Madison.'

Rabine bowed low again, his hand to his chest. 'My prince.'

Sara continued, indicating Levi, 'And my bodyguard, Levi, without whom neither Prince Madison nor I would be here. This is my chancellor, Rabine.'

'Allow me to express the thanks of our people for their safe return,' the chancellor said.

Bowing always made Levi uncomfortable, and he felt himself

flushing and gave what he presumed would be a suitable response. 'I seek no thanks or reward for doing my job other than pointing me in the direction of the stable. I'd like to feed and brush down my horse before finding myself a spare bunk in the barracks.'

'Oh, I'm sure we can do a little better than that, can't we, Chancellor?' Sara said in a clipped tone.

Rabine's mouth curled briefly in disapproval before he clapped twice, the sound echoing against the stone. Two young pages appeared at his side. He motioned one to take the two horses, his fingers flicking as if trying to rid himself of an annoying fly.

'He will see to it. This one,' he pointed at the other page 'will take you to *suitable* lodgings. Highness, the royal suite has been kept in constant readiness.'

'All these years?'

'Of course. We knew you would return eventually.'

Rabine bustled off after her, his short legs pumping to match Sara's long stride. Levi handed over the reins of the horses and followed the other young page in the opposite direction.

As palaces went, this one was modest. The wide stone passageway provided a common access to rooms and chambers carved into the mountain. Passing the open doors, Levi couldn't see any expensive draperies, gilded furniture, or massive portraits of dead people. He'd not even passed any servants staggering under steaming, heavy platters of gold or silver, despite it being the meal hour. It was almost, but not quite, rustic—more a fortress, a place of purpose rather than show.

Levi had a feeling that here everyone also had a job that contributed something to the community rather than a title and a role that had to be constantly defended. 'So where is everybody?' he asked the page.

The young boy turned his head, continuing to walk. 'Those that aren't at mess are with the herds. You would have seen one of the great mammoths in the elevator hall?'

'You mean there's more of those?'

'Hundreds. It takes many men to escort the herds from the highland pastures to the stables. Their fleece is thicker in winter, so when we shear them it's important the animals are kept warm, particularly the young ones.'

'You mean you keep them inside?'

'Only in winter. The stables are behind the living quarters.'

Levi remembered the size of the beast below and tried to imagine—

'These are your quarters, sir.' The page ushered him through a carved wooden door. Inside was a good-sized room: a single bed with a brown shaggy cover that looked a lot like the coat from the mammoth downstairs, a simple wooden chair, and a sideboard with basin and a jug for washing. Basic, but definitely a step up from the barracks dorm and thirty snoring, farting soldiers. He dropped his saddlebag kit in one corner. The page gathered it up, his nose twitching. 'I'll have these washed for you, sir.'

Levi nodded, noting the only window opened onto the broad common walkway. 'They certainly need it, thanks. So, where are the queen's chambers from here? I need to speak with her.'

'I'll ask the chancellor to schedule a meeting for you. Perhaps tomorrow.'

'Tomorrow?' Levi grunted and sat down on the edge of the bed. He sank into the deep mattress, the shaggy coverlet luxurious. Postponed fatigue stole over him as he pulled off his boots and lay down. 'Tomorrow is fine.'

He didn't hear the door close.

A LOUD KNOCKING WOKE HIM. He didn't have the energy to get up. It felt like he'd been asleep for only five minutes.

'Come.'

The door swung open, and a young girl in a brown shift carried in a platter of meat and a tossed selection of fried vegetables, along with a ewer. Levi eased himself up, the smell of the rich gravy drawing him over to the table.

He sat and poured himself a goblet of red wine from the ewer. 'Thank you.'

She nodded and pulled open the curtain. Outside, the moon had risen over the high peaks, its light picking up streams of mist attempting to form into cloud.

'What time is it?' he asked.

'It's gone midnight, sir.'

Midnight? I must have been out for six hours or more.

'Do you usually serve a meal at this time of night?'

'No, sir. The queen herself ordered it for now.'

The maid left, and he set about demolishing the meal. As he drank the last of the wine and was weighing up whether to find the privy or collapse back onto the bed, there was another knock. This time he answered it. Sara stood in the doorway, a man in colourful robes just behind her. He stepped back, belatedly remembering to bow as she glided through. The man, caught in the slipstream of rustling skirts, followed, dragging a trolley piled high with thick dusty books. The room seemed much smaller with the three of them and the huge trolley at the centre.

Sara noted the crushed bedcovers. 'I thought you'd be asleep, so I sent the meal for you first.' She indicated the man with her. 'This is our physic. Remember I told you about him?'

'The one with all the remedies for ancient curses. Have you told him about our—'

'Only that *you* have a separation problem.'

'Me?'

'Yes, of course. That's why we're here.' He intercepted her warning glance and decided to change the subject.

'How's the prince?'

'Fine. Resting. He'll be safe now.'

'Any sign of Nicolai's men?'

Sara shook her head. 'He wouldn't dare attack us yet. It would send entirely the wrong message to those he wants to join him in his war against the barbarians.'

'He won't give up. You do know that? He can't claim the throne in his own right while your son lives. If he doesn't mount a frontal attack, he'll infiltrate one of his black assassins into your ranks. They're experts, impossible to detect, and it'll only take one of them to get through.'

'So what do you suggest?'

'Dispatch royal envoys to the other kingdoms warning them; tell them what Nicolai plans to do and entreat them to join you in a coalition to avoid all-out war. A conflict won't benefit anyone except Nicolai. They'll see that, surely. After that, encourage them to join you in taking the fight to him. Draw him and his army out onto the plains. You'll have a better chance out there than laying siege.'

'I'll consider it. In the meantime, I'm sure you want to be free of your "situation," I think you called it.'

'Absolutely.'

The man in the robes took this to be a cue and opened his voluminous jacket to reveal a multitude of pockets crammed with vials and bottles. He took his time in selecting one and eased off the cap. A noxious smell filled the small room. Both Levi and Sara recoiled, holding their noses.

'Phew. What's that stink?' Levi asked.

The man looked surprised as he made a space on his trolley and sprinkled some of the powder into an iron bowl recessed into the wood. He used his finger to sweep it into a cone. 'Sorry, I always forget. My nose is inured to these compounds. It will not take long. Your arm, please.' He made an impatient gesture, and Levi hesitantly held out his arm, remembering the melders and their leeches. The physic produced a long thin tube sharpened to a point at one end and, without warning, plunged it into a vein pulsing above Levi's elbow.

'What the hell!'

Behind him he could hear Sara chuckling.

The narrow tube filled rapidly. After removing it, the physic dribbled a little of the contents onto the small cone of stinking powder on the table and handed Levi a cloth to staunch the wound.

All three watched the blood bubble and react with the powder. The physic nodded as if this confirmed something.

'I'm assuming you don't have access to the antidote from the sourced infection?'

Levi bit back a sarcastic quip. It would not be helpful here. 'No.'

The physic directed his next comment direct to Sara. 'As I suspected, the alchemy is too strong. I would need some of the source material to come up with an antidote.' He shook his head.

'Is there nothing you can do?' Sara's voice was tinged with desperation.

The man refastened his coat, the bottles sewn within it clinking together. His expression was pensive. 'There is a plant. It grows much further up the mountain. But this late in the season,' he shrugged, 'it will be difficult to find. It doesn't like the cold and lies dormant during winter.'

'Do you have any that has been dried or extracted, something that might help in the meantime?' Levi asked.

'It is only effective while fresh. Dried or as an extract, the plant becomes toxic.'

'And if it's fresh?'

'The results will not be... pleasant. But if you survive—'

'If I survive?'

'—it will go some way towards neutralising a melder separation curse. You still won't be comfortable if the separation becomes too great, but unlike now, it will be tolerable. Ultimately, though, if left untreated it will drive you mad if the separation becomes prolonged.'

'And that's better because?'

'It gives you time to locate the source material before it kills you.'

'What?' Sara snapped.

The physic looked taken aback. 'Yes, Highness. If the curse is not broken, then both joined parties will die within months. Three at most.'

A heaviness thumped into Levi's heart. 'Three months?'

'At most,' the physic added.

Levi looked at Sara. Her face was white, full lips pinched.

'No, physic. Neither of us knew,' she managed.

'Where might I find this plant?' Levi asked, a quaver in his voice.

'The other side of Silver Lake. You must gather it before the deep snows come.' He looked meaningfully at Sara. 'There will be no time to go around.'

'You mean we have to go across the lake?'

The physic sucked in his cheeks and nodded sagely. 'Yes, if the freeze permits. Though I must tell you the first ice crust has already formed on the lake, so time is moving quickly.' He regarded Levi gravely. 'I would not wait another night. You should take this.' He riffled through his pockets and produced a white bottle slashed with an irregular gold stripe. He removed the elaborate stopper and carefully spooned the blood and powder mixture into the opening before inserting the stopper once more. 'This may help you locate the plant. Hold it up to the sun; the light will strike the gold, and its reflection will point the way to the plant. When it turns pink, you will be close. I think there is an illustration here somewhere.' He picked up one of the thick books and flopped open the cracked cover, flipping through the pages.

'Ah, here.' He turned the book so they could see. The page contained a stylised sketch of a plant with a curvy stem, a profusion of jagged leaves, and a star-shaped flower at the top. The elaborate border of the page was decorated with lines and flourishes.

'I'll have my apprentice make a copy for you. It shouldn't take long; he's quite the artist.'

Levi nodded. One plant looked much the same as another to him. He pointed at the gold slash on the bottle. 'This is *kintsugi*, is it not?'

The physic looked up sharply, his eyes narrowing with suspicion and evaluation. 'You know of it?'

'Some. My master calls it the Golden Journey, representing an opportunity to embrace our wounds—our brokenness—by turning them into something beautiful. He taught me it follows on from the Zen tradition of Wabi Sabi—impermanence and imperfection—because the shape of us is impossible to see until it becomes fractured.'

'That is correct. Repair leads to transformation. I would like to meet this man, your master, one day. Personally, I think of *kintsugi* as a reconciliation with the flaws and accidents of time, the gold emphasising that all breakages have a philosophically rich merit. I think you will be able to work with this bottle successfully.' The physic bowed and handed it and the sketch reverently to Levi.

The bottle felt cool and smooth between his hands, its golden seam gleaming beneath the oil lamps. He tucked it and the sketch into his waistband.

'So what do I do when I find this plant?'

'Place it inside that bottle with hot water. Once it has steeped, drink the tea.' He turned to Sara. 'Will there be anything further, Highness?'

'No. Oh, yes. Could you ask the chancellor to join me in my chambers?'

He bowed again and left, closing the door quietly behind him.

She waited a moment before whispering, 'Do you think it's true? That the curse is fatal?'

'We have to assume it is. That makes it even more important to recover the source material from Nicolai, and to be able to do that, I first have to find this plant.' Frustrated, he flicked a finger against the sketch the physic had given him.

'That would be a "we," given that you can't travel more than a few leagues without me before you fall off your horse.'

Levi fumed, his yes wending its way out through clenched teeth.

～

THE PAGE CAME to fetch him an hour later and conducted him swiftly to Sara.

She handed him a thick, shaggy brown cape.

He held it up in front of him. 'Do you use the mammoth's fleece for everything?'

'It's the warmest covering we have—anyone has, for that matter. It is well prized and the staple of our treasury.'

Levi swept it around him, securing it at the throat. The sensation was of snugness and warmth. It exuded a faint smoky odour, like it had been washed and dried in front of an open fire. She hurried him down the hall.

'It's just us?'

'Yes. I had to be firm with Chancellor Rabine. He wanted to send a full regiment. I reminded him that his primary purpose is to protect Madison at all costs. Secretly, I think Rabine loves being told what to do.'

'He should be right at home with you then,' Levi muttered.

Down the passageway, he heard Valour's whinny and turned to follow it.

'Not that way. Come. I had Rabine prepare everything.'

Sara led him in the opposite direction, turning down a tunnel that led deeper into the mountain. 'I heard you speak to the physic of your *master*? I was under the impression you were a soldier. Though, as I recall now, you were also a yellow skin—a thief—when we first met.'

Levi grimaced. 'I was in the army for many years. One day I woke up and realised Nicolai had turned me into an assassin—murderer— so I petitioned a *kintsugi* master to take me on. However, Nicolai found out, bought up the chop debt incurred by my ex-wife, and forced me to become a journeyman. You know the rest.'

'I'm sorry.'

'No, I should have told you. It didn't seem important at first, and later, well, it's been a busy time.'

'And none of my business.'

'That too.' He paused, looking away, and cleared his throat. 'I was also ashamed.'

'Ashamed?'

He shrugged. 'Proud men suffer it more, I'm told. I hate it that Nicolai bested me. Bent me, yet again, to his will.'

Sara stopped, and he turned to face her. Her gaze slid away, settling in a dark corner of the hallway before returning to regard him fully 'No. I'm the one who should be ashamed. I knew where Nicolai would probably be keeping the antidote, and I didn't tell you after we'd rescued Madison. Nicolai's chambers were close to where we were. I wanted to get Madison to safety.' Her face flushed.

'As I recall, we barely had time to escape as it was. The main objective was to save your son. We did that. There was no time for anything else, regardless of what either of us might like to imagine.' He paused, reflecting. 'You know, it's odd. Every now and again I get the feeling there's something I need to do or get. I had it when we were escaping the palace, as if I was running out of time.'

'If what the physic told us about the melders' curse being fatal is true, then we are.'

They continued on in an uncomfortable silence, their footfalls hollow in the confined space until they reached a barred double door. Rabine emerged from the shadows, his oversized stiff robes inhibiting his deep bow.

'Everything is prepared, Highness. I have instructed the men that you'll be gone for a day and a night. After that, I have your permission...' He let the words hang, and she finished it for him.

'To come and find us.'

This seemed to settle the little man. 'Is it true you are travelling to the Silver Lake?'

Sara made a clucking sound. 'There's only one person who could have told you that.'

He bowed. 'The physic and I have a close relationship. I must warn you, Highness. There is talk in the streets of harpies.'

Sara snorted. 'Harpies are only legends, like the Widow.

Designed to keep children in their beds when the first snows might tempt them outside.'

'Legends often have a kernel of truth—'

'Enough! No more talk of wind spirits and old women's ghosts hungry for hot blood. I know the stories as well as you. In fact, I remember it was you who used to tell them to me at bedtime. They scared me back then.'

'As you wish. Ah.' He tapped his head with his index finger. 'Almost forgot. The physic asked me to give you this. A sketch he promised, I understand.'

Levi took it and flipped it open. It looked to be an exact copy, complete with the same intricate border. He tucked it inside his jerkin.

Rabine bowed and backed away. 'Safe travels then, Highness.'

Sara nodded her dismissal and pushed open the doors, revealing a natural deep cavern inside the mountain. As Levi stepped inside, the ripe stench of the close enclosure overwhelmed him. Huge, open pens lined the rock walls, and inside each, a great mammoth was tethered. Some of the beasts had been shorn, their skin pinkish and raw, yet already brown stubble was growing back. Most were feeding from deep troughs at the front of their pens. They all swayed to a somnolent beat from a drummer squatting in the middle of the floor.

'You get used to the smell. The drumbeat keeps them calm.'

One of the beasts chose that moment to grunt and deposit a pile of green dung so high it would bury a horse and rider. Men in leather aprons with curved shovels rushed in, dragging a green-stained cart behind them.

'Their manure is valued as fertiliser as well. Some even say it has aphrodisiac properties.'

'I'll take your word for it,' Levi said, rubbing his nose. 'Why are we here?'

She gestured towards the rear of the cavern where two shaggy beasts were standing in front of another of the drawbridge contraptions.

'You don't mean...'

'They are very gentle and can run faster than a horse through the snow. They are also our only means of crossing the lake. The fleece is waterproof, another reason why it is so highly valued.'

'We're riding *them*?' Levi's voice was tight. The beasts were almost as high as the cavern's roof. 'How do I even get up there?'

Sara made a motion with her hand, and one of the leather-aproned men waved from the top of the nearest one—and jumped. It took Levi a moment to realise the man had hold of a rope. It whirred, spooling out from a pulley above.

'There is a large spring attached to the pulley. The downward journey captures the energy and loads the spring. The pulley preserves it until it is activated. Come, I'll show you.'

She led the way to the rope from which the man had descended. Taking it in her hand, she pulled it out and down with a sharp tug. The rope whirred and retracted quickly, drawing her up until she was at the top. Levi, still unsure, allowed himself to be led to the next mammoth, and after some encouragement grabbed the rope and pulled it out and down. The rope tightened, dragging on his upraised arm as it hauled him up, his face ploughing through the beast's long fur. Once at the top, he skittered on hands and knees along to what might pass for its neck.

'You steer with the feet, so try lying back instead of sitting up. It's more comfortable that way too.'

He glanced over. Sara had her feet positioned on the bumps behind her beast's woolly ears, and he tried to mimic her. Lying back on the fleece certainly was more comfortable; she was right about that.

Below, men were lined up on either side of two massive ropes connected to a wheel that held the drawbridge shut. Sara yelled, 'Release!' and moving as one, they fed the rope out, lowering the drawbridge in creaky stages. When it was down, Sara's beast lumbered through the opening. Levi hung on as his mammoth followed.

Sara called back over her shoulder, 'You don't need to do anything. He'll follow her. They are mated, and theirs is a matriarchal hierarchy. The females are in charge.'

'Why am I not surprised?' Levi muttered, hanging on against the slow roll of the bull mammoth beneath him. This high off the ground, the feeling was not dissimilar to clinging to the top of a ship's spar during a sloppy sea. He hadn't liked that much at the time either.

Outside, the night was still. The earlier mist had scattered, and now heavy clouds pregnant with snow idled across the sky, as if deliberating where they would land their load. Levi snuggled down into the cloak. Sara was right, the ride was more comfortable this way, particularly if he didn't need to guide this beast. He found himself drifting within the deep warmth, lulled, now he was used to it, by the regular rolling gait. His eyes became heavy, setting up a cycle of light dozing and sudden awakening until the sun peeked at him from the horizon on the other side of the plain.

Levi straightened, reassuring himself that the swaying backside of Sara's cow was still in front. Breathing easier, he took in his surroundings. They'd travelled uphill for most of the night, of that much he was sure. There was no real road, only a track one broad footfall wide that would be obliterated entirely once the first snows came. The terrain across the gently rising plateau was unremittingly the same: stunted growth, a cross between low brush with olive-coloured leaves and aspirational spiky grass clustered haphazardly in stunted tufts, while, in between, bare earth gave way to lichen-covered granite. The terrain would have been hard on Valour's hooves. The thick hide on the beasts' feet seemed immune to the sharp rocky edges.

He sat up, craning his neck. In the distance, he could make out a shimmer against the harsh backdrop. He hoped it was the lake. If the physic was correct, they needed to find this damn weed before the serious snow started to fall. He touched the bottle in his hide shoulder pack, still unsure who would be the one to taste the tea.

Overnight, the clouds had ceased their scudding journey and now hovered, waiting, their undersides grey and ominous, the air thick with the smell of impatient snow. Mentally Levi urged his mount on, but with a jerk, they came to a sudden halt, throwing him to one side. He scrambled for a fistful of fleece and hauled himself back up. In front, Sara's mammoth had stopped. Levi's drew level, snorting something to its mate.

'Everything all right?' she called across.

'Fine. Looks like the snow is coming.' He pointed up, the gesture superfluous.

'The lake is just ahead. We'll swim the animals over where it's narrowest, but it'll still be quite a distance. If we get separated, use your feet to guide him. He should know where to go, but just in case, here's a quick lesson. Ready?'

Levi nodded, leaning back and positioning the bottoms of his boots on the bumps behind the ears that she had shown him earlier.

'Tap the ball of the foot for faster, the heel for slow. Stamp both feet hard to stop. To steer, take your feet down to here,' she brought hers down to the bottom bump and pointed, 'and press down with the foot for the direction you want to go. Use your left to go left, and right for right, got it?'

He suspected this was one of those times when the instructions sounded easier than it might be in practice. He nodded anyway.

'The pressure will determine how sharp you want him to turn. These beauties may look cumbersome but can turn faster than a cavalry horse, so be careful. You can get thrown off, and without a rope, there's no way to get back on. Try it while we're with you.'

Levi tentatively used the balls of his feet, and the beast rumbled forward. Stop was easy, the turns not so. Travelling straight seemed like the best option. He resolved to keep his mount glued to the back-side of Sara's.

She continued. 'Once we're in the water, you'll need to hang on even tighter. They inflate themselves in order to float more easily. That can make your seat less secure. They roll quite a lot in the water, like a shallow-keeled ship.'

'What about feed? I noticed in the stables they had mountains of dried grass in their feeding troughs. There doesn't seem to be anything out here for them.'

'They store food and water in their bodies. They can go for days at a time without either. We'll be back well before then, but there will be grazing on the other side.' She gave a final glance at the clouds and re-settled herself on her mount, using the balls of her feet to move off. Levi followed her through a dip, and when he crested the ridge on the other side, the lake became fully visible, its vast area stretching away in all directions. The wind was stronger on the exposed ridge, and Levi huddled further into his cloak. The lake looked deep, and its surface was beginning to ruffle ahead of the strengthening wind.

Sara turned and pointed at one of the lake's fingers that thrust itself into the woodlands to the left. 'That's the one we need to cross.'

Levi squinted, following the direction in which she was pointing. It was one of the narrowest parts, but it was still some distance across.

'Come on. We have to hurry before the wind gets too strong. It's very changeable here.'

Levi's mammoth didn't wait for a signal but immediately took off, following its mate down the steep slope towards the lake. Levi held on, lurching and rolling with the increased pace. Neither animal hesitated at the lake's edge. Both plunged in with a blast of fetid breath that drifted back over Levi before they sucked in what seemed to be an inordinate amount of air. Levi felt the sides of his animal's body inflate like a balloon, and then they were afloat. Ahead he could see the legs and feet of Sara's mammoth churning beneath the water, moving fast enough to create a wake, its body rolling like a barrel. Levi gripped handfuls of his animal's long coarse hair and wedged the toes of his boots beneath the beast's ears, hoping this didn't signal some other steering instruction he hadn't been told about.

The crossing was longer than he had the stomach for, but shorter than he'd feared. When the massive beasts' feet found the muddy bottom on the opposite shore, he gave a sigh of relief and loosened his frozen grip, looking around. The terrain was similar to the other side, with low bristly bushes, now bending before the rising wind, and a kind of long green grass that the mammoths seemed to favour, as they'd already begun grazing. Levi pulled out the sketch of the plant the physic had drawn, comparing it with what he could see growing along the shoreline. Nothing was flowering this late in the season, and he wondered whether they'd come here more out of desperation and some misplaced hope.

An icy wind gusted off the water, and Levi tugged the hood of his cloak closer around his face. The silvered surface of the lake rippled, breaking in small wavelets against the marshy banks. He dug into his pack, retrieving the vial the physician had given him, and held it up. Overhead, the sun fought for dominance and finally streamed through a break in the clouds.

It caught the glass vial in Levi's hand. A golden beam that the physic had said to watch out for stretched away in front of him.

'There.' He pointed. 'We need to keep moving.'

Sara urged her mammoth on, keeping to the perimeter of the lake. Levi followed, stopping to hold up the glass vial whenever the winter sun was strong enough.

BY THE TIME morning nudged its way into afternoon, the ground had become marshy, but the clouds had dissipated enough to provide continuous sun. In front, Sara rested her mount and waited for him to catch up.

'We need to find firmer ground. The mammoths don't handle marsh well, and this looks like it turns into swamp up ahead.'

Levi squinted into the distance. Long grass poked through low-lying water. It was hard to tell where the lake ended. He held the glass vial up, angling it to catch the light. A shape like a golden arrow flickered faintly across the ground, pointing straight ahead towards the swamp.

'We can't take the beasts in there—'

'Then we'll go on foot. Or, I will,' Levi said.

She swung her leg over, grabbed hold of the pulley-brake line, and slid down. 'You know we both have to.'

Levi grunted and followed.

'Leave the beasts, they'll graze,' Sara said. 'If something happens and we don't make it back in time, then at least the search party will find them and have a place to start looking.'

'Hopefully before we've drowned,' Levi muttered, visually tracking the golden line that disappeared into the swamp. 'Come on then.'

He squelched on, making sure to mark their path for the return journey as he followed the golden arrow. It danced across the spongy ground in front. He fancied that the glow was getting stronger.

'Levi, look.'

He stopped, thankful for an excuse to rest, and lifted his gaze. Brackish water interspersed with swamp grass and patches of thick black mud stretched in front of them. Wispy strips of swamp gas hovered close to the water's surface, pooling at the base of rotting trees.

'Swamp and bog. We can't go through there; it'll be full of sink holes and what we call fast mud.' Levi checked the direction of the arrow. 'But it's pointing that way.'

Sara walked over and squatted down, separating some long tufts of grass. 'There's an animal trail here. It might lead us around the worst of it. What do you think?'

'That's where the arrow is. We should hurry though, or we'll lose the light to get back. I don't want to spend the night out here.'

They started along the narrow path trampled bare in patches by generations of the animals that normally lived here. Levi guessed most of those who hadn't left for the winter would already be bunkered down in hibernation. The path gradually became wet, then sticky, stinky mud before finally submerging altogether. They paused, water sloshing around their ankles. They were marooned, with enough wizened tree trunks to block the view and prevent any meaningful orientation.

The arrow still pointed forward.

'How deep do you think it will get if we go on?' Sara asked. 'My boots are already leaking.'

'Mine too. Hang on a bit; I think I see something just below the water.'

He transferred his weight onto his back foot and sprang forward, landing on a slippery flat rock. Taking care, he turned around and extended his hand.

'Come on. I'm standing on a rock. It's big enough for us both. I can see another one over there. This could be a bridge, of sorts.'

'A bridge? Who for?'

'Right now I'm hoping it's for us.'

She took his outstretched hand, and he hauled her across.

'See.' He pointed. Another rock of similar size was barely visible beneath the murky water. It was another long step away. When they reached it, Levi spotted the next. The rocks zigzagged across the swamp. The further they went, the deeper the water separating the stepping stones, yet the rocks themselves were always flat and the same distance below the surface. Just enough to flood his boots.

He tried to wriggle his toes, but his feet were numb from the freezing water. He was breathing heavily when he felt a tap on his shoulder.

'Levi, look.'

He turned to where she was pointing.

'The last rock we were on a moment ago. It's gone. As well as the one before it. I thought I was imagining it, but this time I took note. The rock disappeared as soon as I took my foot off.'

'Disappeared?'

Levi peered back the way they had come. Only open water.

'It must be an optical illusion. It has to be there; we were just standing on it.'

'I know, but can you see it?'

'No.' He looked up. The sun was into its final phase. Once they lost the light, there would be no golden arrow to guide them and no way to see the next rock.

'We need to keep going then, this way.'

They continued for another fifteen minutes. Levi had no idea where they were, and even less about finding his way back to the mammoths. Once they'd left solid land, there had been no way of continuing to mark their passage. However, he had the distinct impression that they were going somewhere, being led even, to something or someone, and not just for the sake of a plant. The next rock was on the other side of a dying tree. Levi could make out its edge, jutting out past the gnarled exposed roots. He had to hug the trunk to ease himself around it while feeling for the submerged rock with his foot. His boot scraped against the rock, and he hauled himself the rest of the way, pawing for purchase on the slippery surface. Once across, he was about to turn and help Sara when he saw something. He narrowed his gaze and leant out, hanging on to one of the tree branches to get a better view.

Land.

It was an island in the middle of the swamp. A beaten earth path led up from a rickety jetty, winding through garden beds blooming with a multitude of colours. Colours from plants that wouldn't normally return until spring. Behind that was a stone hut with a thatched roof and lazy smoke trails drifting from the chimney.

He swung himself back in.

'Sara. There's land—an island, I think—and there's a cottage. Come on.'

He helped her around the tree, and together they navigated the final series of rocks that stopped thirty metres short of the island. They waded ashore, shivering as they staggered onto the mud. A wind was rising, dragging in the twilight, the sun already wavering on the horizon. Levi held up the glass vial once more. The arrow flickered weakly, stretching towards the cottage.

'The plant must be here. Look.' In the final flush before sunset, the light had turned the glass vial pink.

Chapter Fifteen

Sara, teeth chattering, hurried up the winding path and gave two sharp raps with the iron knocker against the door.

The sound it produced was solid, like the stone walls of the cottage.

Levi knelt beside one of the flowerbeds, sketch in hand, comparing it to the plants. The fading light made it difficult.

Sara rapped again.

'You know there's something not quite right here, don't you?' Levi said, sitting back on his heels. 'I mean, these flowers are all spring blooms. They shouldn't be flowering now. And what about those rocks that led us here?'

'I know. But right now I'm freezing, and that takes precedence. Whoever lives here is about to save their queen from contracting pneumonia.'

Sara knocked again, more urgently this time, waited a couple of moments, then tried the latch. The door creaked open, releasing warmth that she followed inside. The cottage consisted of one room with four blue doors, one in each wall. No windows. In the centre was a round wooden table with three chairs. A single cot covered with several multi-coloured quilts occupied one corner. Opposite, a fireplace cradled a welcoming blaze. Delicious smells bubbled from a blackened pot hanging over the flames. The floor was beaten earth covered by rush mats that crunched soft and dry underfoot as Sara squelched across to the fireplace, holding up her hands to absorb the heat.

'No one here?' Levi asked from the door. He had to duck to enter, then shut the wind out behind him. 'The light has gone. I'll have to check more thoroughly tomorrow.'

'Only you and me, but there's fire and food. Whoever lives here won't be far away.' Sara shrugged out of the hairy mammoth cloak and shook it out. 'In the meantime, I need to get out of these clothes.' She held up the cloak. 'Here, hold this up and look the other way.'

Levi took the cloak and held it up. Sara peeled off her saturated clothing until she was naked, and with one quick movement took hold of the upraised corners of the cloak and used the ball of her foot to spin herself around, wrapping it tightly about her.

'Neatly done,' he said, nodding.

'There's an art to most things. It simply takes practice to bring them into being. Having six ladies' maids watch you dress several times a day helps too.' She grinned, wringing out her clothes before laying them out in front of the fireplace, pretending not to look as Levi shrugged out of his hairy cloak and saturated clothes, using a quilt to wrap around himself.

'I vote we eat,' Sara said, taking down two of the bowls and ladling some of the stew into each.

Levi wandered over to the door on the back wall. 'What's with the four doors, do you think?' He tried the latch. It was locked. He tried the other two doors. 'They're all locked.'

They exchanged a look before he rushed back to the one they'd come in and waggled the simple latch, trying to drag it open. It refused to budge.

Fumbling through his clothes, he located the pouch with the thin metal strips that he'd used to open the lock in the palace.

'It won't go in. It's like the locking mechanism has been blocked.'

Sara came over and tried the door for herself. 'I get the feeling this might have been a trap.'

Levi kicked the bottom of the door in frustration. 'And we've walked straight into it.'

'Well, we're stuck here for now. We may as well eat.' Sara padded over to the table and sat down in front of one of the steaming bowls of stew and took a bite. Chewing, she said, 'You know, there is something odd.'

'Something else, you mean?' Levi said, joining her.

'Yes. There are three chairs, three bowls, and three spoons, but only one bed.'

There was a gust of cold air behind them and the slam of a door. 'Keen eye—for a queen.'

They turned in the direction of the voice. An old woman dressed in black from bodice to boot stood with her back to the front door. She moved towards them, leaning heavily on a bent wooden staff. 'Queens don't usually see the detail; they're too often taken by life's larger tapestry.'

'Who are you?' Levi asked.

'Who am I?' She coughed out what might have been a laugh. 'You're in my house. I should be asking you that.'

'You appear to know who I am.' Sara gathered her dignity, securing it and the cloak more firmly about her.

The corners of the old woman's mouth stretched, and she nodded. 'Indeed I do, *Queen* Sara,' she used the stick to support her as she turned to face Levi, 'and her faithful dogsbody, Levi Monk.'

Levi's face hardened, and Sara gently laid her fingers on his forearm.

'As your queen, I demand you tell me your name and why you are keeping us here.'

'Fealty must be earned, not expected, missy. You are not my queen, and names, well, they are powerful and should not be given lightly, but you may know of me as the widow.'

Sara sat back, the spoon clattering to the table. One hand moved to her chest, the fingers curling into a childish ward against evil.

The widow snickered and shuffled over to the pot, stirring the contents before taking down the third bowl and carefully filling it with the thick sauce, leaving the chunks of meat behind.

'Eat. You are both weakened by the journey and the cold. Afterwards we will talk.' The widow reached up to one of the shelves above the fire and took down a loaf of home bake, dumping it in the middle of the table before sitting down.

'You were expecting us, weren't you? That's why there are three of everything. You led us here? Why?' Sara went to grab hold of the old woman's arm, but her fingers went through it, coming away cold, like they'd passed through icy smoke.

Sara clenched and unclenched her fingers, restoring circulation before she spat out, 'I should have asked, *what* are you?'

'I said we will talk later.'

'Should we eat this? It could be poisoned,' Levi whispered.

'She's eating it.'

'Yes, but I also saw what happened when you tried to grab her arm. She's some sort of wraith.'

Sara met his eyes, raising her brows. 'A wraith that eats stew? She brought us here for a reason. If she wanted us dead, I'm guessing we already would be.'

The widow's chin hovered above her bowl, gaze darting between them like a balding predatory bird's while she continued to slurp from her spoon with noisy relish.

Sara helped herself to some home bake and dipped it in the rich sauce. The stew was thick with vegetables that she hadn't eaten since last summer.

The old woman finished and sat back, pushing her bowl away, the rough scrape of wood against wood loud within the silence. She stabbed a crooked finger at Levi's bowl and smiled. She had no teeth. 'You have supped with the widow. Do you know what that means, Levi Monk?'

'Indigestion?'

She snickered again, wagging the same crooked finger at him.

'To sup with the widow is to be in her debt,' Sara answered. 'It's part of an old nursery rhyme. "...Sup with the widow and the devil keeps you long."'

'Ah, your queen is clever as well as pretty, Levi Monk.'

'Why don't you tell us what this is all about?' Sara snapped. 'I am not intimidated by childhood fairy tales.'

The crone's words came out slow, heavy with portent. 'All legends have a kernel of truth.'

The words dug deep. *Someone had said just that recently... Rabine.*

'Ah,' the widow cackled, 'I see you have worked out a "who;" now only the "why" remains.'

'What is she talking about?' Levi asked.

Sara's thoughts tumbled over each other, meeting denial at every turn. *Rabine? Is it even possible? I can't believe he would... But why?*

'Rabine, my *trusted* chancellor, turns out to be more devious than I thought,' Sara said.

The widow clapped her hands, obviously delighted. 'And...'

Sara nodded. 'The physic was working with him. It was he who sent us here.'

'But why?' Rabine could have just left us out there on the plain. Nicolai's men would have made short work of us.'

'It was the army who responded to my purple smoke, and the army stands loyal to the crown. Rabine would not have dared intervene. No, if this is a plot, it would be necessary for me to be declared lost, presumed dead, with only a couple of grazing mammoths to mark the spot where we'd disappeared.'

She could see from Levi's expression that he'd caught up.

He spoke the one word that she hadn't been able to. 'Madison. He's going to return Madison to Nicolai, isn't he?'

The widow clapped her hands again, rocking back and forth in her chair, chortling. 'Now you have the "why." Chancellor Rabine has grown used to power in your absence. Like all greedy men, he now considers it his and will do anything to keep it.'

'Including selling his future king to Nicolai.' Sara found the words almost too painful to voice. 'Oh, I was such a fool for leaving him and coming on this... foolhardy quest.'

Levi placed a hand on her shoulder and gave it a light squeeze. 'You had no choice. The curse would have killed you within the season.'

The widow grunted. 'Is that what he told you? The physic?'

'Yes.'

She cackled again. 'He lied. The melders' curse only binds.'

'Bastard,' Levi muttered. 'What I don't understand, is how did all this happen so quickly? It's only been a few days since we rescued Madison. There hasn't been time for all this to happen.'

'Ah.' The widow dismissed his words with a wave of her hand. 'Her mountain kingdom was the only place where she would feel safe, and Nicolai knew it. As regent, he'd already had dealings with Chancellor Rabine and knew the man's weakness for power. All it took was a couple of messenger pigeons to set it up, just as Rabine did to arrange my contract for you two.'

Sara's mouth firmed before she said, 'If Nicolai holds Madison, he automatically becomes regent of the high kingdom, which means he will also have command of my army. If we join his war against the barbarians, then the rest of the nobles will follow.'

She leant back in her chair, thinking, arms folded, legs crossed, her upper foot tapping the air. Finally, the foot stopped and she sat forward, switching her intense focus to the widow. 'What is still not clear to me is why we are here, in this hut with you, sharing stew and home bake? You just said you accepted a contract from Rabine. Why are we not dead already?'

The widow ran her tongue across the slit of her mouth, eyes bright, nodding encouragement, as if willing Sara to discover the answer.

'Tell me, damn it, witch. I command you.' Sara slammed the table with the flat of her hand and then bit down on her bottom lip, as if this might block the anger from escaping further.

The corners of the old woman's mouth stretched, turning the lines in her cheeks into deep crags. She hooted with laughter, belying the bitter malevolence that shone in her eyes. 'Command? Me? And what will you do if I choose not?'

Sara closed her eyes, damping down the rage bubbling around the image of Madison being returned to Nicolai. 'Nothing. I will do—and can do—nothing.'

'That's right. You can do nothing *to* me. But you can do something *for* me. To repay your debt.'

'What debt?' Levi spluttered.

'Your lives. Should I choose not to kill you, when the contract was to do so.'

Sara looked up from the table directly into the widow's enlarged black pupils. 'What do you want?'

The old woman stared back, and without breaking her gaze said, 'Nicolai. I want you to bring him here.'

'Nicolai?' Levi asked. 'Why?'

'That does not concern you.'

'It does if you want our help.' Levi stretched out his legs, hands cupping the back of his head.

She snorted. 'We all have our curses. Mine is that I cannot leave this place. In my arrogance, I once came here seeking the widow and her power.'

'The widow? But you are—'

'Trapped. When I came to this hut, the one you know as Nicolai was the widow. He tricked me into exchanging places with him and escaped.'

'What foolishness is this?' Sara said. 'Surely you aren't saying that you are really Nicolai, my brother-in-law?'

'That's exactly what I am saying. Didn't you notice a difference in Nicolai's behaviour a year before your husband died so mysteriously?'

She had noticed a hardening of Nicolai's nature about then. She'd commented on it to her husband, who'd scoffed, "Nicolai has always been surly about the crown. He's never gotten over the fact that he was born second. He hates not being first."

'Who is he then, if he isn't Nicolai?'

'A malevolence. A spirit thief. I do not know its name.'

'And you want us to bring him—it—back here?'

She showed her toothless gums. 'Yes. I am anxious to return the favour.'

Sara stared at the widow. *Could it be true?* What she'd just heard both confirmed old suspicions and horrified her. An imposter, only one step from the crown, with Madison the only obstacle. Without her to stop him—

'I agree,' she said.

Levi lurched forward, 'Now wait a minute—'

'For what? What are our options otherwise? We've tried all the doors. Even if you could force her to open one of them, where would we go? The way home is blocked.' She leant forward, her finger jabbing the tabletop. 'I shouldn't have to tell you, Levi, that if we refuse, our lives are of no further consequence to her.'

'Before you agree so quickly, what of this?' He unfolded the sketch of the plant the physic had given him.

The widow took the parchment, nodding. 'A fine drawing. What would you have me do with it?'

'This is the plant that is supposed to offset the worst effects of the melders' separation curse. It's why we came. If we are to do this, I want it.'

'That is not why you came. You were sent, remember, by her physic? This,' she shook the page, 'was only to get you here. There is no plant that does what you say. The glass vial that showed the way was designed to bring you to this hut, not to a plant.' She flicked the sketch back across the table.

'No plant?' Levi repeated, as if the information was too much to absorb. 'We came here, through that out there, for nothing?'

The widow stared back at him, a smile hovering about her thin lips.

Levi snatched up the sketch, crumpling it in his fist, and threw it into the fire.

Sara sprang to her feet, the chair crashing to the floor as she used the soup ladle to scoop the balled paper from the flames. It rolled out onto the floor, black-patched and smoking, the edges red rimmed with embers. She stomped them out.

'What are you doing? You heard her.'

'Just because she said it doesn't mean that I believe her. This plant might still exist. For me, it represents hope.' She smoothed it out and stuffed it into the pocket of her cloak before picking up the chair. 'Hope is important to me. Right now, it's all I have.' She took a breath and sat. 'Now, if by some miracle we make it back here with Nicolai, I have one condition.'

'Condition?' the widow parroted.

'Yes. I want you to make a life pledge that should you succeed in resuming your body as Nicolai, you will not harm my son, and what's more, vow to protect him into his majority.'

'You seek a life pledge from the widow? This pile of frigid smoke has no life to bargain with and even less honour.' Levi's tone was incredulous.

'I'm not asking it of her. I'm appealing to what remains of the man. I remember my husband telling me when we first met that while Nicolai was devious, if you ever got him to agree to a pact then he would honour it. So,' she swivelled to face the widow, 'will you?'

Sara waited, watching the old crone's black eyes darting as she processed the request. Finally, she looked up, finding Sara's gaze.

'Very well. I simply want my life back. What is left of it. Note well, though, if you fail to return with this spirit thief, I have the power to summon your son, and I promise that he will not find the journey here as pleasant—or his time here as long.'

Chapter Sixteen

No one said anything, the silence crowding them. Sara considered the weight of the widow's words, wondering whether she'd gone too far. *There is no guarantee we can deliver Nicolai. He's secure in the palace, protected by hundreds of men at arms. Can I justify the risk to Madison? At what point does the price become too high? Yet, if I don't, Madison will be lucky to reach his next birthday before some "accident" befalls him.*

It was Levi who broke the silence and put practical voice to her fears. 'It will take many days to get back to Nicolai's palace. We may not arrive before harm befalls the crown prince. Plus, I am not confident we could remove Nicolai from his stronghold so easily and then make the long journey back here ahead of his men. It was difficult enough last time.'

'You do not need to. Watch.' The old woman eased herself to her feet and shuffled over to the door on the back wall of the hut. Retrieving a large key from the pocket of her black dress, she inserted it into the lock. It turned with a resounding clunk, and she pulled the door open.

Sara started, her breath catching in her throat. Through the open doorway she could see one of the courtyards of the palace, courtiers rushing with scrolls in their hands, servants carrying water gourds, couriers arriving and grooms taking delivery of their steaming horses. Sara could even hear one of the mares blowing hard after what must have been a long ride. She worked out that the doorway opened into the stables. 'What witchery is this?' she finally said.

The widow stared out at the scene as she spoke. 'This hut sits on a nexus of time and energy lines. Instead of time being a sequential line, here it can be folded in on itself so you do not need to travel the many days to Nicolai, simply get him across this threshold. I have spent long days getting this opening in just the right place.'

Sara and Levi stood and cautiously approached the open doorway. While the courtyard was brilliantly lit with torches and warming fires, neither that light nor heat penetrated the hut; it was like watching a scene projected and captured inside glass.

'They cannot see us from that side.' The widow waved at a groom inches from their faces as he forked some straw into a nearby stall. 'Only the keyhole is visible from over there.'

'How is this possible?' Levi muttered, his hand reaching toward the busy scene outside. The widow swiped it away.

'Do not be foolish. Do you want that groom to see a hand emerge from a blank wall? You must make the crossing later, while the palace sleeps. I will also give you this.' She handed Sara a sewing needle threaded with a long length of black cotton. 'Pierce Nicolai's skin with this needle. Its tip is impregnated with a drug to make him compliant. Then sew a patch on his skin using the thread. You'll be able to lead him by the thread. He will follow as long as it remains unbroken.'

Sara carefully slid the needle into the lapel of her jacket.

'There is one more thing,' the crone said.

'Only one?' Levi quipped, still peering at the scene on the other side of the doorway.

'Nicolai stole something from me. You need to take it from him. It's how he resists my summons to return here.'

'Where will I find it?' Levi asked.

'It never leaves his person. He wears it in a small red pouch around his neck. It must be removed before you attempt to lead him back, otherwise he will not be able to cross. Its power will not inhibit you though.'

'Secrets and more secrets,' Sara said, trailing her fingers along the rough plaster wall of the hut, pausing before one of the other blue doors. 'Where do these other doors lead? More distant worlds?'

'Those doors have never been opened. Legend has it that one leads to hell, the other, heaven. However, unlike this one and the front door, once one of those doors is opened, everything and everyone in the room is sucked through it. There is no way back.'

'So which is which?' Sara asked.

The widow regarded her out of the corner of her eye. 'No one has ever been brave, or foolish, enough to find out. Would you like to? I have the key here, but you'll understand if I wait outside.' She held the same long brass key out to Sara, who shook her head. The old woman cackled.

THEY WAITED UNTIL MIDNIGHT, leaving the door to the courtyard open while the palace settled into its nightly rhythm. At least the time had allowed their boots and clothes to dry. As the hour grew later, most of the torches were allowed to burn down along with the warming fires, until only a few remained for the scattering of retainers still on duty.

'It is time,' the widow finally said, handing the long brass key to Levi. 'Walk straight through and do not look back until you are on the other side. Take note of the keyhole's position in the wall before you leave, otherwise it will be difficult to find on your return. Most of the guards have been stationed on the wall watching for the invaders. The kingdom is already on a war footing.'

Sara stood, brushed herself down—mindful of the needle in her lapel—and came over to stand beside Levi, whispering, 'I still have difficulty believing any of this.'

'Then I'll go first. Watch. See what happens. I can't see how this could get any worse.' Levi took a step forward, his foot rippling the smooth surface of the portal as if he were entering water. His leg, body and finally the trailing leg and foot followed. Once the surface ripples settled, Sara could see him standing on the other side, looking back at her like some bizarre mirror image. He raised his hand as if to offer help across a rough patch of ground.

The widow nodded to her. Sara took a deep breath, and with her heart hammering took the first step across the threshold. It wasn't so much through as into. There was a sensation of chilling cold, followed by a soaking that didn't quite make it to wet, and then her nose filled with the familiar smell of warm horseflesh and clean straw. Stable smells.

A puff of cold breeze through the open door stirred a wisp of hair about her face, and she shivered. When she looked back at the wall, she could see no doorway or opening, only a slight brush of shadow that, when she peered closer, might conceal a lock between the panels of rough wood.

Levi was crouched beside the open door leading to the courtyard. She went over to join him. He whispered, 'You know your way around here better than me, Sara. Which way?'

She pointed, and they darted out of the stable, keeping to the shadows at the edges of the buildings as they crept along dark alleyways, stumbling over uneven cobblestones.

She heard Levi curse as he tripped over something that scuttled away behind them.

Sara stopped to take a breath, leaning a hand against the alley wall. Its surface felt slick and slimy, and she wiped it on her filthy clothes. 'Are you all right, Levi?'

He grunted something about rats as big as cats before adding, 'How far now?'

'Nearly there. We can't risk anyone seeing us. I might have bluffed my way through last time, but knowing Nicolai, he will have shut every barn door after we bolted with Madison.'

'Do you? Know Nicolai, that is? Do you believe what the widow said about stealing his body?'

'Here, where everything feels, smells, and tastes normal, no, I don't. It's inconceivable. Yet the confounding paradox is that I have to because it's the only chance any of us has. Particularly Madison. Come on.'

They padded to the end of the alley. Sara peeked around the corner. In front of her was the fountained courtyard that opened to the main staircase leading to the royal chambers. Water tinkled, splashing against the stones in the soft light.

She pointed to the staircase, and Levi nodded. Hunched over, they sprinted across the open space and into the shelter of the servants' access. The way was clear, dimly lit by guttering torches. 'Those torches are just about out. They'll be coming to replace them soon. We'll need to return via the main staircase to avoid them. Oil lamps light the other stairway.'

'Let's hope Nicolai cooperates then. I don't fancy having to carry him across my back like a bag of chaff.'

They hurried up the steps, pausing at the top. 'After his brother's death, he took over the king's suite. The chamber is at the end of that corridor. There'll be guards.'

'Thanks. Any suggestions?'

'Only one. The king's suite is connected to the queen's chambers by a door in the back wall. As the queen's rooms aren't currently occupied, there's a good chance that it will be locked and not guarded from that side—but I know where the key is. Or used to be. I recall you visited me there once. You ruined my breakfast with purple sprinkles.'

It's like a lifetime ago.

'It was to prevent you from being poisoned.'

'As it turned out, I was safe from that particular threat, at least.'

'See. It worked.' He chuckled.

The tension lessened with their banter. She led him away from the broad royal promenade to a mezzanine that overlooked darkened reception rooms below. Huge paintings of dead royals glared down at them from the high wall. Sara had hated the dark, muted palette. Before Anthony died, she'd delighted in wearing the brightest colours —before black had been forced upon her. She halted Levi with an upraised hand at the first corridor leading off the mezzanine. 'My chambers are down there.'

Cautiously, she looked around the corner, pulling back hurriedly when a door opened midway down, splashing a pool of light into the corridor. Sara shooed Levi back the way they'd come, both sliding beneath a long table barely wide enough to support the massive display of flowers atop it.

They crouched there listening as the quick patter of footsteps approached. Sara chanced a look up. A maid bearing a chamber pot carefully made her way past without a glance their way, the smell from the pot trailing behind her.

When the sound of footsteps had faded, Sara eased her way out from under the table and crept back to the corridor intersecting the mezzanine. The door the maid had emerged from was now shut, but a ribbon of pale yellow light was still visible beneath it. Hugging the opposite wall, they slipped past and down to the end of the corridor.

Each corridor leading off the mezzanine graded the bedchambers in order of rank; the first corridor was for the king, then hers, along with any royal family and senior nobles in service of the crown.

'The room the maid came out of belongs to the chancellor. He has a fondness for too much food and rich wine that upsets his digestion.'

'I could tell,' Levi whispered, holding his nose.

She tittered like a schoolgirl. *Can we do this? What if Nicolai isn't in his chambers? Or, more likely, has a bed companion? And what if it isn't a lady?* It was rumoured Nicolai slept on both sides of the sheets, the rougher the better.

It was unlikely Levi would be able to subdue two men without attracting the attention of more.

They paused outside the double doors at the end of the corridor. She pressed and slid sideways a decorative tile on the wall, revealing a recess and two keys within it. She held them up. 'I was always losing the damn things. This hiding place didn't do me much good when Nicolai locked me in before packing me off as a marriage tribute.'

'I remember.' His words emerged slowly.

She paused, keys in hand, as an intense wave of memories flooded her, carrying fleeting images of what had happened since she'd last stood at these doors. The hand holding the keys trembled, and she consciously steadied it before selecting one and sliding it into the lock. It turned as she remembered, smoothly and quietly. Pushing open the doors, she pressed the other key into Levi's hand. 'This is the one for the internal door to the king's chamber. It's over there, the last panel on the wall. This side of the balcony.'

Sara shut the doors, leaving them unlocked. If all went well, they'd be leaving this way. She picked up a taper and flint, striking sparks until it caught. She cupped the flame, shielding the light. The room looked different, less hers. The bedclothes had been stripped, the mattress turned on its side to air and the adjoining dressing room emptied of expensive gowns.

'Sara,' Levi hissed. 'Douse the light. I have the lock.'

She blew out the taper and hurried over to him. Past the balcony, the town stretched away, the peaceful lights from ships in the distant bay winking with the movement of the waves at odds with the churning turmoil of her stomach. The lock made a loud clunk, and she jumped. She'd forgotten how loud it had been. How sometimes she'd wait in bed, dreading the sound from the king's key when he'd come to her chambers drunk.

Levi opened the narrow panel a crack. No light emerged from the other side, and he pushed it open a little more.

The sound of light breathing travelled to them through the pitch black. Levi eased into the king's room. Sara followed. Both knew the consequences if they were discovered here.

Focusing on the dark shadows in front of her, Sara pictured the room in her mind. A massive bed and a night table were next to the internal door. The balcony access that spanned the length of the room was closed off, the heavy drapes drawn. The sound of breathing was coming from this side of the bed. She reached up to her lapel and, careful of the point, slid the needle out, the black thread trailing.

She took a step towards the shadowed hump lying on the bed, the needle poised and ready.

Is that a Nicolai shape? Is it big enough?

A burp followed by a loud fart interrupted her speculation. She froze. The sounds had come from across the room. They waited, pinned against the dark, before Levi pulled her to the ground. They crawled over and hid at the side of the high bed. The figure on the mattress above slept on, the breathing regular and soft. *Too soft.* Sara remembered one of her maids gossiping that Nicolai snored so loudly, you could hear it from the mezzanine.

Nicolai must be awake? Then she remembered that the king's chamber was the only one fitted with a commode alcove. *What timing! Between the chancellor and Nicolai's digestion, I'm betting there will be one less cook in the kitchen tomorrow.* From across the room, she heard a curtain being thrust aside and a door creaking open. Light flowed out with it, but the glow that made it to the ceiling was dull. *Likely only one candle. Enough to light his way to and fro. This side of the room should remain dim.*

Shuffling steps followed, then a huffing exhale as the mattress shifted. The sleeping figure above them stirred, muttering something. A bedmate, but at least it sounded like a woman and not one of the guards. The candlelight puffed out, and the darkness returned. Sara remained huddled beside the bed, waiting for Nicolai to fall asleep. Gradually the darkened shapes in the room assumed meaning as her eyes adjusted.

Several minutes passed before Sara became aware of a shuffling of bedclothes, the mattress moving as Nicolai's weight shifted, the woman muttering, roused from sleep as Nicolai rolled on top of her. They did not speak as they rutted, the only sounds the movement of the two bodies against the mattress and Nicolai's quickening grunts. The woman, Sara suspected, was the victim of forced copulation, a place of resigned acceptance that she knew too well.

Sara waited until Nicolai's breathing quickened and moved up, onto her knees, the needle between her thumb and index finger. When Nicolai peaked, she drove the needle into the back of his unprotected neck like a miniature spear. His back arched, though whether from pain, surprise, or ejaculation, it was impossible to tell. He flopped down, collapsing onto the woman beneath him.

She gasped. Sara could tell she was about to scream, sensing the dark shape hovering over Nicolai's shoulder. Sara threw herself forward, hands frantic, clamping them over the woman's mouth. She bucked, but with Nicolai's weight on top of her she could do little but try and bite Sara's fingers, head tossing from side to side. Levi dragged Nicolai off. Relieved of his weight, the woman renewed her struggle, her breathing loud and irregular like a horse nearing the end of its endurance.

Questions rattled around Sara's brain like dice in a leather cup.

What would they do with the woman? Had the guards outside heard anything?

Sara whispered desperately into her ear, 'We're not here to harm you, either of you. Please be still.'

She repeated it, and gradually the woman on the bed settled.

Levi eased himself away and lit a candle.

Nicolai's body lay limp, mouth slack, but his eyes were open as if wondering what had happened to the rest of him. The needle protruded from the back of his neck, the black thread trailing down his undershirt. A leather strap was looped around his neck.

'We'll need to gag and tie her up,' he whispered before dragging down the luxurious canopy above the bed. He ripped it into thin strips and secured the woman's ankles together, doing the same with her wrists.

Sara used one of the pillow slips to gag her, tying it behind the girl's head with a secure knot.

'Sara, can you give me a hand with him? We need to sew the patch. Use the back of his hand; he'll be easier to lead.'

Sara released her hold on the woman, giving her a reassuring nod and a tenuous smile as she sat back on her heels, easing out her cramped hands, rubbing the areas where she'd been bitten.

The woman was young, barely out of her teens, long blonde hair wild and tangled about her head, blue eyes wide with fright, nostrils flared. She'd have a story to tell tomorrow.

Sara eased the needle out of Nicolai's neck and quickly reinserted it in the skin on the top of his hand.

'We'll need to dress him first,' Levi whispered, picking up some of the discarded clothing from the floor. Together they dragged on the minimum: soiled leggings, shoes, and a vest splattered with a large wine stain across the chest. 'Don't be too fussy,' Levi said. 'Once he's up, we can cover him with this.' He held up a full-length blue velvet cape heavy with gold brocade.

'If we're going to lead him, then I'll need to sew the patch on.'

She took Nicolai's hand and deftly drew the thread back and forth, repeating the stitch to create first one black square and then across it at right angles to form a black patch.

'Let's try it out,' Levi whispered taking the remaining thread and tugging it. The string grew taut. Nothing happened. Nicolai remained lying where he was.

'It's not working, pull it harder' Levi said.

'No, it'll break. Wait, what's this?' Sara tugged at a leather strap looped around Nicolai's neck, revealing a small red pouch. 'That must be what the widow spoke about. It's supposed to stop her from recalling him. We need to remove it.' She tugged it off and slipped it over her own head, tucking the pouch beneath her shirt. Levi tried again, giving the thread a tentative tug.

Nicolai's forearm flexed at the pull, his body following the tensional direction of the thread. They helped him off the bed, standing him up.

Sara sighed with relief and draped the cloak around Nicolai's shoulders securing it tightly at the neck.

She lit a lamp from the candle flame and made her way to the interconnecting door, turning at a sound behind her. Nicolai was still standing by the bed, but Levi was rustling through drawers, tossing clothing and papers to the floor. Sara rushed over, tugging at his sleeve. 'Levi what are you doing? We have to leave.'

'I'm not leaving until I find the original material to break the melders' curse. It has to be here. These are his private chambers.'

'Levi, there's no time. We don't know how long the drug will work for, and soon the corridors will be filled with servants. They rise well before dawn. We have to go. Now.'

'You go. Take him with you.' He yanked on another drawer with too much force. The dresser toppled to the floor with a crash.

An urgent voice came from the other side of the double doors. 'Highness, are you all right? Do you need assistance?'

Levi hurried over to the doors, feeling for the key. There was none. Muffling his mouth behind his hand, he imitated Nicolai's smarmy tone.

'No. Stand down. The wench just needs some taming.'

He riffled through a jumble of items on an exquisitely polished *escritoire* before moving onto another chest of drawers.

'Levi, please,' Sara whispered. 'No one wants to get rid of this curse more than me, but it needs two of us to get him out of here. Please. Hurry up.'

Levi paused, hands still deep inside the drawer. Finally, he straightened and threw the handful of silks he was holding to the floor. 'There never seems to be enough time for this, does there? But you're right. There are more important issues. Again.'

They led Nicolai over to the connecting door. Sara passed the girl on the bed and placed a shushing finger to her lips. At worst, the servants would find her there in the morning, but hopefully the real Nicolai would be back before then. Explaining what had happened would be his problem. She followed Levi, then shut and locked the door behind them.

Nicolai, or whoever was inside this body, seemed, thankfully, incapable of speech under the influence of the drug. Thoughts of his cruelty besieged her as she passed familiar memory triggers in her former chamber. She hadn't been imagining things after all; Nicolai had changed, but ultimately it had been the man's greed for more power that had brought him to the widow in the first place. *Can I really trust him not to turn on Madison and me again? If indeed what the widow said was actually true.*

Regardless of everything, she would have to be careful once they returned to the hut. But first they had to get there. And afterwards? What of the curse? She couldn't live her life depending on a man to be constantly within hailing distance. She fervently wished they'd had time to search Nicolai's chambers thoroughly.

Sara dispelled the chasing thoughts and cracked the door leading to the corridor, whispering over her shoulder, 'All clear.'

She slipped through, and Levi followed, keeping the black thread on a short rein so the three appeared to be walking together within the lamp's tight circle of light.

The palace was quiet and dim; even the strip of light beneath the chancellor's door was now extinguished. Sara led the way. Rounding the corner to the mezzanine, her footsteps were barely a patter across the intricate mosaic that ran in a broad ribbon along the wide balcony.

They approached the grand staircase. Oil lamps hung at regular intervals down the steps, splashing light towards them and out into the courtyard beyond. From the servants' stairs adjacent, she heard men speaking in low voices. *Replacing the torches, as I suspected.* They would have to use the main stairs. Everything appeared deserted, so they started down.

'Take his other arm. We need to be careful he doesn't fall,' Levi said.

Sara scampered around to the other side and hooked her arm through Nicolai's.

'Take it slow,' Levi hissed.

They descended, Nicolai's steps clunky and uncoordinated, as if he were a life-sized automaton made from clockwork machinery. The sound of approaching laughter and voices echoed up the stairs.

'Someone is coming,' Levi whispered. 'Two, possibly three.'

Sara looked back up the staircase. *Too late to go back.* She tugged the heavy velvet hood over Nicolai's head, fluffing the furred edges out so that it shadowed his face. She did the same to her own and then hooked Nicolai's arm over her shoulder before resuming their descent.

Three men appeared at the bottom, their conversation stalling abruptly when they saw the trio descending. She recognised two of them. Minor nobles.

'Someone has had a night in their cups,' she heard one of them mumble. The other two snickered.

Sara elbowed Levi, who moved his free hand to conceal the thread and called down, 'Our master is unwell. The physic warns that it could be highly contagious once the bowels loosen.'

Levi glanced meaningfully over at Sara, who, after a beat, lowered her head inside the hood and made a loud blurting sound with her lips.

On cue, Levi shook his head and wrinkled his nose, looking behind Nicolai. 'I fear that has now happened. I suggest, kind sirs, you stand well clear, lest this horrible disease infect you and your families as well.'

Sara made the wet sound again, and the three men took a step back before scattering to make use of the servants' stairway.

'Come on,' Levi said, grinning.

They descended the remainder of the steps and joined the dark safety of the alleyways, finally pausing at the circular courtyard outside the stables.

'See anything?' Levi whispered.

'No.'

They waited, moments dragging. A few torches cast flickering light across the courtyard and the wall beside them. From inside the stable, she could hear the horses moving about inside their stalls; an occasional snort or nicker was all that disturbed the quiet peace of the night. In the distance, she could make out the palace wall and on top the silhouettes of soldiers moving back and forth in front of their fires, patrolling the walk.

'Come on.' Levi started across the courtyard, leading Nicolai. Sara followed, her gaze darting in all directions. Once inside the stables, the familiar smell of hay and horse settled her. They were close. Levi exchanged Nicolai's thread for the lamp and held it high, searching for the keyhole along the back wall.

Everything looked the same. The uneven surface was mottled with shadows, any of which might be a keyhole. They could search all night and still not find it.

'The widow said to make note of where the keyhole was,' Sara said.

'That is not helpful now.' Levi's voice was hushed, heavy with tension.

Sara cocked her head, listening. 'Shh, someone is coming.' The sound of something being dragged against the cobblestones intruded. It was coming closer.

'Quickly, over there.' She led Nicolai over to one of the empty stalls, securing him in a darkened corner. She crouched beside him. Levi extinguished the lamp and joined them. The dragging sound came closer, and now she could hear someone whistling quietly and out of tune.

'What is that?' she whispered coming to a half-stand, stretching her neck as she strained to see.

Levi pulled her back into the shadows. She lost her balance and fell heavily against some riding tack on the wall. The whistling stopped abruptly. A circle of light edged their way, the dragging sound now cautious.

Sara flung off her hood and unpinned her hair, allowing it to tumble to her shoulders. The light came closer, intruding into their corner of darkness. Sara turned her back, and shielding Nicolai, dragged Levi towards her, planting her mouth over his. He struggled for a moment, then relaxed into the kiss. The light picked them out of the dark. Levi broke off the kiss, shielding his eyes with his hand.

'Hey, fellow. Off with you now. Is there no privacy even here among the horseshit and straw? Take this and go.' Levi pulled out a coin from his pouch and flicked it with his thumb. The man scurried after it.

'Sorry m'lord. It's only old Tom. Be leavin' you to it, sir.'

They waited until he had gone before easing apart. She avoided Levi's eyes, pulling up the hood of her cloak, an afterburn from the soft crush of his lips still tingling against hers.

'Sorry, that was the only thing I could think of,' she said finally.

Levi cleared his throat. 'It seemed to work. That guy, Tom, looked to be a cripple. One foot was dragging.'

'I remember now. He mucks out the stalls. I heard he was a soldier once.'

'Some deaths are quicker than others,' Levi muttered.

'Come on, Levi. We have to find that lock, and now we have no light.'

Sara led Nicolai over to the wall, stumbling over a bucket, causing her to release the thread.

'What was that?' Levi hissed. 'Are you all right?'

'I'm fine. I'll give you a hand.' Sara left Nicolai where he was and helped Levi search, running her fingers lightly across the rough boards at about the height where she remembered the keyhole to be.

'Here.' She reached out for Levi, grabbing his wrist, and guided his fingers to the small depression in the wall. 'You open it. I'll lead Nicolai through.' She turned, arms extended, groping for Nicolai through the dark, finding his shoulder and then tracing her fingers down his right arm to the dangling thread. Wrapping it around her index finger, she drew Nicolai over to where she'd left Levi. The lock on the hidden door clunked.

'Got it,' Levi said.

Excited Sara moved a little faster, the thread tensioning. Mindful of the bucket she stepped sideways to avoid it but Nicolai with his clumsy gait did not and he tumbled over, the thread connecting them snapping as he fell to his knees.

'Urrrgh,'

'What was that?' Levi asked.

Sara crouched, sweeping her arms wide, as she tried to find him. 'Nicolai fell. The thread snapped.'

Her hand found Nicolai's velvet hood. He swiped it away.

'Uurrgh.' Louder this time.

'He's waking. The drug is wearing off.'

'I'm holding the door open. Push him over this way and I'll grab him.'

Sara cursed beneath her breath and swung her fist through the darkness on the same arc as before, crunching into ribs. Nicolai was standing.

'Whaa-aat?'

The sound came out as a wail. Confused and angry. If it became much louder, he'd wake up more than old Tom. She stepped behind where she estimated him to be and, using all her weight, pushed, feeling him stagger forward. He yowled like he was trying to yell for the guards. He turned; his movements sluggish. She pushed again, and he staggered forwards a few more steps.

'Where are you, Levi?' Sara called.

'Here.'

Raising her boot, she shoved him towards where the voice had come from, unleashing all her frustrations. Nicolai grunted and stumbled forward. There was a crash and then nothing. In the distance she could hear shouting and the sounds of running boots against the cobbles.

'Sara! Sara, he's through. We got him. Come on.'

The dark shape of Levi's hand appeared before her. She grabbed it, and he dragged her next to him. She scrunched her eyes into slits, trying to penetrate where the doorway should be. The wall remained.

'I can't see...'

He thrust her forward. Her hands rose up in reflex to protect her, but she kept going, legs running to catch up she lurched into the stone hut. Levi came through moments later.

The sudden silence and light assailed her. She found it hard to make anything focus and then to make sense of what she was seeing. Nicolai was bound inside a silken web like a cocooned insect in the middle of the room. The widow cackled and danced around, clapping her hands.

The doorway to the stables was still open. Sara could see lanterns and men searching. Old Tom appeared, pointing at the corner where he'd seen them.

'Maybe I should have flicked him more than a copper piece.' Levi came over to stand beside her, his arm snaking around her shoulders. She flushed, remembering the touch of his lips, and in a subtle movement took a step sideways. The arm slid away. She missed his solid reassurance as soon as it had gone.

Inside the silk web, Nicolai glared at them, his hands groping towards where the pouch had been.

Sara held up the red pouch. 'Looking for this?'

Nicolai roared like an animal, the noise rattling around the hut.

The widow stopped her frenetic jig and shuffled over, her toothless grin wide. Sara passed the pouch to the widow. She tugged the drawstring apart and peered inside, nodding. 'Watch now.'

She stepped close to Nicolai, placed her hand over his heart, and began chanting in a low voice. Nicolai struggled within the binding, his mouth stretching as if in great pain, as if something jagged was being torn bodily from him. Then he wailed, the sound long and protracted. If it was a blade, it would have sliced through them all. Sara held her hands against her ears and shut her eyes.

Then.

Silence.

Opening her eyes, she jumped back. Nicolai was now free, and the widow was bound.

Nicolai smiled. It was Nicolai's face, but somehow the eyes were still the widow's.

'Is that... you?'

'If you mean am I once again myself. Yes.'

It was odd to hear that reviled voice and feel relieved. She could feel Levi hovering and tense near her elbow, not convinced. Not yet.

'In a few moments, those bonds holding it will dissolve. I suggest that we all take our leave before that happens.' Nicolai placed the long brass key on the table. 'This is rightly hers now. Use the front door.' He added with a crafty smile, 'It is not locked. Take this.' He reached inside the red pouch and took out the contents, tossing it to Sara. 'You'll need it to get back.'

She caught the ball clumsily between her palms. It was gold, round, and jagged with an intricate pattern of what looked to be precious stones.

'Throw the sphere into the air once you get outside. It will lead you back to the edge of the swamp.'

'You will remember your pledge? About Madison.'

Nicolai bowed his head. 'In that one thing, my brother was correct. I always keep my pledges—once made.' With a grin, he strode through the door to the stables, slamming it shut behind him. Sara noticed that the silken bindings around the widow were disintegrating, drifting to the earthen floor with no more substance than smoke. She was almost free, her wordless screams beginning to fill the small room.

'We better go too.' She hustled Levi to the front door. It swung open at her touch. Light spilled from the hut. The garden beds outside were now fallow, the magnificent blooms and fruits of only hours before were now rotting brown husks.

Once they were across the threshold, the front door slammed behind them, the night closing in.

Sara weighed the heavy gold ball in her hand and then lobbed it into the air, expecting it to fall with a thud at her feet. It hovered, bobbing like a buoy in the sea before drifting out over the swamp. It glowed with a strong golden light that spread in all directions.

'That's it, let's go before this gets any weirder,' Levi said. Sara followed him through the water.

As they stepped onto the first rock at the edge of the swamp, they heard a long, drawn out 'No-o-o-o-o,' repeated over and over from inside the hut. Crashing and smashing followed. By the time they reached the third rock, there was a wrenching screech, as if something deep-seated were being pried free. Sara spun about, pointing. 'Look! The hut. It's coming loose from its foundations.'

As they watched, the stone hut hovered an arm's length above the ground before imploding, contracting into its southern end before disappearing completely.

'She must have opened one of the other two doors,' Sara said, her hand covering her mouth. 'She mustn't have been able to bear the thought of being trapped there again with no prospect of escape.'

'I wonder which door she chose?'

'I can guess,' Sara said, 'but I suspect ultimately they were one and the same. Only the experience might be different.'

Levi touched her arm. 'Come on. That flying ball is on the move again. We can't afford to lose sight of it.'

THE SUN WAS RISING by the time they squished out of the swamp, their feet saturated inside the heavy boots. The metal ball fell to the ground, and Sara picked it up, brushing away the mud, and held it to the light. 'These gems are real.' She tucked it into back into its pouch and slung the strap over her shoulder beneath the heavy cloak.

'At least we're returning with something of value.' Levi's voice was resigned, then he shrugged. 'So I guess we're stuck with each other for a while longer.'

'Don't worry. Once things settle down, we'll get the original material back one way or the other. In the meantime, don't get too far away.'

He gave her an uncertain grin, deepening the dimples on either side of his mouth. Her mind returned to the feel of that kiss and the hopelessness of ever experiencing it again.

'The mammoths are still here, at least.' Levi pointed at the animals grazing beside the lake.

'They, at least, are loyal.' Sara's voice was wistful, as she thought of Rabine's betrayal and that of the physic. Trust was a lot like the thread they'd led Nicolai with. It was strong, and yet if tugged the wrong way, incredibly fragile. Someone else had said something like that, but she couldn't think who.

Levi trotted off, calling back over his shoulder, 'I'll go fetch the beasts.'

She nodded, watching him go, her fingers moving unconsciously to her lips, remembering again. *Impossible. Levi is a commoner. Worse, a yellow skin. There is no way.* Yet, if they were bound by this curse, could that indeed be a blessing? An assurance of someone always being there, for her. On her side. For once. Someone she could actually, really trust. But in public only as her vassal, a bodyguard. But what of behind doors? Could there be more? Could he—would he? He was so proud.

She paused her aimless pacing. Head cocked. *What was that?*

Something, no, someone... was calling. Very faintly. Levi was still heading towards the mammoths, slowing now to a walk so as not to spook them.

Did I imagine it? No. There it is again. 'Saaaaarraaaaa.' The word was shackled to the wind, almost but not quite smothered by it. She looked around, listening. A low-pitched screech followed, like the cry of a distant bird. A bird in pain. She turned towards the sound. It was coming from the centre of the lake. Squinting against the wind and reflected light that bounced off the surface of the water, she could make out a black speck. It was heading towards her, getting larger, flying fast. Its screech was now audible above the wind, until finally joining with it, the sound becoming a long drawn-out yowl. To Sara's ears, it sounded like a cried distortion of her name, as if being called from a very long way off.

'Saa-rrr-aaaaa.'

She glanced over at Levi. The two mammoths had both stopped grazing and were staring out into the middle of the lake. They'd heard it as well, and if their stomping feet were any indication, didn't like it.

The shape resolved into a large bird, its massive wings spread, coasting the surface of the wind like a small skiff, angling across the current towards the shoreline.

'Saarrraaaa.'

Louder now. Its head was bowed. The wings beat in long, powerful swoops as the wind changed to a new vector. The bird maintained a resolute course, pushing into the wind. It was massive. The plumage was black with slashes of brilliant gold, apart from the head, which was silver, tucked down away from the worst of the rising gale.

Huge talons extended below its body. As Sara watched, the feet came forward, locking in place as if readying to pluck up some helpless prey or attempt a landing. The bird angled its wings and headed towards her, the yellow feet and talons large enough to pick her up.

Her name, now a continuous shriek, was unmistakable. She caught a glimpse of the head as it came up. The face was human.

A harpy.

The mammoths were bellowing now. Any moment, they were likely to bolt. Levi ran towards her, yelling and waving. The wind carried his words away, sending her only a warning sound. He'd seen it but was too far away to do anything.

She ran, stumbling across the uneven ground, an ominous shadow overtaking her, covering the ground. Above, she could hear the steady beat of the wings, feel the screeching call of her name like chalkstone against a child's writing slate. She feinted to the right and then dodged to the left, feeling a tendon suffer, the shadow veering off.

The harpy's shadow returned, covering her, growing larger. Sara dived into a ditch and rolled in cold, wet slush. The shadow zoomed past. Looking up, she saw it bank steeply for another pass. She peered over the edge of the ditch, looking for a better hide and saw the face of the harpy for the first time. It was old, human, framed by long silver hair. She thought it looked vaguely familiar.

The eyes stared back with recognition and what might have been concern. She knew those hooded eyes. Almost recognised them.

But from where?

The harpy veered away at the last moment and headed towards Levi. Jagged images cascaded through her head, images that didn't make sense, seemed out of time and place but still recognisably familiar, like the face of the harpy. It was like the bird was herding them.

'Levi!' she yelled. The harpy banked again, coming around into a low sweep until it was behind her, the screech beginning anew as it dived.

The wind delivered Levi's shout. 'Drop! Sara, drop down. Now!'

She threw herself onto the long wet grass. The harpy couldn't correct its trajectory in time and swooped past, its wings thrashing against the gusting wind for more altitude. Levi ran over and dragged her up. She chanced a glance over her shoulder.

'It's coming back.'

'When I tell you, run and dive into that.' He pointed towards a cluster of low bushes. 'The harpy's face. I recognise it. I need to find out what's going on. I'll try to draw it away from you anyway.'

The haunting, squealing screech came first. 'Mdi-naaaap.'

'What is it saying?' Sara shook her head, covering her ears against the high- pitched scream.

'I can't tell. Before it sounded like it was calling your name. Best try not to listen.'

That was impossible, of course. The wind had changed direction again and now carried the ear-splitting screech directly to them.

'Maaaad-dnaaaapp.'

'Mad what?' Sara yelled, terror forcing her eyes wide as she watched the harpy angling for another run.

The yellow feet came down once more, long talons arching, ready to snatch one or both of them. Levi must have sensed that Sara was about to run and grabbed her arm, holding it firm. 'Wait! If you move too soon, it will follow you.'

The seconds clicked over. Both of them hunched, as if this might make them a smaller target. The creature crossed the shoreline, swallowing up the distance as its shadow rushed towards them.

'Maaddi kidnaaaap. Leeevi. Saaaara. Havgooooo.'

Levi released Sara's arm, and pushing her aside, jumped up and down, waving his arms at the beast. 'Go! Sara, go now.'

She stood there, staring up, mouth open as if listening to something verging on familiar.

'Sara!'

'Do you hear?' she murmured, still looking up.

'Did you? I said run! For God's sake, Sara, run now.'

'No.' She was shaking her head. Her hair came loose and fell like a curtain across one side of her face. Something clunked into place, as if there were two Sara's and only one of them was here.

'It's talking. I can hear it.' She turned to face Levi, her expression shocked, looking him up and down as if seeing him for the first time. 'Levi. It's Maddy.... We must, we have to go back.'

Levi opened his mouth to say something and was snatched up and into the air. Sara screamed, her fingers tugging ineffectually against the claws of the harpy.

A harpy with Hiro's face.

Chapter Seventeen

Sara's breath snatched in her throat, sharp and barbed like a trapped fishbone, forcing her awake. Coughing, she leant forward, conscious of a large, strong hand thumping her upper back and a voice reciting, 'It's all right,' with each resounding wallop.

It didn't feel all right. She was snagged midway between drowning and suffocation, unable to get enough air. The last thump dislodged something. It slid up her windpipe and into her mouth, furry and slimy. She spat it into her lap and wheezed in pure air, setting off another series of coughs.

'That's it. That's it,' the voice said.

The coughing and retching ceased, and she flopped back against the wall, dragging in more air.

'Don't forget to exhale.' The voice was low and rumbly. It sounded like it should belong to a face from an old black-and-white movie that leaked smoke in lazy wisps from its mouth and nostrils. Sara's head was spinning. It was too large for her neck. Too full.

'Head back, that's it.' A hand cupped her head and eased it back, stretching her throat. 'Breathe easy. I'm going to try and wake Levi. Stay there.'

Levi?

The name sounded familiar, but she had neither the energy nor the inclination to do anything more than sit against the wall and breathe. Distantly she heard the thumping, and the reassuring voice begin again, 'It's all right.' Then the cough, and the spitting. It reminded her of what had been in her throat, and she sat up to take a look. Clumps of gunk bound together with what might have been mucus leaked in her lap. The largest was about the size of a squash ball.

Where the heck had they come from?

'Euuch.' She turned her lower body, rolling the disgusting mess off her lap. It splotched onto the floor, and she shuffled away, bumping into a bank of shelves lined with white bowls seamed with slashes of gold that looked vaguely familiar

The old man was back. 'Ah, good, you're awake.'

'What the hell are they?' She waved towards the mess on the floor.

'An effect of the drug I gave you. How many fingers can you see?'

A large hand materialised in front of her face. Several fingers waggled at her. It was difficult to keep track of them all. 'Three.'

'Almost right. There are four. Do you know who I am and where you are?'

Sara shook her head, closing her eyes. It was difficult to concentrate. All she could see against her eyelids were those slimy choke balls.

'What about him? Do you recognise him?' the voice persisted as the man shook her shoulder. Sara turned her head with difficulty and tried to focus through slitted eyelids. A blurry figure resolved. A man. Seated next to her. He too sat, leaning against the wall. He had long black hair, gathered at the back in what could be a ponytail. It was difficult to tell. In profile, his face was made up of sharp angles, the brown eyes barely open. He was as familiar as the bowls but no more, like someone she might have seen recently, perhaps on a train? She shook her head. Not a train. A journey though. No, it was too hard.

'Give it a moment. Drink this.' The rim of a glass pressed against her lips. Reflexively, she opened her mouth and took a sip, letting the liquid slide down her raw throat. 'Another.' The voice was persistent. She drank a little more, feeling the liquid travel down her oesophagus, leaving warmth in its wake. It soothed her stomach, spreading like a warm golden lake.

Lake.

Sara jerked forward, and the liquid in her stomach threatened to come back up. She gulped it down.

'Madison. Where's Madison?'

He was at her side immediately, the oversized hand and soothing tonality not working this time. 'Easy, easy. Just relax, I'll tell you everything in a moment. Let the remedy settle a little first, otherwise you'll take longer to recover. Let me give some to Levi as well. Just a moment.'

She watched him shuffle across to the man beside her. Levi; she remembered the name now, but the image of him was confused like a double exposure, overlaid on each other, as if from different centuries, neither particularly clear. Nothing made any sense.

Is Madison all right?

Beside her, she could hear the gravelly voice speaking to Levi... *Hiro. Yes, that is his name.*

'Levi. Try to drink some more. That's it.'

'Oh, that's good.' Levi said. 'Whoa, that was some... Hiro, it was you, wasn't it? The face of the harpy? You were there.'

The harpy at the lake. Fear prickled across her chest as she remembered the airborne feeling after being snatched from the ground.

'Yes. And I was also with you at the beginning, in the shop. And then later at the palace. Do you remember?'

'So what happened to you after I barricaded myself in Nicolai's audience chamber?'

'I withdrew back to here. But I kept up the *kintsugi* link with you. Both of you. As I've been to that world before, I can retain memories of both simultaneously.'

More images and scenes shuffled around in Sara's head, sorting themselves into some sort of weird chronology. It was like watching two movies of her own memories concurrently.

Suddenly she jerked forward. 'Maddy. Not Madison. You were that bird, the harpy. You said Maddy was in trouble. Not Madison.' She reached over and grabbed a fistful of Hiro's shirt. 'You said kidnapped! Where is she? Is she all right?'

Hiro eased her fingers away one by one.

'I don't know. I went back through the veil and there was a missed call on your phone from your friend on the island. I rang her back. She said she was passing on a message to say Maddy's grandfather had picked her up, so not to hurry back.'

'Her what? She doesn't have a grandfather.'

'I feared as much.'

'Deb wouldn't release Maddy. Not to a stranger. Never. I can't believe it.' Hiro stroked the grey tuft of hair on his chin. 'I suspect the man who took her is one of Layton's former associates. The type of power they can access has a high level of charisma along with a deep hypnotic ability to persuade others. When I say this, I mean they could convince anyone of almost anything as long as it's rational. I wouldn't blame your friend, Sara.'

'But why would they kidnap her daughter?' Levi asked.

'I suspect they want to trade her for the spheres.'

'What? But we don't have them.' Sara said.

'No. But they must think you do.' Hiro turned to Levi. 'Did you see anyone suspicious, someone acting strangely when you went to the island to find Sara?'

'There was a man. He tried to follow me off the ferry, but he was too slow. When I was on Sara's yacht, I saw him come back on the next ferry looking pretty agitated. I didn't think too much about it at the time though.'

'Why didn't you say something?' Sara yelled, causing her head to pound. 'Do you think I would have got involved with—whatever all that was,' she jabbed a finger towards the gunk on the floor.

'And say what? A man dressed in black missed his ferry stop?'

Hiro reached over, placing a hand lightly on each of them. 'This is not the time for blame. If this man was following you, Levi, it's likely they must have been watching the hospice, waiting to see if anyone visited Layton. Once they discovered where Sara was, it wouldn't have taken long to find out about Maddy. It's a small island, and with their persuasive ability...'

'I don't believe it.' Sara writhed under Hiro's grip, 'I've got to get over there. Find Maddy. The police...'

Hiro slowly released his hold on her wrist. 'I'd advise caution about involving the police, at least not yet. They will only muddy the waters.'

'What are you saying? My daughter has been kidnapped, for God's sake.'

'And what will you tell them? Your friend at the child-minding centre gave Maddy to your grandfather. She will say he had ID and a permission slip asking her to ring you to confirm when he did so.'

'But he didn't,' Sara said, frustration bringing tears to her eyes.

'No. But she will be adamant that he did and is likely to have been given a forged letter from you. It will undoubtedly have a good version of your signature on it too. They are clever that way. Do you see the dilemma the police will then have, how it will complicate— and severely delay—getting Maddy back?'

Sara slumped against the wall, tears streaming down her cheeks. 'But we can't sit here doing nothing.'

'I'm not suggesting that. But there is a process, and joining that flow rather than resisting it will mean we have a better chance of getting your daughter back much sooner, and safer. For all of us.'

Chapter Eighteen

The call came soon after they returned to the other side of the curtain. Hiro picked up the phone and placed it face up on a large sheet of art paper.

Levi glanced at the screen. 'Blocked number. No surprises there.'

He made a final check of the assortment of small bottles that Hiro had laid out. They were supposed to be able to build up an accurate picture of the caller. He wasn't so sure.

Hiro accepted the call, flicking it to speaker, and pointed at the yellow bottle. 'Hello.' Levi popped the stopper and sprinkled the yellow granules liberally over the paper as he'd been instructed.

'You want the girl?' The voice was loud inside the small room. The granules on the paper vibrated. 'I want the spheres.'

'We have them,' Hiro said, nodding at Levi, who immediately emptied the vial with red grains on top of the yellow. The sheet shuddered as if a breeze had lifted one corner, the red and yellow granules moved like magnetised iron filings, forming intricate patterns across the paper.

There was a pause, as if the caller hadn't expected this response. Levi could just make out a low-level conversation at the other end and imagined the phone being muffled.

This guy isn't the decision maker. There is at least one other person involved.

The final bottle contained much finer granules, almost a powder, a riot of colours as if a rainbow had been sucked up and crammed into the vial. As soon as the man started speaking again, Hiro waved his hand, and Levi dumped it all into the middle of the sheet of paper. Nothing happened for a moment, then it began to move, joining the yellow and red lines, shading some sections and delineating others. A pattern was emerging as the man spoke.

'Bring the orbs to—'

'Not so fast, buddy.' Hiro's voice had changed along with his clothing as soon as they'd returned. 'Put Maddy on the phone first. We want to know she's awright.' Like the other times, Levi hadn't noticed when Hiro changed outfits. One moment he was in the long black robe with golden slashes and in the next he was wearing a 1930s suit with grey baggy trousers, a tight matching waistcoat, and a white shirt open at the collar, tie skidding to one side like some woulda-been gangster.

'You'll see her when—'

'No. I told you, pal. Put her on. Now. We need to know she's okay. Proof a'life and all that.'

The man let out a frustrated sigh, and there was more of the hushed hand-covered discussion followed by a shuffling sound. Finally, a hesitant, 'Mummy?'

'Maddy. Maddy, it's me, honey. Are you all right?'

'Mummy. Where are you? I'm scared—'

'Maddy!' Sara went to grab the phone, but Hiro jerked it away, using his other hand to point at the paper. Incredibly, a face was forming.

The same voice came back. 'Satisfied? Bring the orbs to her boat, *Misty Lady*. Midnight tonight.'

'Unacceptable,' Hiro said. 'Give us the girl first, then we'll give you what you want.'

The man sneered. 'You don't understand, do you? This is not a negotiation.' The phone clicked off.

Hiro slipped the phone into his vest pocket and turned the paper to face him, nodding. 'Not bad. Not too bad at all.'

The image was strongly defined: broad cheeks, strong jaw that would wade in first in a bar fight, and a nose that had been broken more than once.

There was no hair, and the eyes lacked colour.

'I recognise him,' Sara said. 'Layton used to call him Batman because he was always disappearing or hanging around and getting in the way. He has grey eyes and oiled black hair, brushed back.'

'Like this?' Hiro used a stick of charcoal to sketch in the details. The eyes stared back at them. Levi felt as if the man could see them.

Levi stared down at the image. 'What were those coloured granules anyway?'

Hiro cleared his throat, his voice seamlessly transitioning to full vowels and clipped consonants. 'Speech is shaped by the articulatory system that involves the resonant cavities inside the skull: nasal, oral, and pharyngeal. This produces a different sound in each of us, with certain similarities that can be detected and mapped. Think of the granules you sprinkled as nanoparticles, each with their own microchips that are wired together. They're not—but it helps to rationalise instead of calling it something as vague as magic. These particles have the ability to link back to, let's call it their "mainframe," to plot their vibrations against the many hundreds of thousands of others it holds in its "databank" along with their faces. From that it builds up what could be best described as an identikit image of the facial and skull structure. Once we have that, the system predicts the type and thickness of the flesh—'

Sara interrupted, frustration peppering her words. 'I don't understand how this,' she waved impatiently at the sketch, 'is going to help us get Maddy back. What difference does it make if we know what one of them looks like? We can't trust those men. I know what they're capable of.'

Hiro turned to face her and gripped her shoulders. 'No, of course we can't trust them. I know. They are men that have sacrificed their conscience for gain. However, if all goes as I predict, we'll use that against them to get Maddy back—completely unharmed—tonight. And this sketch will help. Now, try not to worry, Sara. Easy to say, I know, but it is not helpful to the overall process.' He shot a glance at Levi. 'You both look like you're about to fall over. After what you've been through, you'll need sleep before you're good for anything tonight. I suggest you do so now.'

Sara protested, anxiety overshadowing her fatigue.

Levi knew how that felt and understood also that it was a temporary charge. Denied for too long, exhaustion would radically diminish her ability to make rational choices.

'Hiro is right, Sara. You'll be better equipped to save your daughter once you're rested. Me too.'

'And have eaten,' Hiro added. 'I'll get some food organised. That will help. Levi, you know the way.'

Levi nodded, ushering Sara out and down the hallway to the last door.

He turned the old brass knob, and the door swung open on well-oiled hinges. 'We can rest in here.'

Sara pushed past, arms folded tightly against her chest, barely taking in the high-ceilinged room that opened onto a wide veranda. She spun around to face him. 'Rest? How do expect me to *rest* with Maddy out there somewhere, terrified, held by those... those men? Oh, this is all my fault. I should never have let you on the boat in the first place.' She shook her head wildly. 'I can't believe any of this. It's such a, such a... fucking... mess.'

He walked over and gently laid a hand on her shoulder. She jerked away. Levi continued. 'We can't change what's already happened. What we can do is make sure we get Maddy back safe and sound. I believe Hiro when he says he can do that. But we need food and rest. I know that's probably the last thing on your mind right now, but it's essential to keep our body and spirit glued together. Otherwise we run the risk of the two flying apart. I've seen that happen, and it's not pretty; plus it won't help get Maddy back. You're strong, Sara. I know that from what we've been through.'

Sara sank onto one of the plush armchairs, her gaze fixed on a point between her and the high corner of the room. 'I feel like I'm going mad. That, that place was all so real. I still have the sensation of having a foot in two worlds and not being sure which will hold my weight.'

'I know.' Levi shivered. The room was cooler than the one they'd left, and he squatted next to the fireplace, building a warm blaze out of the stacked kindling and cut logs. When it was burning, he sat back on his heels, leaning against the polished stone flanking the fire, its flames crackling beside him. Sara was still staring into space. He sensed she was seeing her daughter and feeling the burden of guilt. He knew that one too.

There was a light knock on the door. It opened immediately, and Hiro entered wheeling a trolley covered by a starched white tablecloth. In the middle was a single red rose in a long crystal vase. This time he was dressed for room service: white shirt with puffed sleeves, bow tie, black vest and trousers. He lifted and secured the hinged wings on either side of the trolley to make a table and proceeded to lay out plates and cutlery before bending to open a door at one end. From there he removed a steaming platter covered with an ornate silver cover that he removed with a flourish.

'Beef Wellington with beans, carrots, and potatoes. I put this in the oven before I went to retrieve you. Here, I'll carve.' He produced a knife, its long, slender blade slicing through the pastry-wrapped fillet. 'How do you like it, Sara? A little underdone near the centre? Or it's more medium towards the end.'

The smell of the meal wafted over to Levi. He couldn't remember the last time he'd eaten. Really eaten, not dreamt he had. He still didn't know what to make of all that had happened. It was too fresh, and like Sara, he had difficulty separating what was real. It was like this huge meal magically appearing. It would have taken hours to prepare, despite what Hiro had said. It was better just to eat it. Digestion of it—and perhaps everything else—might come later. He dragged over two chairs, positioning them at the place settings. Hiro pulled out Sara's chair. She stirred herself and came over. Levi took the other place and began eating. It tasted fabulous.

'No wine, I think,' Hiro said. 'Not after your experiences. It wouldn't be helpful. I'll go and get some juice instead.'

The door closed softly behind him.

'I'm not even going to ask how this meal happened in, what, ten minutes?' Sara picked up her knife and fork.

'I know.'

They ate in silence until finally Sara sat back, touching her lips to the linen napkin, and aligned her cutlery across the empty plate. 'I keep remembering those awful men and their leeches. The sick feeling that happened when we were too far apart.' She paused. 'You don't think that... I mean, it wouldn't happen now, surely? At best it was a drug-induced trip. A shared dream. I mean, none of it really happened, so those bits can't be real.'

'Hiro said that whatever happened, wherever we were, would manifest here. We'll have to test it out.'

Sara sat back. 'Whatever. Real or not, I'm kind of pleased that Nicolai said he'd look after Madison. He was a cute kid.'

'I suspect that the interactive program Hiro put together builds on aspects of who we are to make it more real. You have a child about that age, a girl not a boy, admittedly, but the name was similar. And I'm a former combatant looking for a way to deal with his guilt. Too much coincidence, methinks.'

'I always wanted to be a princess.' Sara allowed herself a cheeky smile, remembering the haughty way she'd behaved with Levi initially.

'Maybe you got promoted.'

'Either way. It wasn't all I imagined it would be.'

Levi lowered his eyes. 'Things rarely are.'

Hiro returned carrying a large jug and filled two crystal tumblers with freshly squeezed orange juice. He set it down on the table and folded his large hands, beaming down at them like a benevolent uncle. 'I know that this is probably not the best time, but I've been busting to ask. Sara, did you recover the orb and the map?'

Sara looked up at him in confusion, then across at Levi, her hand moving to her mouth as realisation dawned.

Hiro couldn't keep the disappointment from his face.

'There was a gold sphere though, remember, Sara? It led us out of that swamp. What happened to it?'

'You're right. I put it back in its pouch and slung it around my neck just before the harpy—Hiro—came.' She patted down her sides and then her back. 'There's something here.' She tugged on the leather strap, bringing the pouch to the front and taking out the gold ball.

Hiro reached over and gently took it from her, holding it to the light. He rotated the sphere, the intricate pattern of gems embedded in the gold glimmering with a myriad of colours.

'This is it. How about the map? It could be anything. Anything at all.'

Sara shook her head, hands going through her pockets. 'That's all I had. No, wait, what's this?'

She dragged out the crumpled sketch of the plant.

'May I see that?' Hiro reached out a hand.

Sara passed it to him. Hiro dragged over a small table, opening out and smoothing the large page out across it. Parts of it were blackened and illegible.

'I pulled it from the fire. It's a drawing of the plant that was supposed to remove the melders' curse,' she said.

'Ah, yes. Sounds most unpleasant.' Hiro didn't take his eyes off the page, stroking a greying goatee that had appeared on his chin. 'A plant, you say?'

'Yes.' Levi half stood, reaching across the table to point. 'No, you've got it upside down.'

Hiro glanced up, spinning the paper around. 'Perhaps, but let's pretend it's not for a moment. What do you see?'

Levi tried to look objectively at the paper. He shook his head.

Sara cocked her head. 'If you don't focus on the plant but the border, this line,' she traced it with her finger, 'twists and turns but seems to run continuously around the page.'

'But what does it mean?' Levi asked. 'If it's supposed to be a map, there are no reference points or landmarks.'

'Layton never allowed me to see the original. Before he gave it to me, he layered on a level of what he called "impressionable security," which is supposed to conceal what's underneath by something that resonates with the environment. It apparently is impossible to predict what form it will take.' He spun the sketch first one way and then the other.

'How can we tell?' Levi asked.

'Layton gave me a solution that would remove the security covering.' He strode to the door. 'I'll go fetch it.'

He returned almost immediately, once again wearing the long robe with the gold slash, an atomiser bottle in his hand. He carefully sprayed the illustration until the ink began to run, but instead of dripping from the page, it rearranged itself.

'It's working,' Levi said.

They watched while Hiro mopped up the excess before holding it up by the corners.

'What is that?' Levi asked, peering at the wet sheet of paper.

The sketch of the plant had gone, as had the elaborate border—apart from the single line that Sara had identified. However, it now ran straight, separating handwritten notations that ran down the page. The centre of the page was badly scorched, parts of it blackened.

Levi pointed to the notations. 'These look like dates on the left of the border, and on the right what could be city pair codes—you know, the ones that airlines use.'

'What could it mean?' Sara asked.

'Let's not be concerned with it now. You two need some sleep. We can figure it out once we have Maddy back.' Hiro walked to the door, gingerly carrying the wet sheet of paper between thumb and forefinger. 'I'll wake you when it's time.'

≈

THE BREEZE WAS cool off the water. Sara shivered in the bow, pulling the brightly coloured shawl more tightly around her. From the middle of the dinghy, Levi rowed steadily towards the line of yachts in the middle of the channel, while Hiro fiddled with some packages he'd brought with him.

No one had spoken since they'd left the jetty.

The wash from the departing ferry lifted the dinghy. Ahead she could make out the familiar lines of *Misty Lady* riding gently at her mooring in the narrow channel, silhouetted momentarily by the moon. She looked so peaceful midway between the two islands, like the other yachts they silently passed, dark and deserted. She and Maddy had been the only live-aboards in the line of moored yachts.

Despite everything, she had slept. And slept deeply. Now, however, the anxiety had returned, cascading over her until she felt drenched with guilt and dread. Hiro may be right saying that worry was not helpful, but that didn't stop it happening.

As they drew alongside the yacht, Tripod bounded up to the rail, his one front paw resting on it, ears pricked, tongue lolling. He gave a single excited bark when he saw her, and she smiled for the first time that day.

Levi brought the dinghy around to the stern and tied off.

Sara helped Hiro transfer the packages onto the yacht.

'Careful. They're delicate. Or at least what's inside is.' Hiro stopped her as she went to turn on a light. 'Let's just get by with the moon for illumination, shall we? We have to assume these men are already watching us. Let's not make it too easy for them. Don't worry, this will be over soon.'

Tripod trotted over and gave her a lick, glancing from her to Levi as if to ask "Where's Maddy?" Finally he gave a suspicious sniff of Hiro's knee-high buccaneer boots and greatcoat before flopping at Levi's feet.

'You've made a friend, I see,' Hiro muttered, staring down at Tripod, who met his gaze with a slight tilt of his head and an ear twitch. After a time, Hiro looked away. 'I've always found dogs to be an excellent judge of character.' He peered into the darkness. 'Can you make out anything, Sara? Something out of the ordinary?' His mouth stretched into the semblance of a grin. 'As if there were such a thing.'

'Like what? I can't see very much. What time is it?'

'Eleven. If all goes well, we won't need to see to find out where these bad boys are. Levi, pass me that container, the long mailing tube. That's it.'

Hiro popped the red plastic cap off the end and drew out a rolled document. Sara recognised the identikit-type image of the man on the phone. Under the uncertain moonlight, the face looked even more sinister.

'Sara, can you do me a favour and rip this handsome chap up into small pieces for me? Small as you can make them. Levi, give her a hand, would you?'

'Rip it all up?' Levi repeated.

'Yes, about postage stamp size should do.'

Hiro placed the small torn pieces inside a large metal bowl that he'd dug out of one of his parcels. When they were finished, he mumbled some words and struck a match, setting the paper fragments alight. They flared red, burning greedily before collapsing in on themselves and dissolving into fine grey ash.

Hiro's gaze drilled into the night as he lifted his chin, puckered his lips, and blew lightly. Gradually Sara became aware of a breeze puffing up the channel. Hiro held the bowl high and off to one side before upending it. The light ash was captured by the wind and lifted, scattering in all directions across the channel.

'Now, we watch.'

'For what?' Frustrated, Sara looked up. She was entrusting her daughter's life to this man. A man who, despite everything, could still be insane.

'The ash will seek out its original image and glow back red to us,' he intoned. 'There!' He pointed at a dim red glow hovering above the shoreline of Karagarra Island fifty metres away. 'That's where the man is hiding. Can you take note of the position, Levi?' Hiro handed him what looked like a compass from the package.

Levi held it in front of him, glancing between the spot where the red glow was fading and the quivering needle on the compass. 'Got it.'

'Good. Now, I suggest we go below. There's not much time.' Hiro herded them down the steps, and they clustered around the galley bench. Moonlight reflecting off the ruffled water of the bay trickled through the narrow windows, casting distorted shadows and shapes. It was a little spooky, and the sound of the other two breathing into the darkness didn't help. She considered using the torch on her phone to find a beaker for some water. Her mouth was parched.

'No lights,' Hiro muttered as if he'd heard her thoughts. 'Not yet. Levi, how do you feel about taking a little pre-midnight swim?'

'Not my first choice, but now you've mentioned it, I'm guessing you want me to go over and keep an eye on our friends.'

'Or more precisely, Maddy. If this goes wobbly, I'll be relying on you to pull her out. Are you all right with that, Sara?'

'Of course.'

Hiro glanced at the illuminated dial of his watch. 'Good. It's now eleven fifteen. I recall you saying your previous job description required you to swim some distances underwater?'

Levi nodded and began peeling off his skivvy, jeans, and boots.

'I'll use the compass to come up downwind and circle around behind them.'

'Excellent.' Hiro dug around in his remaining package. There was a quiet click, and a light appeared briefly in his hand. Another click plunged them back into darkness. 'Waterproof, same as the compass. Shielded beam. Let's synchronise our watches.'

The narrow beam of light came back on, illuminating the two watch faces, the pale backwash from the torch picking up the prickled gooseflesh on Levi's well-muscled torso. Sara could make out several puckered scars across his abdomen.

'Sara, let's go topside and pull down that rolled canvas cover I saw. What do they call it?'

'Bimini.'

'Yes. We'll make it look like we're creating a windbreak. Once that's done, they won't see Levi go over the blind side.'

She followed Hiro up the companionway, telling Tripod to stay. He was a big dog and tended to get underfoot when something needed to be done. Together she and Hiro busied themselves with the cover, then tied it down. Once it was up and secure, Levi crawled onto the deck and slipped over the blind side without a sound.

Sara knew how cold that water was. She'd slipped and fallen in—what, only a few nights ago? It seemed like a lifetime, and in a horrible way, it was. A lifetime that would max out at three months for all of them, including Maddy. Sara was determined to claw that time back for her daughter, whatever it took, but first they had to save her. Somehow, having Levi over there within snatching distance of Maddy made her feel a little easier.

'He's swum much further underwater.' Hiro's voice floated through the darkness. 'It was part of what he used to do for a living.'

'I know; he told me. Special Forces, or something.'

'It's the "or something" that he's not proud of,' Hiro said softly.

They waited in silence, side by side on the moulded seat, the phone between them, Sara ticking off the seconds, willing it to ring. 'What are they waiting for?'

She touched the screen and it lit up in response. The time flashed, 11:25, before Hiro turned it face down.

'No lights.'

'What's the difference? They know we're here. This is supposed to be the exchange point, isn't it?'

'We are targets sitting here. There's no sense making us stand out any more than we have to. It will also preserve our night vision.'

Her frustration spilled over. 'How can you be like this?'

'Like this, what...?'

'So bloody inscrutably calm—it's infuriating. And while we're at it, where did that wind come from?'

'Wind?'

'With the ash? I saw your lips blowing. It was dead still over the water before that.'

'I work with what is already there. My master called it dancing with the flow.'

'The flow?'

'Yes, the constantly moving energy of the moment. It's a matter of stepping into it and exaggerating, building on, or shifting what is there already. I sensed a breeze blowing on the other side of that headland. It was simply a matter of encouraging it over here.'

'Simply? Nothing is simple about you, Hiro.' She paused before adding, 'And what about these outfits of yours?' She flicked the great-coat he was wearing. 'How do you do that changing thing? It just seems to happen from one blink to the next.'

Hiro's smile was rueful. 'Men like me attract enemies, Sara. People who think I have something they want. People like Eric Layton. I made a miscalculation there. Constant changes in my appearance and how I present myself usually keep me under their radar. Undetectable. Mostly.'

'How?'

'Our bodies rely on electrical signals from the brain to the nerves and back again. This creates a unique energy signature, like a magnetic field. By altering the frequency of that field, I can influence how others perceive me. If they can't recognise me, can't tune in, then I remain safe.'

'You're saying you don't change outfits at all, but somehow change what we're seeing? How is that possible?'

He shrugged. 'Possibility is limited only by the extent of our awareness.' He glanced at his watch. 'It's almost time. I think you, as the mother, should answer the phone.'

Sara fumed. His side-stepping of her question annoyed her, but another part of her realised she'd only been trying to distract herself. For the moment, she mentally filed what he'd told her under D for delusional. Hiro continued.

'When they ring, ask to speak with Maddy again. Insist on it. We need to make sure she's there and all right. Hopefully when they bring her to the phone, Levi will also be able to sight her.'

Silence settled between them, the only sound the constant wash of the wavelets against the side of the hull and the occasional disturbed cry of a night bird.

She started when the phone rang. Snatching it up, she tapped on speaker.

'Hello.'

'Do you have it?' The voice was different this time. More cultured.

'Y-yes.'

'Hold it up.'

'What?'

'Hold the spheres up. Above the canvas. So we can see them.'

She glanced at Hiro, who rummaged through the package at his feet and handed her two ball-shaped objects similar to the orb.

Sara's mouth opened, about to ask where had the other one come from.

Hiro shook his head, silently mouthing "Copies."

Hesitant, Sara held the balls above her head.

A light stabbed out from the left, its beam long and blindingly white. It was a searchlight, mounted on the foredeck of a sleek motor-boat moored twenty metres out from Karragarra's beach.

The beam bounced across the tops of the small waves towards them.

It was so bright. Sara brought her gaze down just as the beam swamped them. It hovered there for a moment and then it was gone. She opened her eyes again and dropped the metal balls onto the seat beside her before picking up the phone again. The powerful beam was now directed down and off to one side, but its ambient spill enabled them to see as if it were daylight. When she spoke, her voice sounded far more confident than she felt.

'Satisfied?'

'I'm sending over a basket. Put them in. We need to check them first.'

'No. *First* I want to speak to Maddy and make sure she's still all right, otherwise these things go straight into the water.' Sara picked them up and held them over the side. Slowly she brought her hands back inside the boat and unclenched her fingers. The sharp edges of the inset stones had made imprints onto her palms.

The man cursed, and she heard more mumbling and then a shuf-fling noise as the phone was passed to someone else. Maddy came on. 'Mummy?'

'Are you all right, sweetie? Have they hurt you?'

'No, Mummy. They said I can come home soon.'

'Yes, honey. Very soon.'

She heard a high-pitched whine, and a blinking light rose off the beach.

'It's a drone,' Hiro said, nodding. 'Clever.'

It headed directly for them. As it approached, Sara could make out a small pouch secured by four lines from its corners to the bottom of the drone like an inverted parachute. It hovered just above their heads, the pouch dangling in front of their faces.

'What about Maddy?' she said into the phone over the buzzing noise of the four rotors.

'We'll send her over in the inflatable raft once the drone is on its way back.'

'Send her now.'

She heard the man snap out a command. A man-sized shape dumped something small into it. In the background she could hear Maddy's voice. The beam from the boat's spot shifted. Sara shaded her eyes from the dazzling light.

'It's Maddy. I recognise her dress. She's in the boat.' The phone was slippery in her hands.

'Now, put the orbs in the basket. Wait.' Sara heard the phone being muffled and the hint of a cultured voice. The man came back on. 'You'll get your daughter once we have it.'

'You said when they were halfway.'

'You misheard. I said put them in the basket. Now.'

Hiro's eyes were hooded. He met her gaze and nodded. She placed the jewelled balls in the suspended sling. The drone rose immediately and headed back to shore, its load swaying beneath it. When it had covered most of the distance, one of the men pushed the inflatable into the water and started the outboard. Tying down the throttle handle, he lined the craft up with *Misty Lady* and let it go. It puttered towards them on low revs.

'It's riding very low in the front with only Maddy in the back,' Hiro murmured.

Sara cupped her hand to her mouth. 'Hang on, honey. You're nearly here.'

Ten metres from the shoreline, something surged out of the water and grabbed Maddy, dragging her, screaming, into the water.

'What's happening? Maddy!'

'It's Levi,' Hiro said.

'Levi? What the hell is he doing with Maddy? He's going to drown her.'

Levi spun the inflatable around, opening the throttle and shoving it back towards the beach before side-stroking towards the yacht, using his other arm to support Maddy's head.

The men on the shore scrambled as the inflatable headed back towards them, the drone pitching wildly before falling into the sea. The man on the motorboat also dived in, thrashing through the water away from the inflatable.

'What are they doing?'

'Forget them. Levi knows what he's doing. Help your daughter into the boat.'

Levi was already alongside, supporting Maddy as she scrambled over the side of the yacht.

'Get down!' Levi shouted. 'That inflatable was stuffed with—'

A huge explosion lit up the night. Sara threw herself onto the deck, clutching Maddy to her. Water cascaded over them; the yacht lifted before thumping back down with the aftershock. Small rocks and sand peppered the yacht, sounding like hailstones against the fibreglass hull. The bright blaze from the searchlight had gone out.

When it had stopped, Sara peeked over the rail. The boat still rocked wildly. On the beach, pieces of the raft were still burning, creating enough light for her to see the massive hole the explosion had made. It took her some time to realise that the bomb had been meant for them. That Maddy was to have been killed. A mantra of "no witnesses" repeated in her head, something she'd heard Layton say more than once, but hadn't realised—not wanting to know—its true meaning. She couldn't believe anyone would so be callous as to sacrifice a child. If it hadn't been for Levi...

'Where's Levi?'

Hiro pointed. Levi was swimming strongly back towards the devastation.

Houses on both sides of the channel were waking up, their lights winking on, creating silhouettes of their owners' shapes as they moved outside to see what was happening. Even if the men who'd tried to kill them had escaped the blast, with this many people now watching it was unlikely they'd try anything else. One part of her hoped they'd been caught up in the blast.

Levi reached the men's motorboat and clambered aboard. The

man who'd waded ashore tried to get back aboard, but Levi hit him. The man slid off the side of the boat and back into the water. Levi fired up the motor and hauled up the anchor. The boat eased away.

'Go below and grab what you and Maddy need along with Levi's clothes. Hurry. We need to get back to the mainland before the police arrive and start asking questions.'

19

Chapter Nineteen

Maddy was still asleep. Tripod curled at the end of the bed, his single front paw stretched across her leg. He opened one eye as Sara eased out of the big bed and, careful not to wake Maddy, stretched. Daylight had been poking around the edges of the blind covering the casement window for hours, anxious to find a way in. She yawned and tugged the drapes across to cover the gaps before padding across the wooden floor to the en suite. She closed the door, wishing it were as easy to shut out the clamouring images from yesterday that trailed in her wake.

The mirror confirmed her suspicion that she was underdone on sleep and overdone on unprocessed stress. Her wig hung at an angle off the shaving mirror like a bedraggled possum. Bending closer to the mirror, she examined the puckered flesh on her scalp, her fingers gently probing, remembering the explosion and fire when she'd almost lost Maddy the first time. When Tony had died. Because of her. Now, *Misty Lady,* her last link to Tony, her only home for that matter, had also been taken from her. There was no way she could return now. Not even to collect the rest of her things. Not while those men were still around. Tears welled as memories of last night washed through her. Last night had provided a new high-water mark on what had already been a floodtide of the strange and totally weird.

What sort of mother am I? Endangering my daughter's life like this, not once but twice? Danger that will still kill her before Easter unless I'm able to locate the damn cure for whatever curse Layton has infected us with. How she hated—*loathed*—that man.

Turning from the mirror, she spun the taps of the shower, slipped out of her dirty underwear, and stepped beneath the water, lathering up too much shower gel on the sponge, layering the luxurious suds in thick white swathes across her body before allowing the steaming water to slough it off, along with the tears, imagining her sins swirling away with it.

SHE FOLLOWED the hushed voices down the hall, unwilling to bear her own persecutory company any longer; unable to watch innocence sleep while evil prowled the perimeter of her life.

'Sara. You're awake.' The two men sat back in their chairs as she entered, their former quiet words swallowed by the widening space. Between them was a round occasional table, and atop it the so-called map. A map to nowhere.

'I heard you two talking. It sounded private.'

The two men glanced at each other. Hiro, in a highland kilt and leggings, waved at a buffet table behind them where there were several platters of food. 'It's not exactly breakfast, but I'm sure we can find you something nourishing to keep body and soul together. Maddy still asleep?'

'Yes. I'll take some food through for her a little later, but first I want to know what happens next? How can we *fix* this mess? Last night was terrifying, and nothing has really changed as a result.

Those men are still out there, and Maddy will sicken and die from those spores unless we do something quickly.'

'We were just discussing that. Here, let me get you something to eat first.' Hiro pulled up another chair and ushered her into it.

Across the table, Levi's eyes were hooded, his face drawn. She guessed he hadn't slept well either. He gave her a weary smile.

'Levi, I wanted to thank you for last night. I can't remember if I did already, my head is all a bit of a mish-mash, but I do know if you hadn't pulled Maddy out of that raft, she—' Sara's throat thickened, and the words wouldn't come as the memory of the explosion returned.

He looked self-conscious, managing a nod. 'I'm just pleased it all worked out.' He cleared his throat. 'Is she okay?'

'Yes. Thank goodness. Hiro gave her something when we arrived back. She went straight out. Tripod is with her. I'll let her sleep a bit longer.'

Hiro handed her a full plate of cheese, ham, and assorted greens along with a crusty baguette.

'Whatever it was you gave her in that tonic, Hiro, certainly helped.' She smiled her thanks, tears coming unbidden. She swiped them away with the back of her hand. Hiro gripped her shoulder and gave it a squeeze. 'She's a strong lassie.'

'Sara, I was saying when you came in that this page looks different now that it's dried off. It seems older, more brittle,' Levi said.

She angled her head to get a better view. 'It's a shame the bit in the middle was burnt. I'm guessing it's the key to what's written along the sides.'

'I agree,' Hiro said, resuming his seat. 'It's logical that Layton would have left some kind of instructions for you underneath the protective coating.'

Sara speared slices of cheese and ham, sandwiching them between a chunk of torn-off bread. 'Levi, you said you thought these notations were... what did you call them?'

He shifted in his seat. 'City pairs. I spent some time in logistics early on in the army, moving equipment and men around.' He waved a finger above the first entry. 'This JFK-CDG for example looks like it could be John F. Kennedy airport in New York and the destination Charles de Gaulle airport in Paris. The other column is obviously a date. Maybe the date of a flight?'

'Or something on a flight?' Hiro ventured.

She swallowed. 'Wouldn't he use a flight number if that was the case?'

'Possibly,' Levi said, 'but I think this is more specific. See how the arrival code of the airport is the same as the next departure point? And the dates are sequential. I believe that this could be the projected operational schedule of one particular aircraft.'

'You mean Layton hid the other orb on a plane? Why would he do that?'

Hiro scratched the silver day-old growth on his neck. 'When he came to me with this, he said he'd had to hide the second orb in a hurry. Something about "they" had discovered he had it.'

'By "they" I'm guessing you mean those men from last night.' Sara's voice hardened as she remembered how close they'd come to killing Maddy.

'Most likely. I imagine Layton bribed someone for this operating pattern, intending to go back to retrieve the orb himself when he had things under control, but by the time he felt safe enough to do so he'd became too sick to travel.'

'The only thing we don't know is what airline and which specific aircraft.' Levi tapped the blackened section in the middle of the page. 'This might have been able to tell us.'

'There might be a way to retrieve it, but it's risky,' Hiro said.

'Risky how? If it's anything like last night, count me and Maddy out.'

'No, Sara. Nothing like that. It's risky because if it doesn't work, the page will be destroyed completely. The process I have in mind should briefly return the page to its original, to when it was written.'

'How briefly?' Levi asked.

'Seconds only, perhaps even less given the treatments this paper has already been through. After that it will spontaneously combust. Spectacularly.'

'Too bad if you're a slow reader,' Levi quipped.

'How spectacular is spectacular?' Sara asked.

'Put it this way, you wouldn't be able to be in same room with it. I do have a space, though, which might be suitable, but we need to find a way to read the information in the seconds before it's incinerated.'

Sara snapped her fingers and pointed. 'Live feed. We mount a video camera above the page and connect it to a computer outside the fire zone. Then we can record the whole thing and later freeze/zoom in on the image when it appears. Won't do much for the recording equipment though.'

Hiro's eyebrows bunched, and he nodded. 'That might work. I'm just not confident these burnt sections will recover fully. The process relies on retrieving impressions made in the paper, and parts of that have been burnt off. The sections that are only scorched may respond, however.'

HIRO'S FIREBOX, as he called it, was at the back of the house. Concrete floors and ceiling with cinderblock walls. No windows or furnishings other than a metal toilet and hand basin that hinged out of the wall. It reminded Sara of a prison or monastic cell, and she wondered what Hiro did in here, but didn't ask as she wasn't sure she'd like the answer.

They laid the page out on the floor, mounting the video directly above it on a wheeled frame complete with spotlights all trained onto the paper below.

Hiro squatted beside it, placing a four-litre paint can and a six-inch house painting brush within reach. He was now wearing a white tee shirt, paint-spattered overalls, and sneakers with fluorescent pink laces. 'You two better go outside now. Leave the door open. I won't have much time once I finish.'

'Don't trip over the wires when you're running out,' Levi said, taping down the last portion of the video cable. Sara followed him out. Maddy was outside, kneeling on a chair, peering at Hiro's image on the monitor. Tripod was flopped beneath the desk. As they approached, the dog's ear twitched in their direction, but other than that he didn't move.

Sara placed her hand lightly on Maddy's back, giving it a rub. She looked up with a broad grin. Hiro's tonic, "to take the edge off," appeared to have worked a treat. Maddy still remembered what had happened to her, but it was as if she was describing a movie she'd seen rather than something that had the potential to traumatise her. Even when she'd described the swim back to the boat with Levi, there was more excitement in her voice than fear. Levi tugged playfully on the girl's ear as he came up to them.

'Toot, toot. You ready with the fire engine noise I showed you, Maddy?'

She giggled and gave a long siren-like howl.

'That's it. Now let's watch while Hiro does his trick. Ready?'

She nodded, grinning.

On screen, they watched Hiro dip the paintbrush into the can and slop the contents onto the paper, quickly slapping the brush back and forth, covering the entire surface with clear lacquer. As they watched, the edges of the paper blackened, a curl of red working its way towards the centre. Hiro finished in a hurry, threw the brush to one side, and sprinted, clanging the metal door shut behind him as a white-and-red fireball exploded. The monitor went blank. Moments later, Sara heard a louder explosion that reverberated through the floor. Maddy, head back, howled her siren noise again.

'That would be the paint can catching,' Levi said quietly.

Hiro panted up behind them. 'Did you get it?'

'We don't know yet. I'll play it back,' Sara said.

The images rewound, Sara slowing down the progression until they became stills.

'There.' Levi touched the screen. 'Can you zoom?'

Sara expanded the image, and Hiro leaned in towards the screen. The original burnt sections remained illegible, apart from one or two words which were now visible.

'What is that word there?' He muttered. 'Seat?'

'Looks like it.' Levi pointed to another area. 'And over here maybe "package"?'

'There's some letters and numbers further down, but I have no idea what they refer to,' Sara said. 'Unless it's related to this bit below. Is that 59J?'

'If this is about an aircraft, then that might be a seat number, but I'm guessing row 59 would be way down the back. Layton doesn't strike me as an economy class kinda guy,' Levi said.

'No, he always insisted on first. Business class absolute minimum,' Sara said.

Levi looked up, tapping a thumbnail against his teeth. 'If I wanted to hide something, I'd put it where there was going to be no connection with me, so not my allocated seat or even class. I also would put it where I knew I could easily retrieve it but where there would be no risk of it being thrown away with the trash. So, what if he waited until the lights were out and then wandered down to find an empty seat in economy to secrete the orb somewhere in row 59, seat J?'

'That narrows it down,' Hiro said. 'But we still don't know which airline, much less what plane.'

Levi clapped his hands together. 'That's it! Sara, can you scroll back up to those numbers and letters we saw before?'

Sara steadied the image, zooming in on the area where Levi was pointing. 'Each aircraft has a unique registration called a tail number. I'm betting that's what these letters and numbers are. Layton gave us the tail number for the aircraft he was on.'

'How would he know that?'

'It's painted in big letters at the rear of the fuselage, near the tail, hence the...'

Sara nodded. '...tail number, got it.'

'And that will identify the airline and the specific aircraft?' Hiro asked.

'If I'm right, yes, it will.'

Levi copied the registration number down on the back of his hand. 'If the aircraft is in the air now, I should be able to locate it. There are websites that use live radar to track planes worldwide.' He pulled out his phone. 'Ah, I forgot, no signal on this side of Hiro's house. I'll go over and check it and come back.'

'I'll come with you. I need to ring my friend Deb anyway and tell her everything is all right. She'll also know what happened on the island after we left last night. Hiro, can you look after Maddy for a bit?'

He grinned at Maddy, and she smiled back. 'I'm sure we can find something interesting to do in my workroom. That all right with you, Maddy?'

She nodded happily. Ever since Hiro had produced two choco-lates and a self-inflating ball from the sleeve of her jumper, she'd been fascinated by him.

'Come on then.' Levi led the way back through the maze of rooms. Sara paused before the heavy curtain leading to the other side of the house, her fingers trailing its heavy edge. Last night when she'd made the crossings, it hadn't been so bad—preoccupation and fatigue had that effect. She'd simply gritted her teeth and sandwiched herself between Hiro and Levi. But now the feelings from the first time she'd made the crossing intruded, making her hesitate.

'You all right?' Levi asked.

'Yeah, fine.'

'It gets easier each time.'

'That's what my first boyfriend said. He was wrong.'

'I'm sorry.'

'No, I mean he was just "wrong." For me... first of many... I don't know why I said that.' Levi gave an encouraging smile, about to slip through the slit in the curtain. She gripped the fingers of her opposite hand, wringing them like wet washing.

'Levi.'

He turned.

'I'm scared.'

'You can hold on to me—'

'No, I mean I'm scared that even if by some miracle we have escaped the maniacs from last night and find this magical cure, I'll still screw up Maddy's life. Oh, I don't know why I told you that either. What's happening?'

Levi guided her to one of the deep stud-backed armchairs. 'That divide over there,' he pointed at the curtain, its edge rippling, 'dredges up our deepest fears. You don't want to know what nightmares flash up for me each time I have to make the crossing, but believe me, they're way easier to deal with if you allow them out. The crossing will drag them into the light if you let it. Buried, they keep growing, their midnight whispers eating away at who we want to think we are until there's only a husk of that left. Take it from me, that only ends one way. I've seen too many good men and women end up sacrificed to their own monsters.'

She was surprised to find her cheeks were wet. Sniffing, she fumbled for a tissue. Levi found one and gently dabbed her face. 'You can sit this one out, you know. I can ring your friend for you.'

Sara shook her head and then blew her nose. 'No, you're right. I'm a runner. Always have been. It's time I stopped. You know, I kind of liked being the queen over wherever we were. I felt strong there.'

'Bring that with you then. Remember, Hiro told us that the program/dream/trip whatever it was took the qualities and experiences that were already within us and expanded on them.' He took her hands and squeezed them. 'That means you are that woman already, Sara. You just have to be willing to accept her the same way as the parts that are scared. All of them go up to make Sara Montgomery, a strong, beautiful, and intelligent woman who has done everything possible to protect her daughter and keep her safe.'

Sara's eyes welled, and the tears came again. She'd been frightened for so long. Alone in a way that didn't have the words to describe it, much less be heard. Even Tony hadn't understood, not really. He'd never known what it was like to scrape enough strands of hope to get through another day. But somehow she knew Levi had, perhaps still did.

She slid her hands free and, with a firming of her lips, nodded. He helped her up, and together they entered the crossing. Knowing a little of what would happen helped, and while the doubts, inadequacies, and negative self-talk still rose, this time they were more shadow than substance. She simply acknowledged them without succumbing.

'All good?' Levi said at the other side.

'I wouldn't say good, but definitely better.'

'Great.' He busied himself with his phone, tapping rapidly.

'Levi, what happens when we locate this plane?'

He looked up from the screen. 'What do you mean? Once I figure out where it is, I'll book myself a seat in 59J and fly over to meet the flight, wherever it is. There can only be a limited number of places in an airline seat that he could have hidden it.'

'No, I didn't mean that. What if... what if the melders' curse, the separation thing is real here too? You wouldn't make it as far as the airport.'

He shrugged. 'We'll have to take that chance. What choice do we have?'

'What about Hiro? Couldn't he...?'

Levi shook his head. 'There are things you don't know about Hiro. One of them is he's what people in the security services used to call a ghost. If the wrong people find out he's still alive, well, it wouldn't end well. He travels way under the radar. That's what the constant changes to his appearance are about.'

'Yes, he told me. Sort of.'

'I still hear a "but."'

'Yes. We need to be sure you're able to make the trip first. Those men from last night are probably still out there looking for us. Remember last time you tried to slip away from me on your horse? When I found you, I could have asked you anything and you would have told me. You were too weak to resist. This curse affects the mind and will as well as the body.'

His haunted glance told her he did remember.

'We'll only get one chance at this.'

'So, what do you suggest?'

'Find out before you go. Do a test run. Now, with me. Maddy and I need some toiletries and underwear anyway; I didn't have time to grab much more than my passport off the boat. There are some shops just far enough away for us to find out if this curse still affects us.'

'If anyone is going, it should be me. You have Maddy to think of.'

'I *am* thinking of Maddy. Plus, they've seen you—at the hospital, and that man on the ferry has as well.'

Levi seemed to wrestle with what she'd said for a moment, then reluctantly agreed. 'I'll let Hiro know. Oh, damn, now my battery is low. Can I use your phone before you go while I figure out this plane location thing?'

AFTER THE HUSHED and subdued sanctuary of Hiro's strange house, the traffic bustle of Anne Street leading down to the James Street precinct was jarring and loud. Levi had suggested she catch a cab (better security), but she'd wanted to walk. There was a David Jones store down that way, and it wasn't too far. This way she'd be able to monitor her reactions as the distance between her and Levi increased incrementally.

Given the strange time slippage on the other side of the curtain, over here it was now only just past ten, the morning sun gathering strength, and she relished its warmth on her face.

On the phone, Deb had been full of the news of the explosion last night. Sara had avoided the issue, saying that they had spent the night with Maddy's grandfather on the mainland. She'd learnt it was better to keep the lies lined up behind each other. It was easier to keep track of them that way.

When Sara checked the news on her phone, the official version was that the police were exploring several leads and were anxious to interview the occupants of a motorboat seen powering away from the scene towards the mainland. Sara breathed a sigh of relief. She'd suspected some of the residents may have seen them aboard *Misty Lady*. Hiro had been right about not using the lights.

Hiro. She snorted to herself. A couple of days ago, she had never heard of him; now he had become integral to their survival. She'd even left her daughter in his care. He had that effect on people. Levi was another enigma. The whole virtual trip had bonded her closer to him than she'd been with anyone, and yet she hardly knew a thing about the man. *Does Levi remember the kiss? Why do I? What is wrong with me? He's a killer.*

But a killer that saved Maddy—and me.

What? In a dream?

No. Last night too. He saved Maddy. That was real.

Now she was arguing with herself. *Is that part of the separation symptoms?*

She took a breath, waiting for yet another set of lights to change at a cross street, and looked back the way she'd come. Last time the discomfort had started as a tingling in her belly, as if something wasn't quite right. It was hard to tell whether the fluttering she was feeling now was that or just nerves They'd certainly had a workout lately.

The buzzer sounded to cross the road, and she stepped off the curb, glancing automatically at the cars waiting their turn for a green light on her left. Something familiar caught her eye, and she looked closer. One car back, a man was staring at her. Not in the way that men usually did; this was more intense. He looked familiar. Then her heart bucked, and she averted her gaze, increasing her pace, weaving through the pedestrians, trying for distance. Behind her, she heard a car door slam and horns begin to blare. She chanced a quick glance over her shoulder. The car he'd been driving was now marooned in a stream of traffic that flowed around the abandoned vehicle. The man Layton used to call Batman was running towards her, along with another man covered by tattoos.

Sara didn't hesitate; she sprinted, running diagonally across busy Anne Street, finding gaps in the traffic stream, punctuated by horn blasts and screeching tyres, abuse trailing in her wake as she increased her stride down the opposite side of the street. Behind her, she heard a more urgent screech and then a hollow thumping sound. A woman screamed. Sara looked back. Batman had been hit by a truck, but the tattooed guy was still standing. Traffic had stopped. People clustered around the man on the ground; someone was on his knees beside him. She thought she could see blood. Batman's offsider was caught up in it. Their gazes locked through the crowd, and he pushed his way clear, shoving people aside. Sara turned and ran, attempting to put distance between them, heart thumping. She turned right, running down the next street and up another, shopping forgotten. All that mattered was getting clear. Behind her, she could hear the heavy shoe slaps of determined pursuit. She caught a snap of him behind her in an angled storefront window, his shoulders hunched, arms crossing his body, elbows out, head forward, chin up all the exposed skin covered with tattoos, even his face and skull, but the man wasn't a runner.

She was. That was something. She used that knowledge to focus on her own form, head in line with shoulders, arms pistoning at ninety degrees, hips to chest, power concentrated in her torso down through her hips to her feet. She wove between other pedestrians, calling out a warning where there was no gap, surging between them when people jumped out of the way. Part of her registered she was heading down Brunswick Street towards New Farm and the river.

Damn. I should have gone the other way. Back towards Hiro's house.

Taking a moment to check on traffic, she sprinted across the road, hoping to circle the block at the next cross street and head back to Hiro's. She missed a stride, stumbled, and almost fell. Something was wrong. Nausea cramped her stomach, and she bent over clutching her abdomen as she heaved partly digested cheese and ham between her feet.

Oh, not now. Not the fucking melders' curse. Not now. I have to head back, get closer to Levi. Which way?

She pushed herself on, staggering about like those wannabe guys at the tail of the pack mid-way through a half marathon. Rounding the corner, she stumbled again and sprawled across the ground, fingernails clawing at the pavement as if to pull herself forward. The heavy footfalls behind her ceased, and the sound of his laboured breathing filled the space. She turned her head to look over her shoulder. Even that was an effort. He towered over her. It may have been her imagination, but the tattoos across his enormous arms and hands seemed to be gyrating. He put a phone to his ear, grinning. Calling in help, no doubt. Soon more of them would be arriving; there was no telling how many or close they were. *Oh God, I feel sick.*

Cars streamed past, oblivious. Sara couldn't see any other pedestrians. The man grunted something further into the phone and slid it back into his pocket. He crouched beside her and took one of her hands. She was powerless to stop him.

He smiled. Several of his front teeth were missing, 'Try anything and I'll cruth your hand. Under-thand?'

She nodded. The hand clutching hers was both rough and slimy. Up close she could make out tattoos of beetles up and down the fingers while his palm showed a coiled red worm. It was hard to think clearly. The images on his hands seemed alive, yet how could that be? *Am I hallucinating?* She remembered the feeling of brain fog when she'd been separated from Levi before but this was different. Her head was clearer, if anything.

Behind her she heard a car screech around the corner and skid to a stop, motor still running. *Here they are.* She gathered her energy and pushed herself onto all fours. The big man turned towards the car as Levi leaped over the bonnet, launching himself feet first at the man, his boots slamming into the man's jaw. Levi rolled away in a tuck and bounced to his feet. He hurried over. 'Are you hurt?' he asked, eyes scanning her.

'I don't think so.'

He dragged Sara's arm across his shoulders and hoisted her up. 'Can you walk?'

'Trying.' Strength returned in gulps. It became easier to breathe, walk, the safety of the car only steps away.

'Watch out.' Levi yelled, swinging around. Too late. The other man had crawled after them and grabbed Sara's bare leg, his meaty hand slippery as it gripped her. She had the sensation of something cold and slimy slithering across her bare calf. Levi kicked the man away and the grip released.

Opening the rear door, he bundled her in, Sara's arms and legs like *al dente* spaghetti. He slammed the door and she collapsed onto the back seat, relief coursing through her.

He hurried around to the front and slipped into the driver seat, dragging the transmission into drive, and they squealed away.

'It's still there. The curse,' she managed.

'Tell me about it. Hang on.' He made a U-turn. 'Pass me your phone.'

Sara managed to haul herself upright. Now they were together again, her strength had returned. She noted they were heading back towards Hiro's. She dug the phone out of her waistband and slipped it into his open hand. Levi buzzed down his side window and dropped the phone onto the road, hearing it crunch beneath the rear wheels.

'What did you do that for?'

'It's how they found you. They had your number. It doesn't take much tech to triangulate the signal for a general location, then, as soon as you hit the street, it would have given them a nice clear location signal for you. I should have thought of it. My bad. Remember they used your number to ring through the ransom demand.'

'Is that how you found me?'

'Similar. As soon as I started to feel the symptoms, I set off after you. Before you left, I took the precaution of synching your phone with mine just in case the melders' symptoms started. That way I'd be able to trace you. Good thing too; I'd never have found you way down here.'

'I just ran.'

'A little too far, it turns out.'

'Batman. He was there too. He got hit by a truck.'

Levi swung the wheel sharply, bouncing into a narrow street, and clicked on a remote. A garage door at the end of the alley glided open, and Levi drove straight in. The door closed softly behind them, and she heard several loud noises as heavy bolts slid into place.

'Hiro's place is a fortress. No one knows we're here, and even if they did, there's no way they could get through the security in this place. Come on now, we need to talk with Hiro.'

Chapter Twenty

Levi led the way through the dark house. There were too few windows for his liking, but he understood the necessity. The house had been built with security in mind, and not only structurally. Hiro had woven in powerful energetic wards to both cloak and protect the rambling house. That was reassuring, but it didn't stop his skin from crawling. He felt them ripple across his back and forearms as he passed each checkpoint.

He was still charged. That made two close calls in twenty-four hours. They'd been lucky both times, but the only men Levi knew who'd relied on luck to get through were now dead. Sara was right. They would only get one chance at getting this right. *I only hope she's up for it.*

They made the crossing through the curtain without incident, and he ushered her into the room where they'd had breakfast, the light bright after the dimness. Hiro was dressed as an old-time airline captain: white shirt, tie, and black double-breasted blazer with big brass buttons and four sleeve braid loops.

He's obviously figured out what has to be done too.

'Ah, welcome back, weary travellers. Tea?'

Levi flopped onto one of the three deep armchairs. 'Please.'

Sara looked around. 'Where's Maddy?'

'Playing in your room with her horse. She's fine.'

'Horse?'

'Only a small one. Miniature, really. She seemed to get a kick out of it. I suspect Tripod was a little more uncertain, but he figured it out in the end. Smart dog, that.' He gave them both a broad wink and passed Levi a cup of tea. 'So, Sara. Levi has kept me up with developments. It seems that this separation curse you two share has added a further complication to retrieving the hidden orb. I only see one option to bring this all to a close, and that will involve flying to retrieve it.' He flicked the lapels of his double-breasted jacket.

'Nice outfit, but I assume you won't be the pilot,' she said.

'Sad but true. But you know, when the jacket was fashionable I made quite a bit of money from these nautical-looking brass buttons. We would cast replicas of them in 24kt gold and then sew them onto the jacket to bring into countries where it was difficult or very expensive to acquire gold, selling them at a premium. Some cultures only trust gold. Afterwards, we'd replace the brass buttons and fly back out.'

'And that is relevant because?' Sara asked.

'Because everyone ended up with what they wanted. As I trust will be the case when you two get back.'

'You're suggesting that Levi and I both go and get it. What about Maddy?'

'She will be perfectly safe here with me. I'm assuming Levi has apprised you of the impregnability of this house along with my particular limitations around travel?'

She nodded.

'Excellent. Then if you leave shortly,' he glanced at the oversized watch on his wrist, 'you'll arrive in plenty of time.' Hiro's grin looked alarmingly like Alice's Cheshire cat. He sipped delicately at his tea.

'Leave for where?' Sara asked.

'Singapore,' Levi said. 'I checked the operation plan that Layton wrote against the live radar website, and it looks like they line up. It's a miracle, because aircraft get swapped around to cover for mechanical and other delays. It's due to fly from Singapore to Sydney tomorrow night. Hiro has managed to pre-book seats 59J and K for us.'

'How prescient of him,' Sara said.

'As you said yourself, Sara, there is only one option left to save Maddy—and us.' Hiro said. 'Don't worry, you'll be over and back before you know it. Jet lag notwithstanding.'

Levi had been watching Sara's face as Hiro spoke. She didn't look happy, but there was resignation there as well. He could relate to both.

'You may want to say cheerio to Maddy and tell her you'll be taking a short trip,' Hiro said.

'Why can't she come with us?'

'After what happened last night and this morning, I'm not sure that would be wise. Maddy is your squeeze point. Layton's men know that. Don't you agree, Levi?'

'Hiro is right. They now know we're in the general area and will be searching even if they can't yet hone in on this place specifically. They'll have CCTV surveillance in place all over the Valley in a couple of hours. Maddy will be much safer here with Hiro.'

Sara's expression stiffened, and for a moment Levi thought she might refuse. Logic rarely prevailed over strong emotion, and Sara had been through a lot lately. He could see she was both angry and trapped by a lack of choice.

'I'll go check on Maddy.'

Levi breathed a sigh of relief and waited until she left the room, closing the door behind her with a thump.

'She's not happy,' Hiro said.

'Can you blame her? I'm amazed she's still functioning as well as she is.'

'Yes, she is a remarkable young lady. Her resilience is particularly high. Maddy's too.'

Levi studied Hiro's lined face. 'So. What weren't you telling her?'

The older man's eyes widened. 'You know me too well. There's no time to get you both new passports, so I had to book the flights in your own names. Layton's men are well resourced, so it's possible they'll have someone official red flag you both. If so, there are likely to be people in Singapore waiting for you—if not on the flight. The best I could do is buy duplicate tickets on as many connecting flights out of Singapore to put them off the scent. That may give you some breathing space, as they won't know which one you'll be on until it's too late. The bad news is once they know what flight you're on, they'll have time to put a welcoming committee in place. The good news is, there's money if you need it, so my advice is to use as much as you need to come up with one of your famous Plan Bs.'

'Right.' Levi rubbed the bristles on his face. He was still jumpy from the adrenaline, and this news didn't do anything to settle him. 'If this works out the way I think it will, we're going to need some new IDs after this. Ours will be burnt. Can you do that?'

'Yes. Given time. You can go to ground here until I can arrange it.'

'Good enough.'

'There's something else.' Hiro said. 'I had someone visit Layton's former office manager. She's willing to sell access to his personnel records.'

'Including photos? That would be a big help if I could recognise them.'

'She says yes. His records were kept on the dark web, but she can get access. I was hoping we'd have them by now, but I'll send them to you as soon as they come through.'

~

'SO, did Maddy really have a horse in the bedroom?' Levi took a sip of his coffee and made a face. He put it back on the table, eyes automatically tracking the parade of passengers hurrying towards the departure gates.

Sara gave a weary smile. 'Put it this way: it felt and smelt like a miniature pony, but I swear it had clockwork innards. As far as Maddy was concerned though, it was one hundred percent horse. I don't know how Hiro does what he does, but he does it incredibly well.'

'Yeah, if Hiro was a cocktail, he'd be one part scientist, three parts shaman.'

'Add ice and shake well, then sprinkle liberally with magic or sometimes BS,' Sara added.

Levi gave her a weary smile. 'I've got to the stage of not being able to tell where one part of him ends and the other begins.'

'Looks like you could use a little barista magic right about now,' she said, indicating his full cup.

'I live in hope.'

He hadn't wanted coffee as much as an opportunity to sit and observe. They'd left Hiro's through a back door layered on the street side with old bricks. Once they'd shut the steel door behind them the bricks blended perfectly to look like a blank wall. From there they'd cut through a multi-level car park zigzagging through several side streets to finally arrive at the Valley's train station. From there it was an easy twenty minutes on the air train. He still didn't have the personnel files that Hiro had promised.

'How are you doing about leaving Maddy?' He noticed her fingers tighten around the bag's handle.

'I don't like it. But what choice do I have? Maddy has had to cope with so much change lately. I feel like she's constantly being uprooted. I don't want that for her. She needs stability, a home.'

Levi nodded, suspecting Sara was also voicing some basic needs of her own.

'It's only for a day or so. Hiro will look out for her; I can promise you that.' He stood and picked up the overnight bag, mentally thanking his Plan B man for delivering on such short notice. Everything he needed had been moulded into regular baggage items or compressed inside others. 'We better get moving; we're on final call and I think they're about to page us.'

They hurried to the gate. Levi had delayed their boarding on purpose. Coming in last meant everyone was already seated and would be facing him as they made their way down the aisle. It made it easier to scope the other passengers. He noted a few who were pretending a little too hard not to notice them and made a note of their seat row to check out later. If Sara and he had been red flagged, there would have been ample time for Layton's men to buy tickets on this flight. *Or am I overthinking this?* As one of his trainers used to like to say, "paranoia is like salt; a little develops the flavour, too much and you destroy the dish."

Sara found their seats in the last section of the aircraft. Levi took a last look around before flopping into the seat beside her and buckling up. Sara was flicking through the entertainment options of the seat back screen. 'You look a little nervous.'

'I have a thing about flying.'

She snorted. 'I bet. You were looking for them, weren't you? Layton's men.'

He made a noncommittal grunt. Sara had a way of reading him that he found disconcerting. *Maybe it's the melders' thing?* Maybe it made them more sensitive to each other.

'Levi?'

She is persistent too. 'Yes, all right.' He took the magazine from the seat pocket and leafed through it. Watches and perfume. *When did watches become a thing?*

'And? God, this is like pulling toenails.'

'I think you mean teeth.'

'No, I mean toenails. Yours, if you don't level with me.'

'All right. I was checking out the other passengers. There are a couple I have my doubts about, but even if they turn out to be the bad guys, nothing will happen on board. They'll wait until we get to Singapore.'

'And then what?'

Levi felt like he was in an interrogation. He snapped the magazine shut and stuffed it back into the seat pocket. 'And then what, what? I don't know. That's how these things work. They try something, we take a step back and counter. It's like a dance with an alternating lead.'

'But surely they don't think we have the orbs with us?'

The plane had completed its push back and was now under power to join the queue for the runway.

'If—and that is still an if—they are onto us, then my best guess is they'll realise were on our way to collect them. They'll do their best to tag us, and when they think we have them then they'll try something.'

'Like?'

He shrugged. 'Something like a snatch and hold, the same as they did with Maddy. We need to stay ahead of that.'

The emergency procedure announcement blared through the speaker system, and he used the interruption to settle back and close his eyes. For the next ten minutes, or at least until the seat belt sign went out, he could relax.

THE FLIGHT HAD BEEN UNEVENTFUL. He'd sat through three movies, two meals, and Sara's four-hour nap, her head floppy and heavy against his arm. She awoke with a start as they touched down. He patted her upper arm.

'It's all right. We're here and safe. You must have needed that sleep.'

She rubbed her eyes, then noticed the wet patch on his shirt sleeve and brushed it with a scrunched napkin. 'Oh, no. Did I do that?'

'Forget it. Everyone dribbles.' He paused. 'Admittedly, not always quite that much.'

She slapped his arm. 'Nothing happened then with those men?'

'No. I took a couple of turns up and down the aisle, but the guys I was keeping my eye on didn't stir.'

Which was technically true, but he'd felt their gazes on the back of his neck after he'd passed, and coming back the other way they'd studiously avoided his eyes. They also didn't have that happy holiday excitement or crushed corporate look about them either. If his estimate was right, there were at least four of them. He checked the time. The next flight, which hopefully had the missing orb hidden on it, wasn't for another four hours. He'd already checked in online and hoped Hiro would do the same with all the other red herring flights he'd booked. It had been an expensive exercise for Hiro, but if it meant Layton's men didn't know their next move it would be worth it.

He smiled to himself. He and Sara had been through a lot together and in a strange way, he felt he knew her at some deep level —and she him. The people he could say that about would make a very short list.

However, they still hadn't talked about that kiss. Not even a mention. Admittedly it had been a strategic improv move, and a good one, but for a moment there, near the end, it had felt real.

'Levi? Are you awake? People are ready to get off. Shouldn't we be going?'

Blood flushed his cheeks. He coughed. 'Just resting my eyes. I'll get the bags.'

Sliding out of the seat, he opened the overhead locker, taking a quick look along the crowded aisle, but he couldn't make out the men he'd tagged earlier. It didn't matter if they really were Layton's men. They'd wait. The best defence was to stay inside a crowd. That shouldn't be too hard inside a major transit hub like Changi Airport.

He eased Sara to the front of him in the aisle and slipped his arms through the backpack straps. It felt reassuring and provided a layer of protection against attack from behind.

The queue shuffled forward, finally moving. He squared his shoulders, redistributing the load. He bent forward and whispered into Sara's ear, 'As soon as we clear the door, take hold of my hand and hang on, whatever happens. If these guys are on the job, then it's likely they'll try and separate us and probably go after you to reel me in. We can't let that happen.'

'You're saying I'm a, what did you call it once? A soft target?'

'What I meant—'

'I get it, Levi, and if you want any chance whatsoever of holding my hand, then you'll shut up.'

'Yes... Highness.'

He heard her snort and imagined an involuntary smile tugging at the corners of her mouth.

Once they'd passed through the plane's doorway, her fingers lightly brushed against his, and he took her hand, their fingers interlacing. They looked like lovers. The disturbing thing was, it felt so natural. Comfortable even. They entered the airport.

'If we get separated, find the biggest crowd and stick with them. Keep to the middle and stay away from the sidewalls.'

'What happens on the sidewalls?'

'You could get boxed in, or they might come in for a pretend group hug and bundle you out through a side door.'

'What for? We're in an airport, on the transit side of the immigration barrier. What good would that do?'

Levi took a breath. 'One quick jab with a fast-acting drug, and you'd be propped up in a wheelchair with one of them facilitating you through immigration and customs. Then you'd become leverage the same way Maddy did.'

'Or I could make sure I hang on to you.' She tightened her grip on his hand. 'Why are we stopping? You said to keep moving.'

Levi stared up at the departure and arrival board. It was too early for their ongoing flight to be listed, but he remembered its inbound details.

'Our next flight is going to be delayed.'

'How do you know? Where?'

He pointed at the arrivals board. 'See the flight near the bottom that says delayed? Once it gets here, that's going to turn into our flight home, but it's already running an hour late. By the time they get the aircraft cleaned and catered, we'll be lucky if that delay doesn't stretch to one and a half, likely two hours.'

'We can't walk the terminal for six hours; we'll be too exposed.'

She pointed at a sign. 'There's a transit hotel inside the terminal. We could get a room... or two rooms there.' Sara blushed.

Levi shook his head. 'As cosy as that sounds, it's too quiet. I've been there before; there's only one way in and out. Let's try the private lounge instead. I'll be able to monitor who comes in, and it's still public enough to be relatively safe. Showers and food too.'

They followed the signs to the Plaza lounge, paying for five hours. Levi led the way to a table against the wall that afforded a clear view of the doors. 'If you're going to shower, I suggest you go now. The longer we wait, the more chance there will be one or more of them will walk in. I didn't see any of the men I marked from the plane, but with so many people outside, it was hard to tell.'

'Shower it is, then,' Sara said.

He waited until she weaved through the maze of tables before he took out his phone. Hiro picked up straight away. 'Problems?'

'Our flight has been pushed back by one, likely two hours.'

'That's very disappointing, but you're good with contingencies, I recall.'

'I do my best. Did those photos you were talking about come through?'

'Yes, I was waiting until you landed before I sent them.'

Levi's phone buzzed. 'They should be coming through now.' Levi scrolled through the file; all headshots, full face and profile. There seemed to be a lot of them. 'That's some photo roll. Any favourites?'

'I like them all, but the last six are standouts. Particularly the one at the end.'

Levi thumbed through the file and examined the last six photos more closely. Four of them matched the faces of the guys on the plane. The final photo, though, was unfamiliar.

'Yes, I agree. Four of them are very familiar.'

'You take care now, Levi. Don't worry, we're all well here.' Hiro clicked off.

Levi studied the faces. The names and details on the file were encrypted. But that didn't matter. At least now he knew he hadn't been imagining things.

He scrolled back to the last photo. He was older than the others, mid-forties, with a shaved, shiny scalp, but it was the eyes that drew Levi's attention. They were a searing blue. Eyes that had glutted on misery yet still carried a lust for more. Levi had seen eyes like that before on men who stalked and hunted the no man's land between war and murder, no longer knowing, nor caring, about the difference. He replaced the phone on the table, gaze quartering the room, checking faces against those he'd now memorised before returning his attention back to the door. Several people were queued at the desk waiting to get in. Levi sat forward. One of them was the guy with the bald dome and the searing blue eyes. He was staring directly at Levi.

Time downshifted to the slow-motion gear that Levi knew so well. The one that always happened before real action threatened. Travellers carrying drinks or plates of snacks drifted across his field of vision, but he maintained eye contact with the bald man who left the desk and slowly closed the space between them. He paused a metre or so from Levi's table.

'Mr Monk. I don't believe we've met in person. Justin Turner.' He stood to attention, clicked his heels, and gave the slightest bow of his head.

Levi nodded in response, his body tense, ready to uncoil, not sure where this was heading. Turner's body language was giving nothing away. He made no attempt to sit or come any closer. Levi tried a mental probe, but it bounced back at him with a jolt. The other man's smile was greasy enough to be a sneer.

Levi tried a different tack. 'I was surprised to see some of your colleagues on my flight. That must have taken some organising.'

Turner grinned. 'I pride myself on my ability to respond quickly to changing situations. In this instance, however, I'll confess to some help from some helpful insiders. Though I must admit I was surprised that you both travelled under your real names. It made our job a little easier.'

Levi shrugged. 'What others would we use?'

Turner ignored the stonewalling. 'Your onward travel arrangements, however, remains a mystery. Forty-eight flights?'

'We like to keep our options open.'

Silence stretched between them. Turner was the first to speak, his voice several degrees colder than it had been. 'I assume you know what I'm here for.'

'Let's assume I don't.'

Beyond Turner, Levi saw Sara returning. He gave a small shake of his head and hoped she'd see it.

Turner's smile was wolfish; the blue eyes remained cold. 'I'm here for the orbs. Give them to me, and my colleagues and I will leave you and Ms Montgomery in peace.'

'You mean pieces, surely.'

Turner snorted. 'I admire your *attempt* at humour.' He turned his head a quarter, not taking his eyes off Levi as he spoke over his shoulder. 'Please don't stay back there on my account, Ms Montgomery. Come over and join us.'

Sara had stopped several metres behind Turner. There was no way he could have seen her coming unless he'd picked it up from Levi. He reinforced his psychic defences, including Sara within them as she slid into the seat beside him.

'Is this...?' she asked.

'Yes,' he said without taking his eyes off Turner.

Turner repeated the introduction in exactly the same manner, adding at the end, 'Forgive me. I choose not to shake hands.'

Levi took in the man's fastidious linen trouser pleats and matching ironed shirt. He didn't look like someone who'd stepped off an eight-hour flight.

'Mr Turner—'

'Justin, please.'

Levi snaked his arm around Sara's shoulders. She shifted closer.

'Mr Turner here was just telling me he'd like us to give him the orbs.'

'I see,' Sara said. 'And have you told him we don't have them with us?'

'I was about to.'

He returned his attention to Turner, tightening his grip on Sara's shoulder, ready to pull her to the floor with him if Turner tried something. 'We don't have them with us... Justin.'

The mask of cordiality slipped from Turner's face. Levi felt something like large hailstones batter against his energetic barrier. It shuddered but held.

Turner gave the smarmy smile again, as if Levi and he had shared a private joke. 'My men are stationed just outside. You are trapped in here and have nowhere to go. Whatever flight you catch, I'll have people waiting. Give me the orbs or face the consequences. Forced retrievals can be painful.'

'Sounds unpleasant. It's a shame we can't help you.'

Turner shrugged. 'In that case, we'll be seeing each other again. Very soon.'

They watched him walk away, gliding like a ghost between tables on the way to the exit.

'What now?' Sara asked.

Levi released his grip on her shoulder and slid his arm free, watching Turner leave the lounge before looking at his watch. 'We've got five hours or so to figure that out, but I think you're going to have to lose that wig.'

~

'SARA, IT'S TIME.'

Levi touched her shoulder and gave it a gentle shake. She sat up with a start and groaned just as they'd practiced, her hands moving automatically to her shaved scalp, the puckered scarring angry and red. His own long hair had been left in the bathroom bin. He'd used other resources from his backpack to change his own facial structure: glasses, false beard, and cheek inserts. Fortunately, they wouldn't have to test it.

'Your wheelchair's here, honey. Better put your mask on now.' He handed her a surgical mask, and she slipped it on. He did the same. Many people were still wearing them in the terminal to avoid respiratory infection. Since the COVID-19 pandemic, they had become a fashion statement, coming in different colours and prints. All he cared about was that it made it even more difficult for them to be identified.

Levi motioned for the attendant to bring the chair over so Sara could access it. He helped her up and guided her into it.

'We have the cart waiting outside,' the attendant said. 'You can both travel on it.'

'I appreciate you arranging this. My partner thought she'd be able to manage, but this airport is so large, it's too far for her to walk after her illness.'

'We get that all the time, sir. It's no problem. This terminal alone covers around 1 300 hectares.'

They exited the lounge and boarded the motorised cart. There were already three others, mostly older, on board. That was good; the more the better. The cart lurched off, its electronic beep clearing a path along the carpeted terminal. Levi glanced behind him and spotted three of the men from Hiro's photo reel striding after them, keeping the cart in sight. With them stationed outside the lounge, there was no way they could avoid being identified. What Levi wanted was an express lane to take them inside the aircraft.

There was no sign of Turner.

Levi willed the cart to go faster.

At the gate, they assisted Sara into another wheelchair. Their three pursuers pulled up fifty metres back, two of them bent over, breath heaving from the long run. The other was speaking urgently into his phone, no doubt relaying their flight details to Turner.

Sara was wheeled to the head of the queue for passport and boarding card checks. Levi mentally thanked the airlines' priority policy for mobility challenged passengers. Sara was playing her part brilliantly with brave smiles and small apologetic grunts each time she was shunted around. Levi took a final look behind him. Turner arrived on a Segway. Even at this distance, his blue eyes were startling. He didn't look worried. Instead he gave a half smile and wagged his index finger. Levi turned back and followed Sara's wheelchair onto the aerobridge.

Once in their seats, he squeezed her hand. 'You're doing great.'

'Are we still holding hands then?' she asked.

There was no further need for the pretence, but he hesitated, feeling a flush at his throat. 'It wouldn't hurt. Every now and again. For appearances. The other passengers will be boarding soon.'

'Appearances. Of course.' She rested her hand on his forearm as he dug around in his backpack, pulling out two pairs of cotton gloves.

'We'll need to wear these too for what I have in mind. Plan B could get a bit messy, and while Hiro can change our IDs, fingerprints are harder.'

'Do you think those men will follow us?'

Levi shook his head. 'I saw Turner outside. He'll have eight hours to arrange a reception committee in Sydney. There are still plenty of spare bodies on Hiro's photo reel that I showed you.'

Sara slipped her hand free, feeling around her seat cushion. 'Where do you think Layton might have hidden it?'

'It's unlikely to be anywhere too obvious.' He bent forward, looking down and around their two seats. 'But from where I'm sitting, there's very few places he could have chosen. Not where it wouldn't have already been found.'

'What if it has?' she asked. 'Maybe some cleaner found it and couldn't believe their luck. Maybe smuggled it out at the bottom of a mop bucket.'

'Let's hope not. And it's unlikely,' he added with conviction, though the same thought had occurred to him.

The first of the boarding passengers appeared at the front of their zone, and he sat back. 'Let's leave the search until we get into the air. I suggest we sit back and try to look exhausted.'

'No effort required there,' she muttered.

Turner's relaxed manner and his "just you wait" wagging finger had stayed with Levi. With Turner's men waiting for them in Sydney, their options were severely limited. Levi pulled out his phone and quickly sent an SMS. A moment later, a reply pinged, showing a thumbs-up emoji.

Plan B was officially go.

AFTER THE MEAL service was cleared away, Levi and Sara searched the seat cushions, seat backs, and pockets, and then swapped places and did it all again. After that Levi made a hole in the stitching of the upholstery behind the seat pocket in case the orb had been secreted into the back of the head rest in front.

Sara flopped back. 'I give up. Do you think it's possible that he hid it someplace else on the aircraft?'

'That doesn't bear thinking about. I can't begin to imagine the number of places we'd have to search, and how suspicious would we look? No, that parchment page was quite specific in showing this particular seat number.' He slapped the arm of the seat with the flat of his hand. 'It's got to be here, or otherwise it's already been found, or gathering dust in some airport's lost and found shelf. If only I hadn't thrown the sketch into the fire, we'd know exactly what he did with it.'

'Don't go there. We'd be in Sydney before I managed to get through all the "if only I hads" listed under my name.'

'Okay. Come on. One last time.' Levi dug through his seat pocket, taking everything out once more, and Sara followed suit.

He shoved it all back. The edge of the laminated emergency card caught on the ragged hole he'd made in the seat back. He jiggled it back and forth, trying to force the card in. Sara's hand closed over his, her index finger tapping the back of his hand.

'Wait. Wasn't there something earlier? Something they said? You know, during the safety demonstration? Like something being under your seat?' She took the card and pointed at the series of ditching pictures. 'Lifejacket.'

'That's got to be it.' Levi snapped off his seat belt and knelt in the aisle, feeling around under his seat.

He made sure no one was watching and removed the hard plastic container, passing it up to Sara.

She spread the blanket over her lap and slid the plastic box beneath it. 'I've got it open. It feels like there's something tucked inside the folds.' She tried to keep the excitement from her voice. 'Something round.' With a determined tug, she pulled her hand free and opened her fingers. The orb and its inset precious stones sparkled beneath the overhead light.

Chapter Twenty One

Sara fidgeted in her seat. Since finding the orb, she'd been waiting for the flight to end, yet at the same time dreaded it landing. They were so close to this all finishing, yet she was terrified that it would all be for nothing with Turner's men waiting to intercept them as soon as they exited the arrivals doors in Sydney. Levi had refused to discuss it, only mumbling something about Plan B before he put his seat back, pulled the blanket over himself, and went to sleep. So infuriating. But in another way, she was pleased. She felt his scrutiny every time he looked at her. She remembered what she'd looked like in the lounge mirror without her wig. The plumped-up apple cheeks made her face look like a dumpling.

So what is my Plan B—assuming his works out?

They had both come so far in what really was such a short space of time. She felt a connection to Levi. Would that just end, like the friends you made on holiday? Bristling with good intentions but victims to their own busyness. And what about Layton and his supposed reanimation? She shuddered at the thought of him somehow coming back to life and shoved it away. There were too many variables for speculation.

Levi moved in his sleep, the blanket slipping from his chest. Sara gently drew it up and tucked it around him, taking in his rugged profile, his expression relaxed for once, almost peaceful. The short haircut suited him, even if it was a bit plastic-scissor-ragged in places. Her heart softened. It had been unreasonable to blame him for getting her into this. Layton had manipulated him as surely as he had her. Perhaps she'd been fortunate that it was Levi and not someone else that Layton had sent. Levi had saved her life more than once. Maddy's too. *Am I confusing my feelings for him? Like with Tony?*

Gratitude isn't love. The words echoed inside her head. She'd repeated them so many times since Tony died. Nor were there any real white knights. She smiled; nor rugged grumpy ones who were really all soft inside. She closed her eyes. Levi's face appeared, scenes flipping across the backs of her eyelids: Levi throwing her to the ground of the tent, rolling her away from assassin darts; snatching Maddy from the inflatable moments before it exploded; coming to the rescue just yesterday in a New Farm street. There were too many. Her thoughts drifted with the low drone of the aircraft, and she finally dozed.

THEY WERE at something called "top of descent" when Levi woke her. Her head was groggy, eyes gritty with dehydration. Levi handed her a small bottle of water, and she gulped it down, dribbling the last drops across her fingertips to pat her eyelids. Only her shaved scalp felt liberated.

Levi had his backpack out and was digging through it. He pulled out two black half-spheres. Lining up the flat edges, he gave them both a twist, joining them, and handed it to her. It was about the size of a tennis ball, the surface slightly yielding like it was coated with foam over a hard interior. He repeated the process with another two and gave that to her as well. 'Do you need to go to the toilet?'

Sara laughed. 'No, thanks, *Dad*. I just look constipated.'

'Then I need you to go. Both of the toilets are just behind us. Drop one of these balls into each of the waste paper towel bins.'

'I assume this is your Plan B.'

'Part of it. Now go. I'll plant a few more further forward once you come back.'

Sara rolled one of the balls between her palms. 'What are they?'

'A diversion, but it won't work if you waste time asking questions.'

Clamping down on her frustration, she tucked a ball into each fist and clambered past him, whispering, 'I hope they're not going to explode.'

'Not yet.'

Control freak. When I get back, I'll demand he tell me what his damn Plan B is.

She waited until the flight attendants went forward and then visited both aft toilets, dropping one of the black balls into each of the waste paper bins, pausing in the second to examine her reflection in the mirror. Her thought on waking had been right. She looked like a particularly bad version of herself. She took out her wig and reattached it. They already knew what she looked like.

Better.

When she returned to her seat, Levi had another eight of the balls ready. As soon as she was seated, he moved along the aisle, opening overhead bins as if he were trying to locate a misplaced bag. Only she noticed him drop one of the balls into the bottom of each locker before moving to the toilets in the next zone.

When he returned, she asked, 'Are you going to tell me what they are now?'

He flopped into his seat. 'Glorified smoke bombs. When I hit the switches, the thin layer separating the compounds on either side of the sphere will pop apart and the chemicals inside will combine, making a hell of a lot of non-toxic smoke. I'm hoping the flight crew will think it's an electrical fire.'

'What will that do?'

'It depends when they go off. If I time it right, then we'll be just turning off the active runway and starting to taxi. After that it will be a race between us getting out the back door and the arrival of the emergency vehicles. I'm guessing we won't have more than three minutes before the fire engines get here. They're on site. The ambos and federales won't be far behind.'

'Whoa, just a minute. By back door, you mean...'

Levi looked meaningfully at the aircraft door just behind them and nodded, handing her the laminated emergency card and tapping the series of pictures for a land-based evacuation. 'If the cabin crew don't open the door behind us, then I will, but I'm betting once the cabin fills with smoke the captain will call an all-out evacuation. In any case, once the armed door is opened, the escape slide will inflate automatically. Then we just slide down and—'

He was interrupted by the announcement for the cabin crew to be seated for landing.

'Oh, oh... here we go.' He gave Sara's hand a squeeze. 'Hang on, and don't worry. This is now all just a matter of timing... and good luck. Just follow me and do what I say.'

Sara stared unseeingly at the emergency card in her hand, mentally recalling the distance the aircraft stood off the ground when they'd boarded. *Does he really mean for me to just jump out and rely on some giant inflatable slide to save us? And what then? We'll be trapped. The airport is a secure area. They will just take all the passengers to the terminal anyway. Turner's men will still be able to intercept us regardless. What is he thinking?*

Outside, everything was becoming larger much too quickly. They were only metres above the ground...

'Levi, I still don't understand—'

There was a massive bump, and they were down. Someone up in

the next passenger zone started clapping but stopped almost immediately. The aircraft slowed under steady braking.

'Here we go.' Levi flipped several switches on a miniature console. Nothing happened for a few moments, then she saw a wisp of smoke emerge from one of the luggage lockers that Levi had opened earlier. No one else had noticed it yet. The aircraft braked harder. Sara felt the pull against the restraint of her seat belt. They slowed even more, then turned onto the taxiway. She peered between their two seats at the flight attendant behind them, who was talking urgently into a handset while scrabbling for what looked like a fire extinguisher beneath the jump seat. Thick white smoke was leaking through the gaps around the toilet door beside her. Levi had been right. It did smell like an electrical fire, but he'd said it was non-toxic.

The first scream came soon after. Beside her, Levi snapped off his seat belt and pointed at the smoke, yelling, "Fire! Fire! The plane's on fire." Sara joined in, hoping this was going to work out.

The flight attendant behind them slammed the phone back into its cradle and opened the toilet door. Thick white smoke billowed into the cabin, joining that from the luggage lockers and forward toilets. The young flight attendant bravely blasted the CO_2 into the aft toilet, but without a fire to extinguish, the pressurised gas only served to disseminate the smoke further throughout the cabin. It was becoming increasingly difficult to see. More screams. Others began coughing. The plane lurched to a stop. Smoke now filled the rear cabin. Other flight attendants appeared, calling for calm, fire extinguishers in their hands, searching for flames. The intercom crackled into life. 'This is the captain. We have a situation in the rear zone of the aircraft, and I'm ordering a precautionary evacuation. Follow the lights on the floor to your nearest exit. Cabin crew, attend your emergency stations. Evacuate! Evacuate! Evacuate!'

Levi grabbed her arm and his backpack. 'Come on. This is it.'

Lines of emergency lights on the floor illuminated. Cabin crew shouted, 'Come this way. There's an exit here. Leave all personal items behind.' And on and on. Sara let Levi drag her. The flight attendant responsible for the rear door immediately behind their seats was pushing the large handle up. The door moved out and swung out, thumping against the side of the fuselage. A sound like a small explosion followed, and a massive ramp blew out, sucking in air. The flight attendant blocked the exit while the double ramp fully inflated and then stood aside. Levi and Sara were first in line.

She waved them through, yelling, 'Jump and sit!'

Wind whipped into the aircraft cabin, carrying smoke out with it through the opposite door. They only had moments before the smoke would start to thin. The ramp stretched below her, the end of it bumping against the tarmac in the rising wind. It was wide enough for her and Levi to go together. Levi was yelling into her ear. She closed her eyes and jumped, extending her legs, bouncing onto the ramp. She'd expected the surface to be smooth, but it was uneven enough to slow her down as she neared the bottom and rolled onto the tarmac. Levi hauled her to her feet, shouldering the backpack.

Sara looked back up the ramp. It seemed like such a long way up. The flight attendant was such a small figure. She was waving for them to clear the way. Other people were coming down the slide now, one after the other. She helped one old woman get off the ramp, walking her a safe distance away. In the distance she could hear sirens getting louder before being crowded out by another noise, familiar but almost deafening.

'Sara! Come on,' Levi shouted at her. He seemed to be caught in a downward wind tunnel, his hair flattened, head bent beneath the massive downdraft. She looked up. A black helicopter hovered just above them.

This is his Plan B?

She rushed over. Levi gripped her around the middle and swung her into the air. Someone with a black uniform, thick gloves, and full helmet with a blacked-out visor reached down and caught her arm, hauling her in. He then hooked his boot around an upright stay, leaning out further in order to reach Levi. Another man, similarly dressed, helped drag them both up while the helicopter's motor surged, clawing back altitude before racing across the airport. The wind through the open hatch and the thumping sound of the rotors made it impossible to hear anything. All Sara could do was hang on and hope they didn't collide with another aircraft as the ground rushed by less than thirty metres below. Levi was grinning. He caught her staring and gave an enthusiastic thumbs-up. With the wind blasting through his hair, he looked more like an ecstatic shaggy dog facing the wind from the back window of a moving car.

She joined the tip of her thumb and forefinger, making an O back at him. Below, all the aircraft had stopped. Perhaps they weren't sure what this was. A terrorist event? Kidnapping? It was a border violation, certainly. From this height, Sara could see the approach roads to the airport. Flashing lights were everywhere: blue, white, orange, and red weaved through the heavy traffic. All headed this way.

The helicopter banked. Sara steadied herself, holding onto part of the fuselage. They had left the airport and were speeding above open, green manicured lawns. Below she could clearly see people playing golf. A man wearing a yellow polo shirt waved.

The pitch of the rotors changed again. They were coming down, but not on the golf course. It looked to be a big park. The helicopter swung around and descended slowly. She hung on and leaned out to get a better look. Below them was a massive prime mover attached to a long open trailer surrounded by blue-and-white police tape tagged in a large circle around it. In the middle of the trailer was another circle with a dot in the centre.

The pilot was bringing the helicopter down on top of it.

As soon as they touched down, the uniformed men piled out. Levi turned to help her down before ushering her towards a minivan with darkened windows parked nearby. 'Keep your head lowered, Sara. It makes it harder for electronic surveillance and reliable witness statements afterwards.'

She clambered inside the minivan. 'Why do I get the feeling that I'm now a criminal?'

'Man I used to know said you're only a criminal if you get caught.'

'You seem to know a lot of men.' She indicted the three uniformed guys bustling about outside. She leant closer to the van's shaded side windows. 'What are they doing now?'

'Making sure everything is tied down. That copter and rig were liberated on the way back to Richmond Air Force base after some repairs. Wouldn't do us any good if someone vandalised it before recovery. The guys won't be long.'

'They stole it?' Sara's voice squeaked. 'Who are these men?'

'Just guys I used to work with in Special Forces. Now they're freelance. All straight-up guys. We've trusted each other with our lives too many times for anyone to keep count. Fortunately, Hiro had the cash to pay them all very well.'

'What, to steal trucks and helicopters?'

Levi's smile vanished. 'No. To keep try and keep you and your daughter alive.' He turned away. 'Sorry, that was a low blow. I'm a little keyed up right now.'

She reached across and gripped his forearm. 'I'm sorry. I know both you and Hiro are doing all you can. And I appreciate it. Really, I do, and no one got hurt. All of this, it's a little overwhelming.'

He reached an arm around her shoulders and pulled her in next to him.

The men finished what they were doing and sprinted for the van, tumbling in. Within moments, the van accelerated away.

'Where are we, anyway?' Sara asked.

'Barton Park in Banksia.' The man's voice was hollow inside his helmet.

The sounds of more helicopters and wailing sirens intruded as Levi asked, 'How long do we have?'

The man who'd spoken previously glanced at a complicated-looking watch on his wrist.

'Three minutes to dust off. There are too many roads to close off and contain around here. Response time should run to six minutes, depending on patrols. They'll focus on the transport rig and copter for a bit after that, checking whether it's boobied.'

Levi nodded.

They rounded a series of corners, the buildings becoming higher, the traffic around them more congested. After another ten minutes, the van slowed and turned off into a multi-storied car park in a busy part of the city. They pulled up on the fourth level.

'That's you over there, Sarge,' the driver said to Levi, pointing at a small grey Hyundai. 'Don't scratch it. It's my wife's. She thinks it's in the shop.' He tossed him the keys.

'Hey, you know me,' Levi said.

'Exactly. I still remember how you totalled that Land Cruiser I hired that time in Kuwait.'

'I'm a reformed man. Thanks, guys, truly. It was a great job. We'll catch up for that drink soon.' Levi fist bumped each of the men on the way out, fielding good-natured ribbing about his fake beard, haircut, and glasses. He unlocked the car as the van drove off and up to the next level.

'Where are they going?'

'To get their own cars. They're parked upstairs. They'll change out of the uniforms, then dump the van on the top level.'

'Don't tell me, it's waiting to be reunited with its real owner as well?'

Levi raised his eyebrows. 'Maybe. But he might need to order some replacement number plates. On the plus side, his van got a brand-new paint job. One of our guys is a spray painter now in civvies, out near Fivedock. Okay, let's peel away some of these layers.'

Levi removed the cheek inserts, beard, glasses, gloves, and mask. He collected Sara's as well before stuffing it all into a large clip lock bag. 'I'll incinerate these when we get back to Brisbane. In the meantime, I'll stow it inside the spare wheel recess in the trunk.'

She heard a phone ringing. Levi answered, his voice hushed, the words clipped. Sara didn't have the energy to turn around. Too much had happened far too quickly. It felt like the world was turning twice as fast as it should, and she was too tired to even try to catch up.

Levi returned, slammed the door, and passed the phone across to her.

'It's Hiro. He's got Maddy for you. I thought you might like to check in with her now we're on the downhill run.'

Sara snatched up the phone, tiredness forgotten, feeling the tears well, uncaring as they overflowed and coursed down her cheeks.

22

Chapter Twenty Two

The dull thrum of the tyres against the bitumen was reassuring.

Sara imagined the wheels devouring the kilometres that still separated her from Maddy and a life that might yet nudge up against the familiar, or at the very least last longer than a three-month curse. Flat, broad acre plains laden with cotton interspersed with scattered scrub and scraggy gum trees slipped past in an unending stream, only becoming real when the car stopped and they stepped outside. Then the raucous caw of crows, dampening silence, and baking heat would rush in, bringing with it swarms of small, sticky black flies.

Sara waved them away only for them to settle back almost immediately.

'They go for where the moisture is, eyes and mouth mostly.' Levi emerged from behind a tree where he'd been relieving himself. *Everything is always so much easier for men, even that.* 'That's why the old drovers used to hang corks off the brims of their hats.'

'Shame I didn't think to get one,' Sara snapped, slapping at the flies hovering near the corners of her mouth. She stalked around the car to the driver side. They'd been rotating every two hours. She opened the door and slipped behind the wheel, slamming the door behind her. Several of the flies followed her in.

She hadn't meant to jump down Levi's throat. It wasn't his fault she had to wait for a town or petrol station to appear before she could relieve herself. He'd even offered to close his eyes earlier while she went behind some bushes. Maybe stress was cumulative and that particular bucket was full.

Levi got in and immediately reclined the seat all the way back, tipping his cap down over his eyes. He'd be asleep in seconds in that irritating way he had.

It had been his idea to take a circuitous route to Queensland, heading west over the Blue Mountains to Dubbo before swinging northeast towards Brisbane, choosing minor roads wherever possible. Sara hadn't argued. While she wanted to be back with Maddy as soon as possible, the last thing she needed was another hour inside a plane, or to risk being spotted by Turner's men on the main highways. Levi said they probably had the capacity to hack the CCTV at road stops along on the Pacific Highway. It wouldn't take them long to figure out she and Levi hadn't doubled back to the airport. The reach of these people, Layton's people, she had to keep reminding herself, was astounding. They were so determined to get those damned orbs. As far as Sara was concerned, once she and Maddy had used them to get rid of the disease, they could have them. She just wanted her life back. Literally.

And what then?

While the road trip had provided some relief, allowing her to breathe out a little, it had also brought far too much space to think about a future that she could no longer even envision. Somewhere, somehow, time had come loose from its tether to her life and now was free to flap and flutter with every new gust of change, making it impossible to plan further than a leap from one adrenaline-charged minute to the next. She was lost to herself, unable to think past survival, the concept of figuring out where she was going after all this ended totally beyond her. Yet she had to. Maddy depended on her.

And then there was the issue of Levi. They were still energetically attached. That much was clear from their close call in New Farm, where the feeling of collapse had overwhelmed her the more distance she'd created between them. How would they be able to live like that forever? Enforced proximity? Both of them unable to be more than a few kilometres apart, the only cure locked inside a palace that didn't exist on this plane. Levi had given her the impression that he hated to be tied down. Another one of the things they had yet to discuss.

And what about her own feelings towards Levi? Did they help or hinder? Were they even real, or just a dopamine reaction to a succession of life-threatening situations?

Is Levi even aware of any of this? Has any of this even occurred to him?

Sometimes, at odd moments over the past few days, she'd catch him looking at her as a man might before he quickly turned away, and yet other times it was like he was hunkered behind a thick emotional shield. Even in the close confines of a small car he gave off an unspoken preference for the numbing rumble of the road. *Our only shared moments are when one or the other hums along to old but known tunes beamed from a local radio station. What are the rules here? Is there a protocol? When is it all right to bring up life instead of simply staying alive?*

She flicked on the radio.

LEVI'S PHONE BEEPED. The only one who had his new phone number was Hiro. He roused himself, adjusting the reclined seat back to upright.

Sara's eyes darted over, trying to see the screen. 'Is everything all right. Is Maddy—'

'Is fine. They both are. Hiro has booked us into a motel in the next town. Narrabri. I'm just loading the address into Maps.'

'He's a regular travel agent, isn't he?' Sara pulled down the visor from above the windscreen to block the lowering sun. She'd been on autopilot for the past little while. Just driving. It felt calming at any rate, even if she'd solved nothing.

The first billboards appeared, and soon they were in the town. She followed the directions of the GPS to the motel.

'Park outside unit twenty-one,' Levi said.

Sara raised her eyebrows but said nothing about how they were going to get the key. Strange, weird, and Hiro all belonged in the same sentence. She turned off the ignition. They got out, Levi checking in both directions before striding to the door. He gave it three quiet taps in quick succession.

The door opened a crack, and with a glance back at Sara, he slipped inside. She followed.

'Mummy!'

Maddy threw herself at Sara, wrapping both arms around her hips.

'Maddy? How? What are you doing here?'

Hiro stepped into view, wearing a white shirt, blue cravat, and cream trousers with pleats sharp enough to slice ice. He was holding Tripod by the collar, the big dog straining, anxious to get to her as well.

'Levi? Did you know about this?'

He shook his head. 'It's all a surprise to me. I thought Hiro had arranged for someone to check us in under their name and then let us into the unit.'

'It's better this way,' Hiro said. 'Turner and his men know you would be returning to my place in the Valley. They'll be waiting for you to show up there now.'

Sara squatted down and held Maddy at arm's length, searching every part of her face. Maddy beamed back.

She glanced up at Hiro. 'But wouldn't they have followed you when you left?'

'They would have if they'd seen us leave.'

Maddy was bouncing on her toes, a sure sign she was bursting with news. Finally, unable to contain herself, she shouted, 'We came here through the magic curtain, Mummy.'

Sara stiffened, imagining the heavy flap of that horrible curtain in Hiro's place and the memory of her earlier terror.

Hiro picked up on her unease. 'The curtain works on the adult psyche, Sara, snagging on all the guilt, fear, and shame that we accumulate over time. Children Maddy's age, thankfully, haven't racked up too much of that. For her it was simply an adventure.'

'You mean... what? It transported you both to Narrabri?' Even saying that felt stupid.

'Close enough. We had to catch a cab to the motel from the Community Centre, though.'

'Community Centre?'

'We were in a play, Mummy,' Maddy chirruped.

'A what?' Sara's head was all over the place. That happened a lot around Hiro.

The old man intervened, 'We went through the curtain at my end. For the portal to work, we have to exit from behind a similar-sized curtain at the other. The Community Centre stage sufficed, though I believe we interrupted the dress rehearsal for a high school production. I couldn't tell what it was, but one of the young ladies singing was disturbingly flat. The advantage, of course, in using the curtain as a portal is that none of Turner's men could see us depart. Or follow us here. When I arrived at the motel, I simply booked two adjoining rooms, telling the man on the desk I'd be using one to interview people and intended sleeping in the other. Maddy was good enough to wait outside with Tripod until I picked up the keys. I don't think we're supposed to have dogs in here, but Tripod hasn't made a sound so far, have you, boy? Time to let you loose now though, otherwise you might get a little frustrated and start barking.'

Hiro released his grip on the dog's collar, and he immediately bounded over to Sara. She hugged him close.

'That dog loves you. A lot,' Hiro added.

'That's because he's special, aren't you, boy.'

Hiro's gaze was thoughtful. 'Yes, I suspect he is. You say he was a stray?'

'Yes. He saved Maddy from a fire. That's how his front leg was injured.'

'Interesting.' Hiro folded his arms. 'You know, every time I look at him, I get the feeling that he once had another name.'

'He was a stray, so that's likely.'

'Hmm, no, I get the feeling it was something a little deeper than that...' Hiro's gaze drifted.

After a couple of minutes, Levi reached over and touched his forearm. 'Hiro?'

The old man's attention snapped back. 'Sorry.'

'Are you all right?' Sara asked.

'Yes, yes. It's nothing. I thought I felt a ruffle in the ether, so to speak. It's nothing.' Hiro brushed his immaculate white shirt down as if trying to clear it of something.

'Are you sure?' Levi asked, now concerned. 'I didn't think you could leave the Valley compound. Without its wards, you could be traced.'

'I took precautions to cover my tracks, don't worry. Before I left, I created an energetic stealth sheath around us. No one can detect us through that.' He clapped his hands together. 'So, come on now, you two. Why don't you show me your prize?'

Levi passed him the second orb, adding. 'This should complete the set.'

'Ah.' Hiro held it up, the jewels sparkling beneath the light. He nodded. 'Well done. Both of you.'

He placed the orb on the bedside table and retrieved the other one from a knapsack at his feet, placing it a hand's width away from the first. 'Now, let's see what they have to say to each other, shall we?'

He flicked on the bedside lamp. The direct beam reflected off the highly burnished gold. 'If they are genuine, they should begin to resonate with each other.'

Nothing happened for a moment, then one of them moved, more a vibration or shudder.

'Did you see that?' Hiro pointed. 'The other one should respond... There!'

Sara was unsure. The light reflecting off the gold and precious stones was almost too bright. She bent closer, willing the spheres to move as if this would make the cure real. After a moment, she saw it. One definitely rocked, and then the other did the same. The cycle alternated, the degree of movement increasing until they finally rolled towards each other. They came together with a solid clunk, the sound reminiscent of a train engine shunting back to connect with one of its carriages.

'They're joined.' Hiro picked up the two orbs; the curve of one now flowed seamlessly into the other as if they'd always been that way. Their new shape formed a stylised 8.

'Look, a rainbow,' Maddy said, her tiny finger pointing at a splay of colours that now shone out from the precious stones, like light through stained glass.

Sara watched the colours brighten further, extending up the wall before fanning across the ceiling.

'How is it doing that? The light is shining from the inside,' Sara asked.

'The orbs are designed to attract and absorb light. One orb represents life, the other death. When joined, they form the symbol for infinity.' Hiro turned the 8 on its side. 'Once joined, their unification effectively removes the veil.'

'You're talking immortality?' Levi's voice was hushed.

'In a sense. The orbs have the power to rejuvenate human cells and remove the cause of any disease or organ deterioration. Similar to what we want them to do for us.'

'No wonder Turner and his men are so anxious to get hold of

them,' Levi said. 'I'm guessing there must be a stack of billionaires out there with cancer or some other disease who would pay anything to cheat death. Much less what they might do with the licensing rights.'

'Speaking of cheating death, there is something I should tell you before using the orbs—' Hiro grunted and doubled over, clutching his abdomen.

'Hiro, what's wrong?' Sara slipped her arm around his shoulders.

He straightened slowly, cheeks sheened with sweat, pain scoring deep lines on either side of his mouth.

'Are you all right?' Levi asked.

Hiro managed a nod and absently ran his fingers through his hair. Sara noticed they were trembling.

'I'm fine. Thank you.' He took a step and pitched forward, his legs unable to bear his weight. Levi caught him, and Sara dragged over a chair.

'Sit him down.' She laid the back of her hand against his forehead. The skin was clammy, and suddenly he looked very old. Something odd was happening to his clothing too. Whole outfits appeared and disappeared, flickering like a faulty fluorescent tube, mismatching items. An Edwardian suitcoat coupled with a flannel checked shirt appeared topped with a sea captain's hat.

'Mummy, is Mister Hiro all right? Why are his clothes going all funny?' Maddy asked.

'He's just a little tired sweetie.' Sara exchanged a concerned glance with Levi. 'Why don't you take Tripod into the other room and have a little play for a min? Mr Hiro needs a rest. I'll come and get you soon, then we'll get something to eat, all right?' She gave her a hug, and Maddy went through the interconnecting door. Tripod followed, his tail low.

When Maddy had gone, she whispered, 'Levi, we need to call a doctor. I'm no expert, but I think he could be having a heart attack or something. Look at him. And what's going on with his clothes? It's like he's lost control.'

Hiro straightened and took a deep breath, trying to gather

himself. When he spoke, his voice cracked. 'It's nothing—' He cleared his throat. '—nothing like that. It's the stealth shield.'

'Is it being attacked?' Levi said.

'Yes. They're incessant... I don't know... how they managed to track us here. I was so careful.'

'It's got to be Turner.'

Hiro's back arched as if in response to a sudden high voltage charge. Even after it eased, Hiro's fingers remained clenched, his fingernails scoring the wooden arms of the chair. His words came in gulps. 'Coming... from different directions. Can only reinforce... one section of the shield... at a time. Can't predict... where the next.' He stifled a cry as another charge arced through him.

Levi held him. Sara could sense his frustration.

'They must be honing in on something,' Levi said, looking around. 'Hiro, did you bring anything with you they might be zoning in on?'

Hiro shook his head. 'Everything was sheathed. Even the dog.'

'Then it must be one of us. Sara, think back. Did any of those guys at the airport touch you, even briefly?'

Sara shook her head, replaying the time at the airport trying to recall even a casual touch from another passenger, or someone at Changi airport. 'No, no one. The only time was when that tattooed man caught me when I was running in New Farm, remember. Just before you knocked him... oh, no.' A memory slithered in of something cold and slimy moving across her calf.

'What is it?'

'There was a tattooed worm on his palm, and beetles on his fingers. They seemed to be moving. I thought I was hallucinating from the separation.'

'Show me. Where did you feel it?'

Sara pulled up the leg of her jeans, exposing the calf. 'Here.' She pointed to a raised rash on her skin. Levi cupped his hand over it.

'It's live. We need to expunge it to cut off the signal.'

'Live? Do you mean *alive?*' She shuddered at the thought of something like that worm under her skin.

'No. From what I recall, the tattoos were at best two dimensional, so it's probably just an imprint. Like a tracking device that activates when magic is around. The orbs must have triggered it when they joined.'

'Levi, use the orbs.' Hiro said. 'Touch her leg with it and imagine it gone.'

Sara turned away as Levi brushed her calf with the joined orbs. There was a shuddery tremor beneath her skin and then nothing. When she turned to look, the rash had faded.

Hiro cried out, his back arching again. 'They still have our coordinates,' he managed. 'We have to get out of here. Somewhere where they can't follow.'

'Hiro, tell me what I can do.'

'Get us... into the bardo. Use the orbs. Hold them out. Set intention.'

Levi raised the spheres. 'Sara. Get Maddy and Tripod. I'm not sure how this is going to go, but we all better hang together.'

'Mummy?' Maddy stood in the doorway to the connecting room, her arm looped over Tripod's neck.

Sara rushed over, managing a tremulous smile that she hoped was reassuring before scooping Maddy up and dragging another chair over to sit beside Hiro. Settling Maddy on her lap, she draped one arm around him and rested the other across Levi's shoulders. Tripod flopped in the middle of them all, his ears twitching with the surging urgency in the room.

Levi held the orbs in front of him and closed his eyes, the furrow between his eyebrows deepening with concentration. A low hum developed, building as the glow from the orbs intensified. The colours swirled. It was like being inside a gigantic light ball. Outside the circle of brightly coloured lights, the details of the room dimmed until there was only the whining hum and the blindingly brilliant lights, whipping around them so fast they appeared to be unbroken lines of spectrum colours.

Sara covered Maddy's eyes. Tripod, lying at her feet, growled, but he remained where he was. There was a flash...

And then... everything stopped.

Chapter Twenty Three

The humming receded. In its wake a deep, whisper-quiet silence settled around them. The whirling lights slowed as well, leaving only a giddy afterglow and ragged shreds of spent adrenaline, like the residue of excitement from a carnival ride nearing its end.

'Mummy? Where are we?' Maddy's voice sounded hollow, as if she was in a cave.

'I don't know, sweetheart. But we're safe. I think. And look, Mr Hiro seems much better now.'

Colour and vitality had returned to Hiro's face, and the deep pain lines around the corners of his mouth had diminished. His clothing had stabilised as well, and he wore the flowing robe with the gold flashes from the *kintsugi* ceremony. It suited him better than most, and she suspected it was an outfit he'd chosen. Sara allowed her arm to slip free of his shoulders, and she gave his hand a light squeeze.

He smiled, nodding in reassurance. 'In answer to your question, Maddy, we're in a place called the bardo. I like to think of it as a waiting room at the railway station. A place to stay warm and safe until our train comes.' He turned his sharp gaze to Levi, adding quietly, 'Thank you. I don't think I could have taken another hit.'

'Can they still find you...' Sara looked around. '...in here?' There was no shape definition outside their little circle. It was like being suspended in grey.

'Not easily, and with any luck, we won't be here that long. I laid down a tether line before Maddy and I left in case something untoward happened. I have summoned it, and once it arrives, we can use the power of the orbs to follow it back to my house. Without it or an established transit channel like the curtain portal, our chances of becoming disoriented and ultimately lost in here are extremely high, as you can see.' He indicated the sombre, impenetrable greyness below, above, and around them.

'Can we use the orbs now, while we're waiting to...' Sara shifted her gaze meaningfully down to Maddy, who was still perched on her lap.

'Of course, of course. It is, after all, why we are all here. But firstly there is one thing I should apprise you of.' Hiro paused as if uncertain how to proceed.

'What's that?' Levi prompted.

'Layton.'

'What about him?' Sara spat.

'The orbs have the capability to be what we might call programmed. That is, they can be calibrated to only respond to specific energetic signatures. After that, they can be unlocked and used more widely. Before hiding the second orb, the one representing life, Layton linked his essence to it.'

'You mean Layton has first dibs on the cure?' Levi asked.

'Essentially, yes. Particularly here in the bardo where his essence is held in suspension.'

'But how?' Sara's furrowed brow held the emotion of her words. 'He's...' She left the word unsaid, conscious of Maddy on her lap.

'Yes. But you'll recall I told you his essence is suspended. Here, in the bardo. It's likely the activation of the orbs will attract him to us.'

'Here?'

'I'm afraid so.'

'I'm not comfortable with that.' She paused, looking meaningfully at the top of Maddy's head. 'For us.'

'I understand. I know it's hard, but I'm going to ask you to trust me again. Will you?'

She nodded. Hiro looked down at Maddy, Sara following his gaze.

'Maddy,' he said.

Maddy looked up from playing with Tripod's ears.

'I think it's time for another game. What do you think?'

The little girl nodded enthusiastically.

'Come here then.' Hiro made space for her at the side of his chair. Maddy clambered over and sat beside him. 'This is an imagination game. All you have to do is close your eyes, that's it. Now, I want you to imagine...'

When Maddy was fully asleep, Hiro eased himself off the chair and stood.

'Is she hypnotised?' Levi asked.

'Not exactly. Hypnotism isn't recommended for younger children. She's more in a deep sleep than a trance. Now,' he rubbed his hands together, 'while she's dreaming of wonderful things, I'll try and find that tether before Layton...'

As he spoke, Sara became aware of a mist gathering in front of them, a thin line of bright light stretching from it to the orb. The mist formed itself into a spherical shape, assuming definition, taking on a 3D quality. She gasped, her hand moving to her heart when she recognised the blunt features of Eric Layton assembling themselves.

Even the slippery smile that tugged one corner of his mouth higher than the other was the exact same. It was a sneer, she realised now, and wondered why she'd never seen it before. At her feet,

Tripod stirred and scrambled to his feet, growling deep in his throat. She tried to quieten him.

'Sara. How delightful... and your child.' The voice held something of the man he'd once been but was distorted, as if being spoken through a long pipe.

'Your child too, much as I hate to admit it.'

'Then don't. I always said she was Tony's. She has accountant eyes.' He turned towards Hiro. 'And the master of the course, or in this instance should I say, master of the *curse*? Or, you will be.' The sickly grin slid into place again, before swivelling on to Levi. 'And Mr Monk, my personal death watcher and general delivery boy.'

Levi balled his fist and took a step forward. Tripod's growl turned into a bark. With a gentle but assertive hand, Hiro drew Levi back, whispering, 'There's nothing there to hit, Levi. Nothing but your own ego. Leave it.'

Tripod continued to bark, straining against Sara's strong restraint. Maddy continued to sleep on.

'Your dog doesn't seem to like me, Sara.'

Layton's ghostly eyes narrowed as he stared intently down at the growling Alsatian. The mocking smile returned. 'And no wonder. If it isn't two-faced Tony himself. From the look of you, boyo, you seem to have lost the plot on the three-day macho stubble thing. Lost count, perhaps? But then you were always lousy with numbers—for an accountant.'

'What are you talking about?' Sara spluttered. 'Are you mad? Tony is dead. You killed him in the fire.'

Layton's mouth opened, aping a pantomimed yawn, 'Why don't you tell her, old man? I can see you know.'

'What is he talking about?' Sara turned to Hiro, her logical mind three skips behind where her intuition was dragging her.

Hiro took a breath. 'He's right. In a sense. Tony's essence, or spirit if you like, is in the dog. From what you told me about the fire, I can only assume that they died within moments of each other and that when Tony saw the danger to Maddy, he must have assumed the dog's body and re-animated it, leading her to safety. I suspected it the other day, but I hesitated to confuse you even more.'

'Confuse me?' Sara barked out a laugh. 'You're telling me my dog is my former lover and you think that might have confused me?' she shouted.

Hiro spoke calmly, which only infuriated her even more. 'At the moment of death, in moments of extreme clarity, some of us are given a choice: to move on, or to stay and help others. In some traditions they are called *bodhisattvas*. Tony chose to stay, at great personal sacrifice, to save Maddy's life and look out for you both.'

The mist that was Layton sounded as if it was chuckling. Fury bubbled up from Sara's feet, coursing through her in a lava wave of rage, hate, shame, and guilt. She threw herself forward, fingers clawing at where Layton's eyes and mouth should be, finding only cold, wet mist that slipped through her fingers, re-forming almost as soon as it was disturbed. From a distance she became aware of arms encircling her from behind, knowing from their touch and his musky scent that it was Levi but not yet ready to give in. She struggled against him, and he tightened his hold until she flopped back against him.

Tripod, now unrestrained, leapt up, his jaws snapping ineffectually at the hated face-shape above him. Hiro pulled him back, whispering some words directly into his ear. Tripod thumped to the floor as if a weight had been applied to his hindquarters. He continued to growl, his ears twitching with frustration, eyes never leaving the misty figure above.

'Such dramatics. I've missed all this,' Layton said. 'But much as it amuses me, I am anxious to move this on. Perform the ceremony, Hiro.'

'I can't do it here. I need your physical body to reanimate, and it's back at the house. We are waiting for a tether to draw us back, though it's taking longer than I anticipated.'

'Why didn't you say so? Create a merge link so it will recognise me, and I'll fetch it for you. I've been in here long enough to know my way around.'

Hiro hesitated, then raised his arm, palm out. A wispy tendril snaked from Layton's mist to encircle it. A moment passed. Hiro stiffened as if he was being probed. Layton pursed his wispy lips and blew, creating a high-pitched whistle. To Sara, it sounded ghostly, and she shivered. The ball of mist moved off before disappearing into the murk. They heard the whistle once more some way off before that too faded.

'Was that wise?' Levi asked. 'Merging with him.'

Hiro's lips firmed. 'I'm not sure.'

Before they could speculate further, Sara saw a faint golden glow moving rapidly toward them. She pointed, but before she could say anything the end of a golden rope floated out of the greyness and coiled itself at Hiro's feet, much like a glowing, obedient snake.

Layton's mist bubble floated back, its mouth sliding into its customary smirk. 'Your damn tether line almost got itself hijacked by a couple of unsavouries. They were following it back to your place. I had to rescue it. There's all sorts in here, you know.'

'Then you've been in good company,' Hiro added dryly, lowering his arm to break the link. He then used both hands to pull through more of the rope and threaded the end through the belt loop of his robe before passing it back to Sara.

It was warm, almost alive between her hands.

Hiro tapped the side of his robe where the line was attached. 'Thread it
through your belt loop at the side of your jeans and do the same with Levi's trousers. After that, take the rope around behind him and loop it back through the belt loop on the other side. Then do the same for yourself and finally me. That's it. This will keep us all together.'

'What about Maddy?' Sara asked.

'Levi will carry her. I'll take the dog.'

Hiro picked up Tripod, whispered some more words into his ear, and the dog slumped into his arms. He turned and spoke over his shoulder. 'Now, once I give the command, the tether line will retract and pull us back to the house. It may be a little rough. Sara, I suspect you may get squashed on the turns between Levi and me. The centrifugal force will be significant, so I suggest you take hold of my shoulders and stiffen your arms. It might help.'

Hiro levered Tripod onto one shoulder. The dog draped over it like some unlikely fashion accessory. Snapping his fingers three times, Hiro gave the tether line a shake. Immediately a pulse passed along the rope, tingling against Sara's hips. She took hold of Hiro's shoulders, looking around and past him. The greyness stretched endlessly away on all sides. The only light was the golden glow from the rope that stretched in front of them before disappearing into the gloom. The line tensioned on either side, squeezing tight against Sara's hips.

'Ready? Here we go.' Hiro snapped his fingers again, and Sara was jerked forward. Levi cannoned into her back, and what must have been one of Maddy's feet slammed into one of her kidneys. She gasped at the pain as they rocked steeply into the first of several turns. It was like a mad carnival ride. Sara tightened her grip against the force that swung her from side to side, her fingers digging deep into Hiro's shoulder muscles, as if this might lend her some measure of control. The greyness blurred, whistling past, the air harsh and chill against her cheeks. After an interminable time, the pace decelerated and then eased into a slow glide. They emerged from the greyness with a pop, re-entering the world of objects, shape, and familiarity. They slid to a stop in front of the bricked-over basement door she and Levi had used to get to the airport. It seemed like a century ago. In front, Hiro twisted one of the bricks to reveal a retinal scanner and a bank of code keys. He quickly accessed the security protocols, and the door swung open.

Relief flooding her, Sara staggered inside, slid the tether rope free of her jeans, and slumped into an armchair just inside the door.

Hiro secured the door and hefted Tripod higher onto his shoulder. For a man who only an hour before had looked near death, he was remarkably chipper.

'Levi, are you okay to keep on carrying Maddy? I don't want to wake her just yet. There are preparations that need to be made that she won't understand.'

'I'm fine, and so is she. Though getting Sara out of that chair might be another question.'

'Come on, Sara, there's no time for that now. We have to keep moving,' Hiro said over his shoulder, striding deeper into the house, his black-and-gold robe swirling about him.

Sara groaned and heaved herself out of the deep armchair before trudging after Levi. She was exhausted. It was an effort to place one foot after another. *Why am I so tired? Could it be the spores? Is this what it feels like? Getting weaker day by day until at last...*

They moved through a succession of rooms and dimly lit hallways. The air was stuffy, as if it hadn't been breathed for some time. The rooms blurred into one another, Sara's field of vision contracting until all she could manage to focus on were Levi's feet. She had to channel all her resources to simply keep them in sight and wished they would stop moving. Finally, Hiro paused outside a wood-panelled door. He pushed it open and ushered them inside.

Sara glanced around the high-ceilinged room. It looked familiar, and with a rush she realised they were once again in the *kintsugi* room with the shelves of carefully placed white porcelain bowls with the gold joins. This was where her weird journey as a queen had started. She missed it, in a way, wondering again at how real it had felt. How attached she'd been to Madison. She hoped Nicolai had kept his word.

'Sara.'

She started. Hiro was staring at her, the grey gaze shining from his eyes. 'It's important to stay focused, especially in this room.' She nodded. Hiro broke the gaze knelt and carefully laid Tripod on the floor. 'I'll go fetch Layton's body. It's in a roll-out chiller drawer down the corridor.'

Sara shivered at the thought, bending to stroke Tripod's thick fur, letting its touch ground her thinking back to what Layton had said about Tony taking over the dead dog's body.

Could that even be true? Her mind rattled through a playlist of memories, a succession of curious instances where Tripod had been a little too clever. Been more. *More than what? A dog? More even than Tony? Tony loved Maddy, but could love do that much? Is it even possible? No, I can't go there. Not now. Maybe not ever.* It was one train station past Really Weird, and if she went there, she wasn't positive she could find her way back. She tapped Levi on the shoulder, eager to return to something solid and real. 'I'm okay to hold Maddy now. You go help Hiro get Layton.'

'Are you sure? You looked beat back there.'

'I know. But no, I'm fine now.'

He left, and the silence flowed in. Parts of this house were like being inside a vacuum. The quiet was both soothing and unsettling, however, strangely, the blanket of fatigue she'd experienced outside was lifting. It was as if she'd left it at the door, like so much dirty washing. Either that, or this room had some weird healing power.

Maddy groaned in her sleep, a tiny smile curling her mouth. Sara hugged her close, burying her nose against Maddy's neck, inhaling her familiar freshness. *After the cure, please God, let her have a normal life.*

No, I won't try and offload that. It's my responsibility. Whatever happens, I'll make sure of it. For both of us. The rest of this crazy, scary minefield would have to wait in the ever-growing unprocessed pile. Maybe forever. Right now, she couldn't think any further than getting Maddy cured and away from Layton, this place, and men who wanted to harm them, regardless of what Levi did or wanted to do. *Let him follow me for a change.*

There was a bump at the door, and she jumped. Levi backed in through the door, guiding the front of a trolley. Hiro was at the other end. Between them, a green sheet was draped over what could only be Layton's body. Sara took a step back. The two men walked over to the high table, and Hiro motioned her over. Sara was careful to give the trolley a wide berth and joined them.

'Are we going to do the ceremony now?' she asked, her voice low, careful not to disturb Maddy.

'Soon. First, I need to tell you both something. When Layton and I mentally linked up in the bardo, I picked something up. Something I'd suspected.' Hiro rubbed his jaw. He seemed unsure of how to proceed.

'What?' Levi prodded.

Hiro sighed. 'I don't think Layton intends re-inhabiting the body he left. Not for long anyway.'

'What do you mean?' Sara asked.

'You both saw what his body was like.' Hiro indicated the shape on the gurney. 'Would you want to move back into that shrivelled husk?'

'But you said the orbs would cure him.'

'Of the illness, but they won't, can't, change his physical appearance. The ravages of the illness will still be there.'

'What will he do then?' Levi persisted.

'Layton has to use that body to transfer back to the physical, but he will then try and assume one of ours.'

'He what?' Sara blurted out, disbelieving.

'You mean he intends to possess one of us?' Levi asked, his voice flat, as if asking someone the time.

'Yes. That came through very strongly before he managed to cloak it,' Hiro said.

A shiver passed through Sara. 'I can't believe I'm saying this, but whose?'

'I couldn't tell; it was only a momentary flash of understanding. It was as if his excitement overflowed the psychic barrier he'd built around himself, but I think it's safe to say he planned for it to be either you or Levi, as you two were his original targets with the infected envelope. Plus, you're both young.'

'What?' Sara staggered back, looking down at Maddy. Levi reached out to steady her.

Sara shook her head, unsure still of what had just been said. 'Are you saying he can do that? Barge into my body and somehow evict me, like, like... some overstayed tenant. Steal me? Are you insane? How could that happen?'

'It can happen when you, or Levi, are undertaking the cure. Think of it as having to leave the room before a fumigation process, or better cleaning an infected hard drive. The orbs will upload and seal off the data, in this case your consciousness, to protect it while they cleanse the body and mind of the illness. Once the curse has been eliminated, the process is reversed and the original consciousness is, if you like, re-installed. Layton intends using that brief window of vacancy to move in. It's a challenging process. The timing has to be exact, so he may not succeed the first time.'

'Meaning?' Levi asked.

Hiro's heavy eyelids lifted as he looked at him. 'He will likely keep trying. One of you will undergo the cure first. If he doesn't make the transition, then he'll try with whoever goes next. Now he even has Maddy as a backup. Then there's me. I'll be managing the process with the orbs for all of us so, necessarily, I'll be last. I have no doubt he'll keep me in reserve as a final attempt.'

'This is like some unending nightmare. Every time I think it's over, it gets worse,' Levi said. 'What do we do? We have to get rid of the disease somehow. I can feel it creeping through me already; I don't know about you.'

'What we have just been through may have accelerated its progress. We have no choice but to proceed, otherwise we'll die anyway. All of us.' His gaze settled on Maddy cradled in Sara's arms.

'Unless...' Levi said, stretching the word out.

'Unless what?' Sara felt like shaking him. Anything would be better than what she'd just heard, but he seemed reluctant to say it.

'One of us dies first.'

'Meaning?' Hiro fired back.

'You said the orbs are linked to Layton, so he'll have to undertake the cure first. Say I go next. Layton succeeds in making the... transfer into me.'

'And?' Hiro prodded.

'You kill me as soon as he does. I'll already be as good as anyway.'

'That's obscene,' Sara said. 'No. I won't do it.'

'Hiro will take care of it. You don't have to do a thing.'

'Except watch you sacrifice yourself. And then live with it afterwards. Forever. I've already been down that road with Tony.' Tears welled at the corners of her eyes. She swiped them away with the back of her hand. 'No, if anyone has to die for Maddy, then it's going to be me. She's my daughter, and this is my mess. It should be me.'

'That's exactly why it can't be. You need to be there—for Maddy. Hiro can't because he's the only one who can perform the cleansing ceremony for the rest of you. No, it logically has to be me.'

Hiro stepped between them, a hand on each of their shoulders.

'As noble as you both sound, there may be another option. I must warn you though, it's no more appealing.'

'It's got to be better than him dying,' Sara snapped, surprised at the effect Levi's offer to sacrifice himself had had on her.

'I'm not so sure. In my option, everyone dies.'

HIRO PICKED UP THE ORBS, weighing them in his hand. With a flick of his wrist, he lobbed the joined orbs into the air, his concentrated gaze following their ascent keenly. Sara and Levi stood on the other side of the table, waiting and watching. Maddy was a dead weight in her arms, but Sara had refused Levi's offer to hold her. For the next few minutes, nothing would prise Maddy away from her.

The orbs spun up through the air, then paused, suspended, before slowly rotating, creating a kaleidoscope of swirling colour that radiated out like a small, colourful sun.

'Layton's spirit will be attracted to the Life orb's activation and will appear soon. Be ready.' Hiro's voice sounded flat, as if the sound waves were being absorbed by something.

He muttered some more words that Sara couldn't make out, and the light intensity increased, the colours moving faster, their spectrum shades bleeding into one another until there was only a blinding, all-encompassing white. Sara shielded her eyes, but the light was everywhere, invading her attempts to escape it.

As it faded, the brilliance left an afterglow against the backs of her eyes, making it difficult to make out detail. When her vision returned, the first thing she saw was Layton's face, floating as before, shrouded in mist, a thin thread connecting him to the orbs.

Above him, the orbs continued to rotate, slower now, their light more a glow, the whole effect reminding her of an engine smoothly idling.

'Hello again, Sara. I can't wait until we meet... in person.'

Sara turned away, her gaze automatically settling on Levi beside her, who smiled in what he must have thought was a reassuring way but only served to heighten her agitation. She was scared that somehow Layton might read her thoughts and what they intended.

'The process is ready,' Hiro intoned. 'Layton.'

The mist ball floated over to hover at the head of the draped body on the trolley.

'Ready,' it said.

Sara could hear the rising excitement in Layton's voice. She remembered other occasions and the way it thickened when— She turned her attention away, forcing it to settle on Levi. She gripped his hand, and he squeezed back, but his focus was on what was happening.

Hiro uttered more words, and a beam of blue light stabbed from the orbs down to the head on the trolley. It jerked beneath the sheet as if a charge of electricity had been passed through it before beginning to vibrate so hard that it set the trolley jangling.

'It's happening,' Layton shouted. 'It's happening; I can feel it.'

Another beam, a pulsing red, burst from the orbs to shine on the cadaver's chest. It flashed alternately with the blue at the head, the overflowing wash of colour reflecting off the gold slashes on the white porcelain bowls that lined the shelves on the walls. Sara had the feeling she was in a nightclub, but one without vibration or sound. A third beam, yellow, settled on Layton's mist bubble. The expression on his face changed from excitement to fear as the mist was sucked into the yellow beam and splattered against the area on the trolley near Layton's pelvis. The body gave a massive jerk, dislodging the green sheet. It slid to the floor as if anxious to escape the desiccated limbs that splayed over either side of the trolley. Sara stared, her mouth open, conscious only of clutching Maddy against her. The corpse twitched twice. The beams retracted.

'Stand back,' Hiro ordered, his voice once again strong. He stepped forward and reached up, plucking the still rotating orbs from the air. Tucking them into a pocket of his robe, he motioned Sara and Levi forward. They formed a tight circle around Tripod, still asleep on the floor.

'Hurry, we don't have much time,' Levi said.

Hiro removed one of the gold-seamed bowls from the shelf behind him and quickly pricked each of their index fingers, allowing the blood to drip down the sides of the bowl. Maddy gave a little cry when he pricked hers, but she didn't wake. Hiro used a small syringe to take a sample from Tripod. Sara gave Maddy to Levi to hold, her arms weakened from holding the sleeping child for so long. Levi settled her against his shoulder.

'What are you doing?' Layton's voice boomed, bouncing around the walls of the small room.

Sara spared a glance over her shoulder. The emaciated corpse was sitting on the edge of the trolley. It still looked dead, but the eyes burned with the same ferocious rage that she remembered. She forced herself to turn away.

From deep inside the house, she heard something bang and then fall.

They exchanged glances. 'We must hurry,' Hiro muttered. Beside her, Levi tensed, readying himself for whatever might happen. None of them knew whether this would work. Sara didn't gamble, yet here she was putting not only her life at risk, but Maddy's as well. Was that better than what Layton had in mind?

'Together now. Ready?' Sara reached up, her fingers finding a place beside Hiro's and Levi's as they lightly cupped the small bowl.

'Wait!' she shouted. 'What about that holotropic software drug-drink thing we had last time? Don't we need that?'

'Only if you want to come back.'

Behind her, she heard Layton thud to the floor. She started to turn. 'Forget him. His muscles are too wasted to support him,' Levi said.

Sara looked anyway. Layton was an untidy pile on the floor, bones visible beneath his wrinkled skin as he tried to drag and claw his way towards them, his voice frantic. 'What are you doing? You must take the cure. You'll die. Don't you realise? You must use the orbs to take the cure.' The voice was the same, but everything else had changed.

The banging sounds from within the house were much clearer now and had resolved into the sound of men. Running and determined men. They were already in the hallway outside. One pounded against the door. Sara fancied she recognised one of the voices as Turner's. From the wide-eyed terror on Layton's disease-ravaged face, so did he. Hiro had removed the wards surrounding the house. Turner had quickly honed in. She turned back.

'Release,' Hiro said quietly, and the white bowl fell.

24

Chapter Twenty Four

Sara woke with a start, unsure where she was and, as her senses flooded in, acutely aware of where she wasn't.

She roused herself, the unfamiliar feel of long robes inhibiting her movement. Across the room she could see Maddy, still sleeping. Tripod was draped across the bottom of her bed.

'Highness. You are recovered. We were so worried.' The florid face of her chancellor peered down at her.

Sara slid her legs over the side of the bed. 'I can imagine, Chancellor Rabine.'

At the end of the bed, a semicircle of white-faced ladies in long silk dresses fluttered.

'Guards!' she shouted, and all the ladies jumped. Immediately two burly men in the purple uniforms of her personal guard barged through the door, pikes at the ready. 'Arrest Chancellor Rabine. The charge is treason. And find the physic. Arrest him as well for attempted regicide. I'll deal with them both later.'

'Highness?' Rabine's oily smile faltered, his desperate gaze flicking between the men at the door and the queen. Finally, he addressed the guards, snapping out, 'Her majesty is obviously not herself. Find the physic by all means and bring him here, at once. The queen is still unwell. She doesn't know what she is saying.'

The men at the door hesitated, unsure who to listen to.

'Am I still your queen?' Sara snapped.

They looked at each other for confirmation and answered together, 'Yes, Highness.'

'Then do as I say. Now!'

They strode into the room and dragged Rabine away, his screams and curses disappearing down the hall.

Sara smothered a smile, then said to her ladies, 'What has been happening since I've... been asleep?'

A tall one with complicated hair bobbed in a curtsy. 'The wizard who came with you from the north remains in the tower room, Highness. Commander Levi is with him. Both you and he were suffering the effects of exposure when you were found.'

'The wizard?' Sara repeated.

'Yes, do you remember? He found you in the swamp and alerted the search party. Both you and the commander were suffering from severe exposure after you recovered the kidnapped princess.' She indicated Maddy. 'He saved your lives.'

Sara nodded. 'Yes. Yes, he did, didn't he?' Was this a life? It would be more of one than the one she'd been forced to vacate.

'Your Majesty?' The tall one was looking at her curiously.

Sara snapped her attention back. 'Where is my dress for the day? I will visit them both. When the princess wakes, bring her to me.'

They bustled around the room, readying her layers of clothing. When she was dressed, Sara swept from the room, a grin stretching across her face.

She did love being queen.

Hiro's plan had worked. Without the drug to tether their bodies, they had shifted fully into this. Their new reality.

People bobbed and curtsied as she passed; she smiled and

acknowledged them, wondering about Madison. Now that Maddy was in this space, would he be as well? Then she remembered extracting the promise from Nicolai, the recovered Nicolai, to look after the heir at the grand palace. She would have to look in on that and bring him back. After all, Nicolai was still Nicolai, regardless of promises made.

She reached the north tower and navigated the narrow circular staircase to the landing at the top. She was breathing heavily by the time she knocked on the stout oak door. It swung open, revealing a room without corners. Banners and tapestries hung from the walls. Through the narrow windows, she glimpsed the plain far below.

'Ah, Sar... Highness,' Levi said, giving a mock bow.

'You'll have to do a little better than that, Commander, if you are to remain in my service,' she snapped back, voice rippling with privilege.

Levi's eyes narrowed as they might if checking for a fault, unsure if she had retained her memory.

Sara's cheeks crinkled into a smile. 'Almost had you, didn't I?'

The men relaxed and resumed their seats, Hiro waving for her to take the third. She arranged her skirts on the simple wooden chair with some difficulty and accepted a goblet of red wine.

'So.' She used her wine goblet to indicate the room. 'Is all this as permanent as it feels? You said there was no way back, that this would be a one-way trip, but is it permanent?'

'As permanent as life can ever be. There are no guarantees. But once we use these'—Hiro tapped the orbs in the middle of the table— 'we will be fully recovered from the spores and the disease they carried. Even better than normal. As we three have been here before, our memories from both realities remain intact. Maddy, of course, will think she has always been here, the same as you two did the first time.'

'And the dog,' Levi added dryly.

'Well, we don't really know what the situation is with Tripod/Tony, now do we? Other than he still shares our journey.'

Sara shifted in her seat. 'Could Turner and his men find us here?'

'No. Even if he knew what we'd gone, he'd have no idea where we've gone. There are many parallel worlds. Besides, the orbs are much safer here. Perhaps we can do good work with them.'

'And you, Levi?' Sara asked, the breath tight in her chest. She tried a smile, hoping it looked nonchalant. 'What of you after this? I have little doubt Nicolai will be prepared to hand back the vial to break the melders' curse. You'll be free to go wherever you wish.'

Levi sat back, glancing over at Hiro before meeting her gaze, his eyes deep and twinkling.

'I don't know if I'm in too much of a hurry to get that vial back if it means I have to leave you.' He smiled, reaching across the table for her hand.

END

REVIEW

Before you go, thanks for being one of those wonderful people that writers cannot do without– readers.

It would be fabulous if you have time to leave an honest review through whatever feedback or review platform you prefer.

If you'd like to leave a personal comment, join the growing list of readers who would like to hear about Jack's next book or be considered to join the team to receive an ARC (advance reader copy) of upcoming books before they are published please go to Jack's website/contact or subscribe.

https://www.jackgarrety.com

STAR GALLERY

It takes a constellation of stars to make a book. Thanks for shining so brightly for me, in no particular order:

Editor: Olivia Ventura @ Hot Tree

Cover art: Claire Smith@Booksmith Design

Promotion and all round enthusiasm
Zali@Bespoke Social Media

Support, encouragement and great feedback
Sue Reynolds & June Kant
Stephen Dedman for advice and title

To my wonderful beta readers and all round lovely people
June Kant, Kathy Stewart, Kirsty Cramer, Hazel Barker, Chris Robbins, Pauline Behrendorff and Beverley Jones

Thanks too to KSP Writers centre Perth for the residency when In the Broken Places was being written

ABOUT THE AUTHOR

Jack lives on the Blackall Range overlooking the beautiful Sunshine Coast with his delightful wife Annie.

In addition to writing Jack is a registered yoga teacher and yoga therapist through Yoga Australia, loves bushwalking, nature, dogs (though he doesn't have one-yet), and is completing a masters in Gestalt psychotherapy.

Jack/Paul also teaches and runs a creative writing course for U3A in their lecture room at the University of the Sunshine Coast.

In the Broken Places is Jack's fifth novel.

https://www.jackgarrety.com

ALSO BY JACK GARRETY

www.jackgarrety.com